About the Author

The author has spent most of her life in the hotel business. She has, therefore, met many people, learnt of their problems and reactions to them. This sympathetic approach shows in her previously published fiction. She lives in the beautiful Channel Islands and, although retired, still enjoys meeting the locals, regular visitors and, of course, her writing.

Sheila Anne Parker

HE NEVER LOVED ME

Copyright © Sheila Anne Parker (2015)

The right of Sheila Anne Parker to be identified as author of this work has been asserted by her in accordance with section 77 and 78 of the Copyright, Designs and Patents Act 1988.

All rights reserved. No part of this publication may be reproduced, stored in a retrieval system, or transmitted in any form or by any means, electronic, mechanical, photocopying, recording, or otherwise, without the prior permission of the publishers.

Any person who commits any unauthorized act in relation to this publication may be liable to criminal prosecution and civil claims for damages.

A CIP catalogue record for this title is available from the British Library.

ISBN 9781785540202 (Paperback)

www.austinmacauley.com

First Published (2015)
Austin Macauley Publishers Ltd.
25 Canada Square
Canary Wharf
London
E14 5LQ

Printed and bound in Great Britain

Acknowledgments

With grateful thanks to my relatives, friends and others who have helped me in my research for this book.

The early morning sun shimmered on the incoming tide which had almost reached the high water mark, but not the body that lay inert on the sand beneath the sheer cliffs.

Serena Beach was a wide beach with a stretch of sand which dropped steeply to a surface of shingle, exposed on low tides. The high cliffs protruded on either side providing sheltered anchorage for visiting or local yachts.

Although it was early May two swimmers, residents from the nearby hotel, swam the width of the bay. It was not until the first emerged from the water, recognised and accompanied the man walking across the sand, that they discovered that the body was that of Matthew Stenton, owner of the hotel.

Chapter 1

Matthew Stenton, owner of the Serena Beach Hotel, pushed back his chair and stood up.

He had just re-read the programme for Monday, Liberation Day. This was the 60th anniversary of that historic occasion, and the islanders had been thrilled and delighted when it was announced, on the 23rd of February, that the Queen and the Duke of Edinburgh would be visiting the island.

Matthew briefly recalled the day the island had been liberated. He had been 15 and together with his parents, had been standing, waving a carefully-hidden Union Jack, near the Weighbridge as the troops came ashore. And now, Matthew thought, although the Queen had visited Guernsey on previous occasions, this would be the first time she had done so on the 9th of May. His hotel and many others had been well-booked but this announcement had meant more bookings, some of the media wanted to stay the previous night while those responsible for security had arrived a few days ago.

However, Matthew had a more personal reason to look forward to the weekend – Peter, his eldest son, would be arriving on Saturday. As he reached for his jacket Matthew admitted it was time he took his doctor's advice, he should delegate more responsibility to the young members of his second family. Monique had been working at his side as assistant manager for some time but there was no reason why Ben, Noel, his son-in-law, and possibly Gerald, his nephew, should not shoulder extra duties. He was glad that Peter would be here for eight days, this would give him several occasions to discuss this with him.

Five minutes later Matthew looked at the smiling faces of residents and several locals but before he could order a drink one of his regular visitors came towards him, a glass in each hand. As he handed over the full glass he said, 'Gin and tonic is your usual drink, isn't it?'

'Thank you. Cheers'

Later, Matthew moved around the bar talking to the residents and locals then, on reaching the open French window, he stepped outside. Pausing, he looked up appreciatively; it was a fine night, ideal for his usual walk.

Matthew strolled through the grounds then, as he approached the path, reached for and switched on his torch and began to climb, paused for a brief respite and then resumed at a slower pace. He would soon reach his favourite spot from where, looking back, he could see directly in the valley, the lights from the two-storied, 40-bedroomed hotel and their private bungalows, and those that illuminated the extensive grounds. This was also a popular vantage point for visitors and locals who would also look out, beyond the beach, to the sea and other islands.

Seeing the beam of light from the torch and therefore aware of his approach, but before Matthew could turn to gaze back, a figure moved stealthily from the shadow of the trees to the other side of the path, and waited.

Chapter 2

Vere Hamilton glanced at his watch, Matthew was late this morning. They usually met at this vantage point, each walking the same distance from their respective homes except that in Matthew's case he had a steady climb from his hotel.

As he moved closer to the newly-constructed fence Vere noticed that some of the palings were missing and the gorse bushes disturbed. He stepped back quickly but not before he noticed something which made him catch his breath – a body lay sprawled at an awkward angle on the beach, some sixty feet below and he muttered, 'Someone's had an accident.'

Vere hurried down the path, wondering why the swimmers had not noticed the body, then realised that from the sea they would not be able to do this, due to the slope of the beach. It was when he reached the sand that a voice called out, 'Good morning, Mr Hamilton. We don't usually see you down here.'

This came from one of the men who had emerged from the sea whom Vere recognised as John Baines, a regular visitor and daily swimmer who came every year for Liberation Day.

'There's a body along there.' Vere indicated the area at the foot of the cliffs. 'I thought I should take a look.'

'A body!' echoed Baines, dropping his towel. 'Would you like me to come with you?'

'Thanks. It might be a good idea.' As they drew closer they could see the body was that of a man clothed in a light-weight suit and Vere felt a strange sense of foreboding.

He quickened his pace until he was standing over the inert form and knew, without turning it over, it was that of his friend, Matthew.

'Who is it? What happened?' asked John.

'It's...it's Matthew Stenton.' Vere indicated the sheer cliff. 'If he fell from up there it could be a broken neck.' Vere bent, noting the badly damaged hands, broken fingers, the unusual signet ring which he had so often admired, and that the top of Matthew's head was encrusted with blood.

Standing, he looked at John and queried, 'Shall I ring for a doctor or the police?' and then, 'No, 999 would be the best idea.'

'Shall I go?' volunteered John.

'No thanks, but I'd be grateful if you ...' and as the other swimmer reached them, 'and your friend would stay here while I go to the hotel and phone.' Vere started walking, almost stumbling across the sand, muttering, 'I'll have to tell Monique. But not yet.'

Vere was aware that Monique was busy dealing with departing guests, but interrupted them. 'There's been an accident. Could I use the office phone, please?'

'Of course.'

It wasn't until he was seated at the large flat-topped desk that Vere realised he was shaking, but in spite of this he dialled 999 and informed the operator that there was a body on the beach, and other relevant details.

Relieved that Monique was still busy, Vere hurried through the grounds and had just reached the approach to the beach when the ambulance drew up and two men jumped out, the driver asking, 'Mr Hamilton?'

'Yes,' and pointing to where the two men were standing, 'It's...My friend's body is over there.' The two men exchanged puzzled glances and were both attentive as briefly and explicitly Vere explained. They all nodded their thanks to John Baines and his friend, then Vere watched as the paramedic knelt, examined the body, and confirmed that Matthew was dead. Noting the injuries and that the newly-constructed fence had been deliberately sabotaged, he reached for his mobile, saying, 'I'm not very happy about moving Mr Stenton's body. I'm going to phone the station.' Vere gasped as he heard the paramedic inform the duty sergeant why he was reluctant to move the body, then standing he told Vere, 'Sergeant Batiste and a constable are on their way. The latter will inspect the broken fence; with so many visitors here for the weekend we don't want a spate of accidents. It looks as though vandals have been causing damage again.'

This may not be an accident, a lot of people knew about Matthew's evening and morning walks, thought Vere as his gaze travelled from Matthew's injured head to his broken hands. Aloud he said, 'I must go back to the hotel and tell Monique.'

'Are you all right, Mr Hamilton? Would you like me to come with you?' enquired the ambulance driver.

'No.' Vere paused. 'Perhaps it would be a good idea if you're there when I tell Monique – well, all of them.'

Both the ambulance men knew the Stenton family and just as Vere and the driver began to move away, the paramedic called out, 'Will you remain at the hotel please, Mr Hamilton? Sergeant Batiste will no doubt want to question you about finding the body and noticing the damaged fence.'

Monique was still in Reception, talking to Pat Le Page, the Head Receptionist. She stared at the uniformed ambulance driver who stood beside Vere as he said, 'I need to see you now, Monique. Could you ask Ben and Noel to join us?'

'What's happened?'

'Call them, please. And can we use the office?'

'Of course. Go and sit down, I'll order some coffee'

'No,' said the driver. 'Hot, strong tea and plenty of sugar.' Then, taking Vere by the arm, 'Come along, sir. Let's go and sit down.'

Monique and Pat watched as Vere opened the door into the office which was immediately behind and could also be accessed from Reception, then remembering the driver's instructions Monique rang the bar where Ben was stocking up, the dining room where Noel was helping with breakfast, and ordered tea for five.

While they waited, Vere thought about Matthew who was still wearing the lightweight suit he usually wore in the evenings. He had obviously walked up to his favourite spot, leant against the fence and it had given way. Strange, considered Vere; on the many, many occasions that they had met there, summer and winter mornings, wet or fine, he had never known Matthew to stand close to the fence, let alone lean against it; and why were his fingers and hands so badly damaged? At that moment the door opened and Monique, Noel and Ben entered, followed by a waiter carrying a loaded tray. The two men glared first at Vere, who occupied the large leather swivel chair normally used by Matthew, and then the uniformed ambulance driver. 'What's this all about?' demanded Ben.

Vere waited until Monique had sat down before saying bluntly, 'There's been an accident.'

'Is it Dad? What's happened?' asked Monique, picking up the cup of tea which had been placed in front of her by the driver, who was now watching her carefully.

Vere shook his head. 'I'm sorry, there's no other way to tell you: Matthew's dead.'

There was a stunned silence as they all gazed at Vere and it was Noel who spoke first.

'You said an accident, but his car is still in the garage.'

'It happened while he was out walking.'

'He goes every morning, that's when he meets you,' said Ben.

'Not today. He was still wearing the suit that he wears in the evenings.'

'This could have happened last night?' suggested the driver.

'Was it a heart attack?' Monique looked directly at the driver but it was Vere who answered. 'I was having my usual early morning walk and was concerned that I hadn't met Matthew. I stopped at the vantage point where he often stopped for a rest, looked down and saw a body on the beach.' Vere drank the remainder of his tea and continued. 'I hurried down and was horrified to discover it was Matthew.'

'Oh my God!' whispered Monique. 'He'd been there all night.' She turned to the driver.

'What's happening now?'

'Sergeant Batiste and a constable are on their way.'

'Is that necessary? How did they know?' demanded Ben.

'The paramedic, who's still on the beach, phoned the station.'

At that moment there was a knock on the inter-communicating door; it opened and Pat said, 'Sergeant Batiste is here.' Before Monique could reply, the driver, who knew Pat, said, 'Thank you, Miss Le Page,' then looking at Vere, 'as you found the body, Sergeant Batiste will want to question you, sir. However, will you come with us now?' and turning to Noel and Ben, 'Do either of you want to come?'

The two men exchanged glances then reluctantly Ben nodded while Noel said, 'I'd better get back to the dining room or Gerald will think—' but before he could continue the door leading directly from the foyer opened and a young man stood in the doorway, glanced at and nodded to the driver, then looking directly at Monique, introduced himself as Sergeant Batiste. 'I'll see you as soon as I get back from the beach, Mrs Latimer.'

Monique nodded. The driver glanced at Noel and asked, 'Will you stay here with your wife, sir?'

Noel looked uncertain but Monique said quickly, 'I'd prefer to be on my own,' and after Noel had left, the driver looked at Monique and decided to ask Pat to keep an eye on her.

Alone, Monique reluctantly moved behind the desk to sit in the large chair, her thoughts confused. She would, of course, tell Gerald, and later the staff would be informed. It was going to be an extra-busy weekend, not only Liberation Day on Monday but also a Royal Visit with all the attendant media and necessary security. She knew all the necessary supplies had been ordered, extra staff organised, but suddenly felt bereft and was about to pour some coffee (a waiter had just brought this and taken the tea tray) when the door from Reception opened and Pat asked, 'Can I join you for a coffee? Albert will let me know if I'm needed out here.'

'Of course, come in.' Monique gazed at Pat fondly, grateful that she had someone so reliable and trustworthy, and briefly recalled the occasions she had confided in Pat whom she regarded as her best friend but knew that no one would ever replace her father.

*****

'What's the matter – a complaint?' If Gerald was surprised to see Monique seated behind Matthew's desk he didn't show it. 'No. It's…' Monique faltered and said quickly, 'It's Father.'

'Is he ill?'

Again Monique hesitated, shook her head and then said, 'We don't know what happened, his body was found on the beach.'

'You mean he's dead? Why didn't Noel tell me?'

'I said I would tell you after breakfast.'

'What was he doing on the beach? Who found him?'

Monique stared at her cousin. How could he ask questions at a time like this? He hadn't uttered a word of sympathy and she certainly had no intention of answering his questions.

With a supreme effort she stood up and told him, 'The police will be making enquiries?'

'The police!' echoed Gerald. 'Is that necessary?'

'That's for them to decide.'

As Gerald let himself out, Monique opened the cupboard and peered in the mirror fixed on the inside of the door to see pale cheeks and huge eyes. Opening her handbag she found her compact, hastily powdered her nose, then the door opened again and Noel told her; 'Ben's back and the staff are assembled in the dining room.' Then, to her surprise, he slipped his arm around her waist and whispered, 'I think you're marvellous.'

Compliments were rare but the double glass doors leading into the dining room were open and Monique could see Hans, his team of chefs and other kitchen staff standing together, the waiters in one group, the housekeeper and chambermaids in another, while other staff whispered amongst themselves. Then as Ben, pale and anxious, appeared, she asked, 'What are you going to say?'

'Do you expect me to do that?'

'I'm sure you're quite capable,' said Noel, briskly. 'Let's go and get it over with.'

After clearing his throat and a couple of attempts Ben managed and reluctantly waited with Monique and Noel as the older and senior members of the staff offered their condolences.

Monique was about to leave when Hans, the head chef who had been at the hotel for 10 years, touched her arm. 'Excuse me, Mrs Latimer, could I have a quick word?'

'Of course. Do you want to come to the office or shall we go to the kitchen?'

'There's no need for either. I'm sure you know everything has been ordered and some food already delivered for the long weekend, however there are some items which should be topped up. Shall I order whatever is necessary?'

'Yes, please,' then thinking quickly Monique added, 'until and unless it's necessary to make alternative arrangements, will you take over the day to day ordering?'

'Of course and if there's anything else I can do, just let me know.'

Turning, Monique saw Pat and beyond her Vere and Sergeant Batiste in the hall. Relieved that neither Noel nor Ben were around, Monique nodded as Sergeant Batiste said he wished to ask her a few questions and suggested, 'Shall we go back to the office?'

'Would you like me to stay?' asked Vere, looking at Monique anxiously when she shook her head and said, 'No thanks, but could you phone Peter, please? I know he's due to arrive tomorrow, but I think he should be told what's happened.'

'Of course, my dear. Is there—?'

'Wait a minute,' interjected the Sergeant. 'Who's Peter?'

'My half-brother who lives in England and always comes for Liberation Day, and other occasions.' Monique looked at a framed photograph on the wall; Batiste followed her gaze and immediately recognised Matthew Stenton and, although grey-haired, a younger man of remarkable resemblance, obviously Peter. Batiste turned to Monique. 'I'm sorry. I should have realised you're all the same family.' Then, looking at Vere, 'Of course you must phone Peter.'

Monique leant back as the door closed, but immediately sat upright when Sergeant Batiste said, 'Detective Inspector Le Tissier is on his way and will want to question you,' and gasped as he continued, 'also your brother and husband.'

'Why? What happened?'

'I'm not fully cognisant of all the facts and I think it would be better if the Inspector apprised you of these.'

'But it was an accident, wasn't it?' and as the Sergeant hesitated, 'Can't you tell me? I have a right to know.'

At that moment there was a sharp knock at the door which Batiste immediately recognised. He gave a sigh of relief, and stood up as a tall sandy-haired man in a dark grey suit entered.

To Monique's surprise the Inspector held out his hand, shook hers, introduced himself and said, 'I'm sorry to meet you under such tragic circumstances, Mrs Latimer.'

'What happened?' repeated Monique.

'I'd prefer to tell you, and also question you, when your husband and brother join us. Sergeant Batiste has gone to fetch them.'

'Why are we all here?' hissed Noel as he entered while Ben demanded, 'Is this to do with Dad?'

'Yes, Mr Stenton.' Then looking from Ben to Noel, who had seated themselves on either side of Monique, the Inspector introduced himself and asked, 'Did you know your father had gone for a walk last night?'

His gaze lingered on Monique's pale face and she answered quietly, 'Yes. He had a walk every night in addition to his regular morning walk. Everyone – that is his friends, the guests, and the staff – knew.'

'When did you last see your father?'

'Soon after 10 o'clock. I'd been in Reception, handed over to the night porter and joined my husband in the bar. Dad came in soon after and, as usual, circulated amongst the residents and locals.' Monique confirmed that her father had been in good spirits, to her knowledge had no financial problems, and that she knew of no one who disliked him and concluded, 'What's this all about?'

'Why all these questions and why are you here?' Ben sounded aggrieved while Le Tissier noted that Noel looked at him reprovingly.

Monique looked directly at the Inspector. 'The paramedic didn't tell us anything. All we know is that Dad was found on the beach; but how did he get there from the cliff path? Was it a heart attack, an accident?' Monique was trembling, her hands clutching her forearms. Noel leant sideways, putting his arm around her shoulders and pulling her close at the same time, saying, 'There's something you haven't told us. What are you hiding?'

'Mr Stenton fell from the path. It's possible he leant against the fence—'

'That's impossible,' protested Monique. ''The old one was replaced earlier this year.'

'It was damaged. Some of the palings were sawn through.'

'What?' exclaimed Monique and Noel together while Ben shook his head and muttered, 'That's ridiculous.'

'Part of the cliff path will be cordoned off while the area is checked.'

'That'll be inconvenient for the guests – and the general public,' grumbled Noel. 'Is it necessary?'

'Yes.' Le Tissier thought of Matthew's damaged hands and head, then glanced briefly at Monique who asked, 'Can…can I see my Father?'

'Of course. We'll let you know when this can be arranged,' and after a slight pause, 'There'll have to be a post-mortem, probably tomorrow morning.'

'What about funeral arrangements?' asked Noel.

'That depends on the inquest which, due to the Royal Visit and Liberation Day, can't be held until Tues—'

'His torch,' interrupted Monique. 'Dad's torch,' then, aware of the Inspector's puzzled expression, she continued, 'He always took it with him. There was no moon on Thursday so he would have used it. It's not valuable but—' Monique faltered, 'Was he still holding it? Was it on the beach or the path?'

'I really don't know, Mrs Latimer.' Wondering if this had been large enough to ward off his assailant, Inspector Le Tissier learnt that it was a square flat pocket-sized torch which produced a powerful light. He thanked Monique for the information and told her that the team would also search for this. His gaze travelling to Ben and Noel, he continued, 'If either of you remember anything else that's relevant to our enquiries, please contact Sergeant Batiste.' Then, turning to the Sergeant, 'Let's go and see Mr Hamilton. I understand he's waiting in the lounge.'

Chapter 3

'He's dead, Dad's dead!' repeated Ben pacing to and fro while Cheryl lounged on the leather three-seater settee, and said languidly, 'It would have happened some time.'

'I know, but not like this. Seeing him lying there on the sand, his hands, the top of his head ...' Ben shuddered and continued, 'and the police asking questions'

'Why?'

'Because of his injuries, the damaged fence.'

'The wood was probably rotten and he fell against it.'

'Oh, don't be so stupid. It was deliberate. The fence was brand new, some of the palings were sawn through, and we're supposed to carry on as usual. The bloody hotel is full of guests, plus bookings for umpteen meals over the weekend.'

'The hotel,' said Cheryl, her eyes lighting up. 'What'll happen to it now?'

'Why do you always ask stupid questions?' Ben glared at Cheryl. 'What are you talking about? What do you mean?'

'Must be worth a lot of money,' mused Cheryl; and then, 'It belonged to your father, didn't it?'

'What are you hinting at?'

'Oh, don't be so dim! It'll probably be yours.'

'I don't want to be lumbered with all that responsibility. And aren't you forgetting something? I do have a sister.' He paused. 'And a half-brother.'

'Relax, forget about it.' Cheryl stood up, stepped out of her dress, and reaching for Ben sank back onto the settee. 'Why waste time talking?'

'Your parents,' protested Ben.

'Are out. Drinks party and then dinner.'

'I can't stay that long.'

'Then shut up and undress.'

Chapter 4

'My father was here during the Occupation,' said Peter Stenton.

'That's interesting.' Roslyn Tempest wondered why Peter's father had not been evacuated with his school. She knew that all British-born people had been deported to Germany: single men, widowers and those whose wives had taken young children to England were sent to one camp while married couples, some with children, were sent to another camp.

Roslyn gazed at Peter, a tall good-looking man. They had just exchanged names, and she continued, 'I've been coming to the island for the celebrations for the last 10 years.'

'It was a long time ago,' emphasised Peter.

'And 60 years on Monday since the islands were liberated.' Roslyn paused and it was Peter's turn to be curious. Was she a holidaymaker or a journalist? He had arrived late that afternoon, still shocked after learning of his father's untimely death and noticed this tall distinguished-looking woman as he stood in the doorway; then the barman had turned, smiled and greeted him by name. Moving to the counter to order a drink, he had spoken to her, the only person sat there, and they had soon been discussing the attractions of the island.

However, further conversation was impossible as a middle-aged couple, both short and rotund, came towards them, both exclaiming, 'Roslyn! How lovely to see you.'

Turning to Peter, the man said, 'I didn't realise you knew Roslyn. Are we all dining together?'

Trust the family Advocate to leap to conclusions, thought Peter, noting the amusement in his new acquaintance's eyes as she explained that they had only just met. He was also aware that the Levriers were regarding him curiously; then Arnold said quietly, 'I'm so sorry and shocked to hear about your father. How's Monique? Have you seen her?'

'I'm hoping to see her later.'

Arnold nodded. 'I know we're lunching together on Monday, however phone or come and see me at home any time, even Sunday'

'Thank you.'

Ten minutes later Peter sat at a corner table in the dining room recalling the unexpected phone call that morning. He had immediately recognised Vere's voice and asked, 'What's happened? Is it Father? Has he had a heart attack?' Vere had explained the sequence of events, his early morning walk, seeing a body on the beach, discovering it was Matthew, his apparent injuries and telling Monique. He said he was phoning from the hotel, at her insistence, and would remain there until Detective Inspector Le Tissier, who also wanted to question him, arrived.

As he ate his first course Peter considered that his father had led a remarkable life; well-liked and respected by the other local hoteliers, and regarded by his staff with awe and affection. Matthew Stenton had worked hard, in fact he had still taken an active role in the running of the Serena Beach Hotel, ably assisted by Monique, his daughter from a second marriage.

For a moment Peter thought of his mother, not only a loving and caring person but also a pretty and vivacious woman who had supported his father in all his ideas for improving and extending the hotel. Peter remembered his mother's sudden illness and death. He had been 14 at the time and seeing his father so devastated and bereft had felt life would never be the same. Peter smiled his thanks as his wine glass was replenished, and the main course of crispy roast duck and seasonal vegetables were served, and recalled that despite the many invitations from school friends, he had centred his attention on his father and the hotel. It was at the end of the summer holidays that Matthew had said, 'I'm sorry you've had such a miserable holiday, I'll never forget how helpful and supportive you've been, spending so much time in the hotel with me. Not many teenagers would have done that, shown so much interest in the business. When your mother died I seriously considered selling it.'

Peter could still recall his exact words. 'You can't do that, Dad! You're the best hotelier on the island, all the others are constantly seeking your advice. You've improved and enlarged the place since Grandpa died, we even have our own bungalow and garden.' (This had been improved and extended over the years.) 'The hotel wouldn't be the same without you.' But what will happen now? wondered Peter.

Six months after his mother died, an attractive young woman staying at the hotel sought Matthew's advice. She had been left a substantial legacy by her grandmother and was considering buying a small hotel. Unfortunately she had no experience, and would probably have to arrange a mortgage on the property and rely entirely on the staff. Would it be a wise and sensible investment? Matthew had admired her honesty and suggested that she should work in the different departments of a hotel, thus acquiring some knowledge, and then reconsider. It was as an afterthought that Matthew told her that several of his staff were taking holidays, and asked if she would be prepared to help wherever necessary.

Three months later Maureen admitted that although hotel life was interesting she no longer wanted to own and run a hotel by herself, she would return to her previous position, as a secretary in the finance industry.

To Peter's and other people's surprise, and in spite of the age difference (she was 13 years younger than Matthew), Maureen became a frequent visitor to the hotel, joining them for an evening meal or Sunday lunch. She was always interested in Peter's education, sporting activities and other interests, and any alterations or improvements to the hotel.

Peter recalled the evening his father said that whilst he was always pleased to have his and Maureen's company, there were occasions when he felt lonely, but his expression had changed immediately when he, Peter, suggested, 'Why don't you marry Maureen?'

'Would you mind?'

'Of course not.'

That was a long time ago, reflected Peter. He had been pleased to see his father happy, running the hotel and later spending time with his new family. Peter had been in England when Monique was born and three years later, Ben.

Meanwhile, seated on the far side of the dining room, Roslyn said, 'I couldn't help overhearing your conversation with Peter. Has his father been ill? Was it a heart attack?'

'I only know Matthew's body was found on the beach, so it could be either,' replied Arnold.

'Peter was lucky to get a flight so quickly,' offered Esme.

Roslyn nodded. 'Especially this weekend with so many people coming for Monday's celebrations. I usually spend a morning or afternoon on that beach, and lunch at the hotel. I may have met Matthew on one of those occasions. Does Peter have any brothers or sisters?'

'Matthew was only 40 when Iris died,' said Arnold, and Esme quickly volunteered, 'He remarried when Peter was 16. Maureen was much younger– 13 years – and they had two children.' Esme paused as the main course was served and then resumed, 'They're both grown up, of course. Monique has inherited her father's flair for the hotel business and although he works in the bar and helps wherever necessary, Ben isn't very keen.'

'Neither is Noel, Monique's husband,' offered Arnold.

'In which department does he work?' enquired Roslyn, and then apologised, 'I'm sorry. I shouldn't be so inquisitive.'

Arnold smiled. 'We've told you about the family. It's only natural you're curious. Noel is the wine waiter. However, changing the subject, and although we've already asked you, will you be joining us for lunch on Monday?' Arnold named a well-known restaurant overlooking the harbour, and continued, 'We'll have a marvellous view of the afternoon activities, but you may prefer to go and mingle with the crowd.'

'Would you mind? I don't want to appear rude after enjoying your hospitality.'

'Don't be so ridiculous,' reproved Esme with a grin. 'You need to absorb some of the atmosphere to help with your article.'

'Thank you, I'll enjoy that. I hope to be out and about during the morning.' Roslyn glanced around the spacious and tastefully-decorated dining room. 'I recognise a number of residents, they were here last year, and whilst I know Peter Stenton returns for Liberation Day, I certainly haven't met him before.' Then, without pausing for breath, 'Ah, he's going. Pity, he's on his own, good company and not bad looking.'

'Really, Roslyn!' remonstrated Esme. 'You don't change. I remember you saying things like that at boarding school.'

'I'm only stating the obvious.'

*****

Peter was standing outside the hotel when Monique drew up and noting her pallor, quickly bent and asked, 'Would you like to come in for a drink, even tea or coffee?'

'No thanks. I'd prefer to go for a walk. But I can't stay long.'

'Right, let's go down to Castle Cornet.' Immediately Peter was around the bonnet and seated, when he continued, 'We can walk out to the lighthouse and afterwards you can go straight back to the hotel.'

Five minutes later Peter hugged Monique and slipping his arm through hers said, 'Let's go.' He had noticed that while she had always been slim, Monique was now thin and trying to keep his voice light he asked, 'Do you want to talk about Dad?'

'Yes, but firstly thank you for coming so soon. Do you know what happened?'

'I'm sure I don't know any more than you.'

'I still can't believe it. All day I've been expecting him to walk in, smiling and with a cheerful—' Monique faltered, '— cheerful greeting. He's walked that path every morning and evening for years. How or why did he fall? He was fine when he went out last night, what went wrong? Not realising who it was, Vere noticed a body on the beach.'

Peter nodded, not wishing to disclose the full content of his conversation with Vere and the inspector. Monique, Ben and Noel would learn all the details soon enough.

Monique stifled a sob. 'There's a new fence on the cliff side of the path and Dad was always very careful but somehow there must have been an accident. Inspector Le Tissier said that part of the path would be closed so they can thoroughly inspect the area.'

'They were there this afternoon'

'How do you know that?'

'I spoke to Inspector Le Tissier when I arrived at the hotel and Vere told me he saw a police presence there. Some of the residents told me that part of the path was already cordoned off.'

By now they had reached the lighthouse, and were looking across to Sark, Jethou and Herm when Monique moved closer to Peter. 'Noel was unsettled before this happened and Ben doesn't care about anyone except—'

'Is he upset about Dad?' interrupted Peter.

'Shocked, upset and went off to see Cheryl, his girlfriend this afternoon'

Peter noted the disapproval in Monique's voice and although curious did not pursue this, but turned to look at the harbour, the various types of craft, and said, 'Even though I come back two or three times a year, I do miss the island.'

'Why don't you come back?' but immediately she had suggested this, Monique apologised. 'Sorry, that's a selfish idea. You probably have friends you'd miss and whilst I'd be delighted, I can't vouch for Ben or Noel's welcome.' They were now walking back towards the Castle, and Monique resumed, 'There's no real reason for you to return. You've a successful business and you're too young to retire.'

'Would you really like me to come back? Surely you have friends of your own age?'

Monique shook her head. 'Not many. Noel doesn't like them or their husbands. When they do phone I'm usually busy. There's Vere, of course, who's always kind and thoughtful.'

'You haven't mentioned cousin Gerald. What do you think of him?'

'Good as a head waiter, otherwise he's rather reticent.'

'I know he's not married. Is there a girlfriend or does he have other preferences?'

'I don't know, even though he's been here five years. Dad rarely spoke about his brother. Did you ever meet Uncle Roger?'

'No, he left the island as a young man. I knew about him, of course, and that Dad never heard from him.' Peter recalled his father's unexpected phone call telling him that someone called Gerald had turned up, claiming to be his nephew. Gerald's arrival had coincided with an advertisement in The Caterer for a head waiter but he claimed he knew nothing about this. However he had recently worked in a Bournemouth hotel in that capacity, could he be considered for the position?

'It's worked out all right, hasn't it?'

Monique hesitated. 'Yes. Dad checked his references but apart from his reticence there's something odd about him.' By now they had reached her car and glancing at her watch she exclaimed, 'I must go!' and as she slid into the driving seat of her Mini, 'The next few days will be rather hectic. I only hope Noel and Ben pull their weight.'

Peter bent and spoke through the open window. 'I'd love to help but I know how they'd react. Anyhow, let me know when you have a few minutes free.'

'Thanks.'

Peter straightened, watched Monique drive off and began walking, thinking about his conversation with Inspector Le Tissier. He had been shocked to learn that some of the palings in the new fence had been sawn through and unable to suggest anyone who could be responsible. Peter recalled his reply to the next question, that he had no knowledge of any family financial problems. He had told Le Tissier that Arnold Levrier had been his father's Advocate, but that he did not know any details about Matthew's Will. At least I won't be involved in any unpleasantness about this, thought Peter, but quickly decided that this was an unfair reaction. Matthew had given him a substantial cheque when the opportunity occurred for him to buy the hotel he was renting. He knew that his father had inherited The Serena Beach Hotel, which was much smaller at that time, while Roger (Gerald's father), who wasn't interested in the hotel, had been left a generous legacy.

By now Peter had reached the Albert Pier and paused to look across at the church and, as he reached the pedestrian crossing, up Fountain Street at the partially demolished Market then, as he started walking again, his thoughts returned to his father's Will and the future of the hotel. He knew that Monique was capable of running it but doubted that Ben would want to continue working. He would probably prefer to have the money, however, could Monique afford to buy him out? All this was supposing the hotel had been left to them. And what about Noel? It was a pity he had never shown any interest in the management side. It was as Peter approached his hotel that he thought of Gerald again; he would probably be expecting something. Monique's suggestion that he should return to the island flashed through his mind, he could arrange to spend two or three months here if she needed his help and advice then, as he entered the foyer, Arnold Levrier was there and greeted him. 'You look worried, Peter. Do you want to tell me about it?'

Peter glanced into the bar, saw Esme and Roslyn deep in conversation but said, 'It can wait.'

'I don't think that's a good idea. There's an empty table in the corner, we can sit there.'

'I'm probably seeing problems that will never arise,' said Peter but briefly explained, noting Arnold's sombre expression.

'Obviously I can't discuss the contents of Matthew's Will but I am aware of Ben's dislike of work and Noel's attitude towards the hotel, that he only agreed to continue to work there to please Monique, and has been looking around for something else, for some time,' added Arnold.

Peter nodded and explained that he was prepared to remain in the island indefinitely. 'I'll do whatever I can to help Monique.'

'I have the feeling that Ben and Noel will try and persuade her to sell, in which case she'd certainly put up a fight.' Arnold paused while the barman placed their drinks on the table and then resumed, 'I've had numerous compliments from friends and clients who have dined or stayed there, consider it the best hotel in the island.' Then, picking up his glass, 'Would you really consider returning to the island?'

'Ben and Noel may not like it, might think I'd interfere with the running of the hotel but there's no good reason why I shouldn't buy a small property. I'd let it be known that the move is with a view to eventual retirement. I'd have to spend some time here supervising any alterations or improvements.'

Arnold gazed at Peter with admiration. He was obviously very fond of his half-sister and concerned about the hotel. 'What about your own hotel in England? Would you sell it?'

Arnold and Esme had stayed at Peter's hotel in the Cotswolds on many occasions, found it to be very comfortable and the food excellent.

'No. I can afford to buy something here and although Gareth is capable of running it on his own, I could commute whenever necessary.' Peter drained his glass. 'I'd love to buy you another drink but your wife and her friend are looking at us again.'

'Would you care to join us?'

'No thanks. It's been quite a day and I have several phone calls to make.'

As they both stood, Arnold was aware of heads turning in their direction. Peter was still well known locally. Several businessmen who had been dining, or had called into this popular bar for a drink, had come over to their table and expressed their condolences on hearing of Matthew's death. Arnold had also noticed that Roslyn kept glancing across the room. Was she curious as to why they had chosen to sit at a separate table, or interested in Peter? Then he said: 'If you hear anything new, phone me.'

'Thanks,' and with a smile to the two ladies who were still looking at them, Peter moved towards the door when an equally tall man turned away from the counter and called him by name. 'Hullo, Peter! It's great to see you, but not under the present circumstances.'

'Emile, Emile Girard! It's years since we met.' Peter and Emile had been friends since their school days at the College and usually met when Peter was on the island.

Emile drew Peter into the hall. 'I was sorry to hear about your Dad. I was out there last week and saw him. I thought he was looking remarkably fit, and looking forward to seeing you. Do you know what happened?'

'Le Tissier couldn't tell me very much but I do know that the post-mortem's tomorrow. As you probably know he was found on the beach.'

Emile nodded. He also knew that some of the palings in the new fence had been sawn through, and that Matthew Stenton's death was now being regarded with suspicion, and asked: 'Have you seen Monique? How is she?'

'Distressed and shocked. Says she prefers to be kept busy. I hope to see her again tomorrow if she has time to spare but it's going to be a hectic weekend.' Then, glancing at Emile, 'I thought you were going to retire.'

'Yes, but due to a shortage in the Force and the Queen's visit on Liberation Day, I'm staying on until the end of the season.'

'You're too young and fit to retire,' then with a grin, Peter continued, 'You'll probably find something else less strenuous.'

Emile looked thoughtful. 'If you were living here we could possibly set up our own business but this isn't the right time to voice my ideas.'

'Which I'd like to know. I'm here for eight days, at least. Join me for dinner.'

'It'll have to be the latter part of the week.'

'Friday?'

'Thanks,' and as he returned to the bar, Emile recalled Peter's final words: 'Monique would like me to come back.'

It was later, as he walked past Elizabeth College and continued up the Grange that Emile's thoughts turned from their school days to Iris Stenton's death. Although shocked and distressed, Peter had spent all his free time with his father, helping in the hotel wherever necessary. Peter had later accepted Matthew's second marriage and the two children, but that had been a long time ago.

He recalled that Monique had, after college, worked in France and London, returning to become Matthew's assistant manager, and wondered what would happen now. Emile muttered, 'I'll probably hear more on Friday when I see Peter.'

Meanwhile, Peter was in his room. He had phoned Gareth: everything was running smoothly. His thoughts turned to Ben who was a frequent visitor to The Sparrow's Nest with Cheryl Laval, who spent even more time there. He knew that this was one place where drugs were available and hoped that Ben was not being encouraged to indulge.

On the other hand, why had Emile – who was a Senior Officer involved with investigations into the importation and distribution of drugs – volunteered this information?

Chapter 5

After a restless night Peter's thoughts were again of Monique. He knew she was quite capable of running the hotel; it was Ben and Noel's attitudes that concerned him.

After Maureen's death, Matthew, aware of these, had met him on several occasions in England and on the island to discuss the future of the hotel. Peter knew that Arnold Levrier had been very helpful at the time and that now, following Matthew's death, he would do everything possible to help Monique. There was also Vere Hamilton who regarded Monique like a daughter, and would be prepared to help her in any way. At that moment the phone rang and Vere was asking, 'How are you this morning? Have you any plans for today?'

'I hope to see Le Tissier later this morning. Monique and Noel are coming in before me.'

'I can't believe that Matthew would fall, even though the fence—'

'Are you suggesting that he was pushed?' interrupted Peter and before Vere could reply, 'Were there any marks on his jacket? Bruises on his body?'

'Nothing obvious, but that's for forensic and the pathologist to find out. However, would you like to come to lunch?'

'Thanks, but not at your place. It's too near the hotel.' This was not exactly true; it was a 15-minute walk, and a wooded area between the two properties. 'I don't want Ben or Noel to hear I've been in the vicinity.'

'That's no problem.' Vere then named a restaurant on the West Coast, and a time.

*****

'Mr Reardon's on the phone for you, Monique. Are you taking any personal calls this morning?' As usual Pat's voice was quiet and polite.

Monique hesitated and then said, 'I don't really want to talk to anyone and certainly not Godfrey.'

'It's his father.' Pat, being local, knew most of the other hoteliers and certainly Howard Reardon who had come to the island eight years ago and bought a small hotel in a narrow but pretty valley.

'Very well,' and the next moment Monique heard a gruff 'Good morning, my dear. I've just heard the terrible news about your father. How are you? Is there anything either of us can do?'

'No thank you, Mr Reardon. Noel and Ben are here, and Vere is being very helpful.'

'That's good. What about Peter? I know he usually comes for Liberation Day. Is he here yet?'

'My God!' thought Monique, you can hardly move before it's general knowledge. 'Yes, Peter flew over as soon as he heard the news.'

'Pity he ever left the island.' Howard knew of Peter's success and continued, 'He's a first-class hotelier, like your father. We could do with more like him.'

'You have Godfrey,' said Monique.

'When he's not out at that nightclub place, or out in his boat. I should never have bought it,' muttered Howard. 'However, if there's anything we can do, just let me know.'

'Thank you.' Monique leant back in her chair, closed her eyes and scolded herself for unkind thoughts. Howard Reardon was 70, over-weight, short and bald with a pushy manner. He had owned a small hotel in the south of England but after his wife's death – she had managed and run this with a minimum of staff – decided to sell and move to the island. He had bought The Valley View Hotel, retained most of the staff and hoped that Godfrey would, in due course, take over from the capable young manager. Although this had happened, it was soon apparent not only to his father but to the staff and guests, in fact it became general knowledge, that Godfrey wasn't really interested in the hotel, and delegated most of his responsibilities to senior members of staff. But that was no way to run a hotel, thought Monique who, although it was early in the season, had heard complaints about the food and bedrooms. Relieved and grateful for her father's rule that any complaint, no matter how small, should be thoroughly investigated and remedied, Monique reached for another letter of condolence. She was amazed that so many people had sent a card or written a letter, blinking back tears, resolved that she would acknowledge each, personally.

*****

Monique was subdued and again close to tears as Noel drove back to the hotel. Neither spoke until they stopped outside the main entrance when Noel said, 'This weekend is ridiculously busy, far too many bookings. Can't you cancel some?' Monique sighed.

'No, we can't. We've already discussed this.'

'Surely, under the circumstances, people would understand?'

'We can't let our regulars down and we do have our full teams in the dining room and kitchen.' Monique opened the car door as she spoke.

'Greedy bitch,' muttered Noel, forgetting the car window was open.

Oh God, how am I going to cope? thought Monique as she blinked away threatening tears.

Although they both knew no arrangements could be made until after the inquest, Noel had again asked about the funeral and Ben about the Will, but now, as she crossed the foyer, it was Gerald who greeted her. 'How are you after that awful ordeal?'

'Apart from scratches and bruises there were no terrible facial injuries. Dad—' Monique faltered and blew her nose. 'Dad just had a surprised expression on his face.'

It was five minutes later as he placed the coffee tray on her desk that, although he had never met his cousin, Gerald asked, 'Does Peter know? Is he coming for Liberation Day as usual?'

'Yes.' Monique poured herself some coffee, waiting for Gerald to leave. She had no intention of telling him that Peter was here and that she had already seen him. Glancing up she noticed that he was fidgeting with his tie, and at the same time shifting his weight from one foot to the other, so she asked, 'Is anything wrong? Are you worried about the extra-busy weekend?'

'No, we're fully staffed, there shouldn't be any problems. It's—' Gerald hesitated. 'You will let me know about the funeral?'

'Of course. But we'll have to wait until after the inquest, to know that it can go ahead.'

Monique looked desolate and Gerald was about to move forward when the phone rang. Monique waited and he reluctantly left.

Vere's voice was gentle as he asked, 'How are you this morning, my dear?' and before she could reply: 'I'm meeting a mutual friend for lunch. Is there any hope that you could join us?'

'No, I'm sorry. I am rather busy.'

'That's a pity. It would do you good to get away from the place, even for a short time. Perhaps we can all get together another day.'

*****

Alone, Detective Inspector Le Tissier considered what had been noted, having been pointed out to him prior to the post-mortem. Matthew's hands were badly bruised as a result of vicious blows, and there was also bruising and dried blood on the top of his head.

Wooden splinters had been extracted from the wounds and these were being tested, as were other splinters taken from the palings. The marks on the right side of his jaw and neck indicated that he had been struck and that this had occurred before the other injuries were inflicted.

He then wondered who, apart from the family, would benefit from Matthew's death and considered the possibility of a less successful hotelier, a jealous husband (Matthew had still been an attractive man of considerable means), a member of the staff who thought he had been mistreated or even an extremely dissatisfied guest. He knew that Arnold Levrier was Matthew's Advocate. However, due to the long weekend, it would not be possible to see Levrier until Tuesday. On the other hand, Matthew had definitely been pushed and he would be very grateful for any information the Advocate could offer. As he searched for Levrier's private number, Le Tissier wondered if any guests at the hotel had left unexpectedly; this would have to be checked.

To Le Tissier's surprise, Arnold Levrier answered the phone immediately and agreed that Matthew's death, or the manner of it, was a terrible shock. Then, before any questions could be asked, Levrier continued, 'I'm sure you're curious about Matthew's Will. Obviously I can't tell you the contents. However, I doubt that any of the family could be responsible for this tragedy.'

'Do you know if he had any enemies, if there's anyone…?'

'No, Inspector, I don't. Matthew was highly respected by fellow hoteliers, local businessmen, his guests and staff. He'll be sadly missed. I'm glad and relieved, for Monique's sake, that Peter is here.'

Although it was irrelevant, Le Tissier asked, 'Have you seen him?'

'Yes, last night. Esme's school friend is staying at the same hotel, and had invited us for dinner. We arrived to find Roslyn chatting to Peter.' Arnold chuckled. 'Roslyn can never resist a good-looking man. However, if you have any other urgent questions I'll be home tomorrow or, as Matthew was such a good friend, I'll make time to see you on Tuesday.'

'Thank you, Mr Levrier. I wish everyone was as helpful as you.' Le Tissier's thoughts turned to the murder scene and the few items which had been found: spent matches, broken-up twigs, and a round brown button which could be an important clue. Tests were being carried out on dark navy-blue fibres which had caught on the lower branch of a tree, while a search had been instigated for the saw used to cut through the palings.

Owen Mahy, the handyman at the hotel, had been shocked to learn about this and Matthew's death, and accompanied Batiste to the shed when he discovered the saw he normally used was missing.

Other information had come in late the previous afternoon. An agile young constable, roped for safety, had climbed through the broken palings, examined and found bloodstains on the rocks which were on the other side of the fence, also minute particles of skin and fingernails, and it was there, wedged in the crevice of a rock, that Matthew's torch had been found. He had obviously let it go, maybe even jammed it into the crack before he grabbed the rock.

Inspector Le Tissier's expression was grim as he remembered Matthew's injured hands, fingers and other injuries – there was only one way to determine exactly what had happened: organise a reconstruction of the crime. It was approximately 36 hours since Matthew's death and, as he did not wish to postpone this until Tuesday, permission should be sought for this to be carried out the following day. Le Tissier picked up a length of paling carefully wrapped in polythene. This had been spotted in the undergrowth on the landside of the path some six feet down from the fence by an observant constable.

Le Tissier sighed. This could be an awkward case. There were so many people to question. In addition to the family there were the hotel guests and staff, but before he went out to the hotel he was due to see Peter Stenton who was already here, waiting.

*****

'Did you see Monique this morning?' enquired Vere.

'No. She and Noel had already left. Inspector Le Tissier probably realised it wouldn't be politic for us to be there at the same time.' Peter and Vere were seated on the terrace of a West Coast restaurant overlooking a wide sandy beach, and the former continued, 'Although he won't have a full report until later today, Le Tissier was very informative.'

Peter paused to drink his lager as Vere said, 'I can't understand why Matthew stood so close to the fence. He often stopped about there for a breather—'

'He wasn't the only person standing there,' interrupted Peter. 'The team found two sets of footprints when they were examining the path yesterday. They returned early this morning and Le Tissier was going out to the hotel as I left, to ask further questions.'

Vere leant across the table. 'What actually happened?'

'The first set of footprints belonged to Dad, the second set wasn't very clear.' Peter waited while sandwiches and cutlery were set down and then resumed. 'This isn't easy to say, but it's possible Dad was pushed.'

'So someone was there, waiting? That would account for the other footprints, but who? And why?' Vere's expression was grim. 'Matthew was lying face down when we found him but I suppose they do all sorts of tests.'

Peter nodded. He knew there were bruises on his father's hands and head, marks on his jaw and neck, and that a search was being made for the saw that had been used to cut through the palings, but didn't want to impart this knowledge and upset Vere any further. He also hoped the Inspector would not be too explicit when talking to Monique.

'The inquest will be Tuesday afternoon but you'll be advised about that.'

Vere nodded. 'Inspector Le Tissier has been out to see me – a very nice man – and asked that if I thought of anything relevant I should phone him. However, what's happening about the cliff path?'

'They're still searching the area but hope to open it to the public tomorrow.'

*****

'This is the list of guests who were here Thursday night, also their arrival and departure dates. As you will see they are all still here.'

Inspector Le Tissier scanned the list Monique had just handed him. 'Are you sure that no one left yesterday or this morning?'

'Yes. Pat Le Page, our head receptionist is always very accurate and realised the importance of this information. I checked the list myself.' Monique hesitated. 'Why do you need this, Inspector? Is there something else I should know?'

'We'll keep you advised of any progress we make. However, as I explained on the phone prior to this visit, your father's death wasn't an accident and we need to know if any of your residents or staff were on the cliff path and saw him, or anyone else, on Thursday night.'

'Is that really necessary?' protested Ben while Noel muttered, 'No one in their right mind would tell you that,' but Le Tissier ignored these comments. 'It's merely a routine exercise which will only take a few minutes of their time and I'm sure your guests will be quite prepared to cooperate.' Then, turning to Monique, 'Are they all in the dining room at the same time?'

Monique looked thoughtful and glanced at Noel. 'Are they?'

'One way or another, yes. Some eat early and go into town or for a walk, while others come in later. I would say they're all in between 8 and 8.30 p.m.'

Cooperation! thought Le Tissier, and aloud said: 'Thank you, Mr Latimer. Will you inform your head waiter about this, that we'll start at 8 o'clock?'

'That's Gerald,' said Monique. 'He'll probably complain that he wasn't consulted about this.'

'I will explain to everyone before we begin.'

Monique nodded, picked up and handed the Inspector another sheet of paper. 'This is the list of staff, their positions and the approximate time they've been with us.'

'Thank you, Mrs Latimer. We'll also have to question them, after the guests. Could you or,' glancing at Ben, 'perhaps your brother, tell them? As a matter of interest, how did the staff get on with Mr Stenton?'

'Very well. He was always very fair and when necessary, listened to and considered their grumbles and complaints.'

Le Tissier nodded. 'This shouldn't take long, however do you have any rooms we can use? There'll be three of us.'

'You can use this office. As you already know, it has direct access to the foyer.' Monique looked at Noel and Ben who both shrugged and the former suggested, 'Although the function room is already set up for Monday, we could close the dividing doors and these could be used.'

Le Tissier's gaze travelled from Monique to the two men. 'Thank you all for being so helpful. I'm sorry this is necessary but we do want to catch the person responsible as soon as possible.'

Monique nodded, 'Why would anyone do this?' almost a whisper then handed Le Tissier another list. 'These are the locals who were in the bar on Thursday evening,' and searching for another, 'and these are names of the people who live in the houses set back from the cliff paths on either side of the bay. We know most of them; they often lunch, dine or drink here. It's very handy – they don't need a car, can come down the cliff paths, or even walk along the main road and down the hill. It's not unusual to see them strolling through the grounds and talking to the residents who also like wandering around.'

'I'm not surprised. It's a lovely area.'

*****

'I still can't believe it wasn't an accident!' burst out Monique as the door closed behind Inspector Le Tissier and Sergeant Batiste. 'Who would do such a thing?' and when there was no comment, 'It must have been someone who knew Dad always had a walk at night.'

'Premeditated' was the word that flashed through her mind but wasn't uttered. 'I'll go and tell Gerald about the Inspector's visit this evening.'

Noel looked at Monique, amazed at her composure and competence. 'I'll see you at home in a minute.'

'I'll be longer than that. I must pop into town for some tights.'

'You usually have umpteen pairs.'

'I need some in a lighter shade,' and as Ben stood up, Monique said, 'Will you make sure the rest of the staff are told?'

'Why can't…' began Ben and then grudgingly, 'Oh all right. Then I must go and see Cheryl. She'll want to know what's happening.'

And I want to know what the Inspector told Peter, thought Monique as she drove up the hill. She was glad she always kept several pairs of tights in the car in case of emergencies but there was no need for Noel to know that. She had spoken to Peter whilst he was lunching with Vere, and arranged to meet him at Havelet Bay.

In the meantime, Sergeant Batiste was driving back to the station, talking incessantly.

'Fantastic hotel and what a setting!' he had commented on the gleaming white buildings of the hotel and family bungalows as he drove down the hill; he remarked on the variety of trees and shrubs and now said, 'I wonder what will happen now?'

'What do you mean?'

'I'm thinking about the hotel.'

'I expect Monique will be in charge. She's coping very well under the circumstances.'

'But will Ben and Noel stick it? Then there's the cousin, Gerald.'

'He seems reliable but we need to know more about him, and Noel Latimer.' Le Tissier's thoughts turned to Peter Stenton and he wasn't surprised when Batiste said, 'I wonder if Peter will ever move back to the island.' Although he knew that Peter was concerned about Monique, Ben and Noel's attitude and the future of the hotel, Le Tissier said, 'I doubt it. He has his own place in England.'

Batiste knew that the Inspector usually spent part of his holiday in England and now asked, 'Have you ever stayed there?'

'No, but I know several locals who do.' Le Tissier did not mention Arnold Levrier, who had spoken highly of the hotel in the Cotswolds, or the other Advocates and suddenly asked, 'What do you know about Ben's girlfriend, Cheryl Leval?'

'Her parents are very rich while she appears to be empty-headed, spoilt, selfish and—'

Batiste stopped abruptly as they had arrived at the station.

*****

'How are you?' Peter gazed at Monique with concern, noting her pallor.

'I know it sounds silly but I keep expecting Dad to walk in.'

'That's only natural.' They were standing on the Upper Walk looking across Havelet Bay and not wanting to upset Monique, Peter chose his words carefully. 'I realise it's early days, however do you think Ben or Noel will be prepared to take over as assistant manager?'

'No. They've both been unsettled for some time. Cheryl encourages Ben to do as little as possible, while Noel—' Monique shrugged her shoulders. 'There's something bothering him but he doesn't talk about it'.

'That's a pity.' Peter waited a moment and then asked, 'Has Inspector Le Tissier been out to the hotel today?'

'Yes. He...he told us that it wasn't an accident. He and two other officers are coming back this evening; he wants to know if any of the residents were on the cliff path at the same time. He also wants to question the staff.' Monique hesitated. 'Did Le Tissier tell you what happened?'

'No.' Peter had no intention of telling Monique about the second set of footprints – it was possible they had not been made on Thursday evening – or any other details that had been imparted. Instead he spoke of the general anticipation for Monday and, realising what the answer would be, asked: 'Is there any chance of you coming in to see some of the procession?'

'No. There'll be crowds everywhere and no parking. However, you'll come to the inquest?'

'Of course.'

Chapter 6

'I'll pop in to Dad's bungalow to make sure everything is all right,' said Monique as she adjusted her pearls.

'There's no need for you to bother about that.' Noel knotted his tie and reached for his jacket. 'It was clean and tidy, as usual, when you locked up after the police left yesterday afternoon.'

'I'll just look in. It's on our way to the hotel.' Monique glanced around the bedroom and picked up her handbag. Then, while Noel went to lock the doors from the kitchen into the garden and garage, she checked that the French window from the lounge onto the patio was also locked and didn't hear Noel mutter, 'We're too bloody close to the hotel.'

Five minutes later and with Noel reluctantly behind her, Monique pushed the lounge door open and exclaimed, 'Oh my God! I don't believe it!'

'What's happened?' Noel tried to push her aside. 'Let me see.' He looked over her shoulder at papers scattered over the floor, books pulled from shelves, smashed ornaments and other debris. 'Who did that? How did they get in?'

'I think we should stay where we are,' said Monique, at the same time reaching into her handbag. 'I'm going to ring Inspector Le Tissier.'

'He'll be down here presently.'

'I know,' and gazing at the open French window and broken glass she added, 'but I'm not going to leave.' Monique broke off abruptly and on learning that the Inspector had just left she was soon reporting the break-in and then said, 'Le Tissier, who's on his way, is being advised, but one of us should remain here until he arrives.' Noel looked at his watch and grumbled. 'Gerald will be annoyed if I'm not there.'

'You go on, but tell Pat I've been delayed. She can ring me on my mobile, if necessary.'

Alone, Monique glanced around the bungalow which had been extended and completely redecorated when her father remarried. (He, Iris and Peter had lived in a flat in the hotel but this had later been converted into De Luxe suites.) Relieved that nothing had been disturbed in either of the three bedrooms, Monique was standing in the kitchen and looking across at the dining area when a voice called out, 'Is anyone there?' and a young sergeant whom Monique recognised as Detective Sergeant Batiste appeared in the hall.

'Good evening, Mrs Latimer. You reported that entry had been gained by the French window, has anything been disturbed in the other rooms?'

'No, it's only the lounge.'

Monique indicated the scattered debris as Batiste stood in the open doorway and surveyed overturned chairs and small coffee tables, books, smashed photographs, while pictures hung precariously on the walls. The desk, a late Victorian Davenport had been the main target; drawers had been pulled out and hung askew, the lid raised, while sheets of paper or envelopes were scattered on the floor. Batiste knew that Matthew had been an astute businessman, practical, methodical and now said, 'I can't see a safe. However, did your father keep any cash, valuables or important papers here?'

'No.'

Batiste reached for his radio phone, made a brief call and resumed. 'I realise you haven't been in the lounge, however, can you see, standing here, if anything is missing?'

'I don't think so,' then glancing at her watch, 'what's going to happen? Is it necessary for me to stay here?'

'No. I've just arranged for the SOCO team, who were already alerted, to check for fingerprints or any other clues. Inspector Le Tissier will come straight here before going over to the hotel.'

'Do...do you think this could have anything to do with my father's—' Monique faltered and held on to the doorjamb.

Batiste looked at her with concern and asked, 'Are you all right, Mrs Latimer? Would you like to sit down? Shall I get you a glass of water?'

Monique shook herself. 'No thank you, I'll be all right. It's the shock of seeing all this, the thought that someone could break in. I'll have a little walk around the grounds before I go to the hotel.'

At that moment there was a slamming of car doors and voices, then, 'Evening, Sergeant Batiste. Where do you want us?' Two boiler-suited men appeared in the hall. Batiste greeted them, indicated the lounge, the open French windows, grains of sand in the plain dark blue carpet. He then turned to Monique. 'I'd like to see where we're questioning the residents.' This was unnecessary but Batiste was annoyed that Noel should leave his wife in a place which had just been ransacked. However it would be interesting to explore part of the extensive grounds.

It was a lovely evening, the sky was still blue and cloudless and couples were either sat or strolling. As they walked, Batiste noted and commented on the well-tended flowerbeds and various shrubs, causing Monique to say, 'You're very knowledgeable, Sergeant. Do you have a large garden?'

'No, unfortunately. But if I did, I wouldn't have enough time to look after it so I enjoy other people's gardens, and especially this, it's fantastic. Did your father design it?'

'He had some ideas, spoke to a friend who's a landscape gardener. Dad bought more land, and later on, more, and this is the result, with a stunning sea view.' They both stood for a moment watching a group of swimmers emerge from the sea; then turning, Batiste was amazed that the hotel, family bungalows, staff accommodation and grounds should occupy the whole of the wide valley. He was well aware that on both sides the land rose to several vantage points which were reached by steps and a path, still wooded on the land side.

In places the hedges gave way to grassy areas, gorse bushes and numerous wild flowers.

For a moment his gaze lingered on the wooded hill behind the attractive two-storey building, then he was aware of Monique speaking. 'Shall we make our way back to the hotel, Sergeant?'

'Yes, of course.' Batiste was pleased to see that Monique looked more relaxed and continued, 'You must be very proud of everything that your father accomplished over the years.'

'Yes, I am. He was already talking about next winter's programme: redecoration, refurbishment, etc., and asking my opinion.'

As her voice faded Batiste noticed that Monique had not mentioned Ben, or Peter, who he knew was still friendly with several of the older, more senior officers, and that he usually met them when in the island. It only took a few minutes to reach the hotel where Batiste noted that the large function room was situated at the far end of the main foyer, and adjacent to the dining room. Thanking Monique for her time and cooperation he retraced his steps to the main entrance, curious about the contents of Matthew's Will and reflecting that the whole set-up must be worth a fortune.

*****

Engrossed in chef's proposed menus for the forthcoming weekend, Monique was startled by a quiet cough and looked up to see Inspector Le Tissier who immediately apologised. 'I'm sorry to disturb you, however I've just come from Mr Stenton's bungalow. Can I ask you a few questions?'

'Now? As you can see, I'm relieving the receptionist, and we could be interrupted by the phone, or anything.'

She sounded so formal and businesslike that Le Tissier grinned. 'I'm prepared to risk it if you are,' and was rewarded with a sudden smile. It took only a few minutes for Le Tissier to learn that Vere was the only friend who visited Matthew at home and that Monique was unable to name or suggest anyone who would break in and create such chaos.

'Thank you.' Le Tissier paused for a second and then resumed. 'I'd be grateful if you could let me know, when you or your brother have had time to clear up, if anything is missing'

'Of course, but the French window – can I send the porter—?'

'No need,' interrupted Le Tissier. 'Batiste arranged for the broken pane to be boarded up. Someone will lock up and bring the keys back.' As he spoke, Batiste and another plain-clothed officer walked into the foyer. Three couples emerged from the dining room; two were immediately whisked towards the function room while the Inspector quickly turned and ushered the third couple into the office.

*****

'Who do you think broke in? Is anything missing?' asked Noel.

'I don't know, and that applies to both questions.' Monique finished her grilled lemon sole. 'As you saw for yourself, the lounge is a terrible mess.'

'Why didn't you call me, or at least tell me, at the time?' demanded Ben.

'Monique was too shocked and as you can see for yourself, is still upset,' snapped Noel.

They were sat at their usual corner table in the almost-empty dining room. The few remaining diners were lingering over their coffee, awaiting their turn to be questioned, while other guests could be seen strolling in the grounds.

'Are you all right?' enquired Gerald a few minutes later as he poured Monique's coffee and looked at her anxiously.

'Yes, thank you. I've got over the initial shock,' and as he moved away she looked at Ben and then Noel. 'I'm still wondering what the intruder was looking for. It's not as though Dad had anything of value or kept any cash in the bungalow.' Monique could still see photographs strewn over the floor and wondered what Peter would think. She had asked the Inspector to inform him of this latest development and vaguely heard Gerald, who had just returned to their table, say, 'If you need any help clearing the debris, let me know'

'We're quite capable of doing that.' Ben sounded curt, almost rude, and Monique said quickly, 'Thank you, Gerald.'

Then Pat was at her side. 'I'm sorry to interrupt. Mr Hamilton is on the phone. The Inspector has just finished and joined the two sergeants so I've switched the call to your office.'

'Thank you, Pat,' and before Noel or Ben could speak, Monique was on her feet and across the dining room. With a sigh of relief she lifted the receiver to hear Vere say, 'I had a walk as far as the hotel and noticed a police presence in the grounds. What's happening? Are you all right?'

Aware that Peter had already been informed and that this call was being made on his behalf, Monique recounted what had happened and added, 'I'm fine now. I'll probably sort out the papers and general debris tomorrow.'

'I'll be home all day. If you want to get away.'

So he could tell Peter, thought Monique. It was almost as though they were arranging an illicit rendezvous, all because Ben had infused Noel with his irrational jealousy.

'Thank you, Vere. It's very kind of you.' She had just replaced the receiver when the door was opened and Noel demanded, 'What did the old boy want?'

'He was out walking, saw the police cars and was concerned.'

'He shouldn't be so inquisitive.'

'I think you're forgetting, Vere was Father's friend and is also a family friend.'

Noel looked at Monique's pale but determined face. She really was a remarkable person; hard-working, a fine example to the staff, and he knew she would be upset to learn that he had been offered and wanted to accept a partnership in an estate agency. He realised this was not an opportune moment to tell her; the offer had been made the previous Tuesday and although he had some capital he was hoping she would provide the balance. Pushing these thoughts aside he asked, 'Is there anything I can do?'

Monique thought for a moment then, learning that the staff were now being questioned, she said, 'Perhaps a few words of reassurance with residents who are in the lounges or bar.'

Monique knew they would also have been asked if they had seen anyone in the vicinity of her father's bungalow and added, 'They must be wondering what's happened.'

'Right, if you think that's necessary, I'll go and speak to them.'

Alone, Monique sighed. She could foresee problems. She knew that Noel was unsettled and although he had not told her, she had seen him having an animated conversation with Nevill de Garis, a local estate agent. He had spoken of having his own business on numerous occasions but had no specific qualifications other than his wide knowledge of wines, and fluency in French and German. Her thoughts turned to Ben, who was besotted with Cheryl. Like her father, Monique had no patience with the spoilt, selfish young woman who, not working herself, would encourage anyone else to do the same. At the moment Ben did not have the money to indulge her whims and the idea that Cheryl could quickly dispose of Ben's inheritance made Monique shudder. However the Will would not be read until after the funeral.

A tap on the door and the appearance of Inspector Le Tissier interrupted these thoughts, but his voice was friendly. 'We've almost finished.'

'Did...did anyone see Dad on the cliff path?'

'No, however everyone was very cooperative.' The Inspector sat down and continued: 'The residents are still shocked, especially those who have been coming here for years.'

Monique nodded. 'Some of them arrange to meet up again – an annual reunion – and have asked about the...the funeral. I told them it all depends on the inquest.' Monique looked at the Inspector questioningly.

'Which will be Tuesday afternoon.' Le Tissier lowered his voice. 'I understand Peter will be staying on.'

Monique brightened. 'For which I'm very grateful.' And almost in a whisper: 'I shouldn't say this, but he's more caring and considerate than Ben.'

That's often the case.' Then, standing up, 'However, let me know if anything is missing from your father's bungalow. You could always leave a message.'

'Thank you.' Monique had also stood up and now asked, 'Do you think the intruder could be the same person who...who pushed my father?'

'I can't say. But in spite of the limited number of officers available, we'll continue with our enquiries and will be very grateful for any help or information received.' Then, as an afterthought, 'All the people living near the cliff paths have been questioned and were also very cooperative.'

Chapter 7

Monique gazed at the jumble of personal belongings amongst the upturned furniture and, although she knew there was no one in the bungalow, shuddered. How could anyone create such chaos? Then, steeling herself, she moved further into the lounge, righted and placed the chairs and tables to one side. Bending, she picked up the framed photographs which had been thrown haphazardly around the room and, with a lump in her throat, noted that the glass in most of them was cracked, and pieces of broken ornaments had been trodden into the carpet. Some ten minutes later, after she had hoovered up the tiny china fragments and sand, and dusted, Monique was startled to hear the front door open and a voice called out: 'Are you there, Monique?'

'Yes.' Monique gave a sigh of relief at the sight of Vere's familiar face and asked, 'How are you?'

'I'm still shocked at what's happened. However, I can see you're busy.'

'I've made a start.' Indicating the now open French window, she said, 'Owen replaced the broken pane of glass earlier and apart from that,' she waved towards a pile of papers, 'I'm almost finished'

'Is anything missing?'

'Not to my knowledge. The bedrooms and kitchen/diner weren't disturbed.'

'What do you think the intruder was looking for?'

'I've no idea. Dad didn't possess anything of great value, or keep any cash here, and his personal bank statements are in a small filing cabinet in his office;' and in the same breath:

'Would you like a coffee?'

'Can you spare the time?'

'Of course, but it'll be instant.' Seated in the kitchen, Monique told Vere that Arnold Levrier had phoned expressing his condolences and offering help or advice. 'I'll probably be glad of both after the Will has been read. The funeral arrangements can't be finalised until after the inquest' Monique looked thoughtful. 'The Inspector has returned Dad's keys so I'll have to see what's in his safe and filing cabinet.' With a shudder, 'I can't ask or expect anyone else to do that, not his private papers.'

'No, that's something you can't delegate; but later, if there is anything I can do, please let me know.' Vere reached for the broken frames, selected a photograph of a golden-haired little boy and sighed. 'I hadn't been in the island very long when Daniel and Melinda were killed. Although I didn't know Matthew very well at the time, he was pleased to talk to me, a stranger. He told me that Peter was heartbroken at losing his wife and only child, and I could see that Matthew was devastated.'

Monique nodded. 'We all were. Mother had always been very fond of Peter and I probably shouldn't say this, but I think that's when Ben started to get jealous. Peter had always been very popular when he lived in the island so people were naturally shocked to hear of his loss, constantly asking about him and sending messages.'

Vere nodded, hesitated and then asked, 'How is Ben coping?'

'Upset, angry, and no doubt, like me, expects to see Dad walk through...It hasn't stopped him spending all his free time with Cheryl.'

'And Noel?'

'He's upset but—' Monique paused, 'but I think there's something else on his mind. He's been unsettled for a while and Nevill de Garis has been down to see him twice.'

Vere knew de Garis to be a shrewd estate agent and offered, 'Perhaps he's trying to sell Noel a house so you could live completely away from the hotel?'

'That would be a complete waste of money, especially when we have a lovely bungalow and are here if needed.'

'Maybe Noel resents that—'

'He doesn't really like working in the hotel,' burst out Monique. Seeing Vere's surprised expression, she elaborated: 'He wanted to work for one of the travel agents last year. He suggested we should buy an apartment, that I should work in the finance industry, and was furious when I flatly refused. Then the offer of the job in question didn't materialise which upset him, and he's still restless.'

Vere looked thoughtful. 'Perhaps it would be better if he did work somewhere else.'

At this Monique looked aghast. 'How can you say that? I need him here, not only to work – I need his support. I know I can't rely on Ben.'

Vere knew this to be true and nodded. 'Take no notice of me. I should keep my opinions to myself.'

'I shouldn't have burdened you with my worries, thank you for listening.' Monique slid off the kitchen stool and rinsed the two mugs.

'I'm glad you did, and I hope you feel better for it. And now I should be on my way.'

As he reached the front door, Vere suddenly asked, 'Will you be able to see Peter this afternoon?'

'I'll try.'

*****

Monique was about to push all the papers that were now on a coffee table into a large envelope when she heard the front door open again, and picking up a dangerous-looking paper knife, she called out sharply, 'Who's that?'

'It's only me. I wondered if you needed a hand;' then Gerald was standing in the doorway, gazing around the now-tidy lounge, 'but I see you've done it all.'

'Yes.' Monique was glad she had slid the knife into the envelope; she didn't want Gerald to know she had been scared, and quickly added, 'Thank goodness this was the only room disturbed'

'You're an amazing person.' Gerald looked at Monique with admiration, and then around the tastefully-furnished room. 'You've had to cope with your father's death and now this. Couldn't Ben have cleared up?'

'Probably, but I preferred to do it myself.'

Gerald's gaze lingered on the garden. 'It's incredible what Uncle Matthew achieved: extending the hotel and building these bungalows for the family. It's a pity my father never came back to the island, even on holiday, or kept in touch. We could have met as children.'

Creep, thought Monique, he's after something; and then heard Gerald say, 'In fact, he rarely spoke about it. He was probably settled and happy in England. Anyway, I must get back.' Gerald paused, but only for a moment, and continued 'You work too hard. You should delegate some of the responsibility – there's enough of us: Ben, Noel and myself. We'd all be happy to relieve you of the onerous chores, supervising the staff, ordering—'

'It's too early to think along those lines.' Monique picked up the large envelope. 'We have to take each day as it comes.'

*****

'He's ingratiating and for some reason I don't trust him.' Monique looked at Peter. 'Did you ever meet Uncle Roger? Did Dad ever say much about him?'

'No.' Peter looked thoughtful. 'Wait a minute,' and then, 'He died a long time ago. I was back in England after my two years working abroad. It was whilst I was an assistant manager in Cheltenham. Dad didn't hear until several weeks later, but I can remember thinking that if I'd known, I could have attended the funeral.'

'These were also on the floor.' Monique tipped three photographs on to the table. 'Do you recognise anyone?'

'That's Dad.' Peter first indicated a teenager whom Monique had recognised as her father, then an older man: 'That was Grandpa,' and finally, 'He must be Uncle Roger. He was four years younger than Dad.'

'He certainly had protuberant ears.' Monique shook her head. 'Gerald doesn't look a bit like him, whereas, apart from your height – you're a bit taller – you do resemble Dad.'

'Strange you should say that. It's amazing the number of people who have said the same thing, and I've only been here two days.' Peter paused. 'They're all very shocked to hear the police are involved, but I can't answer their questions.'

'It's the same with the residents, most of whom are regulars. In a way they're more interested in what's happening around here than tomorrow's programme, although they're organised as to where they hope to see the Queen, and the procession.'

'It'll probably be quiet out here,' said Peter, at the same time picking up the envelope and tipping out the remaining photos. Then, pushing the paper knife aside, 'My God! That's an ugly-looking weapon. What's it doing here?'

Monique briefly explained and reverted to the Liberation Day programme. 'We're fully-booked for early lunches and have several small parties booked for dinner – not that anyone will be able to see the fireworks from here.'

'They'll probably go back into town or some might walk along the cliff path to one of the vantage points.' Then, as Monique glanced at her watch, 'How are things with Ben and Noel?'

Monique had already mentioned Gerald's idea of delegation, and now said, 'Just imagine either of them in charge of staff or ordering. Ben is always keen to get away to see Cheryl, while Noel—'

'—is still unsettled. Would it help if I talked to them?'

'Thanks, but no.' Monique stood up. 'I'm sorry I can't stay longer,' and looking at Vere who was sat in the shade with the Sunday papers: 'Thank you for the coffee.'

'You know you're always welcome.'

Vere watched as they walked to the gate and once again reflected it was a pity there was so much discord. Then as Peter returned and sat beside him, Vere found himself saying, 'It's not going to be easy for Monique.'

'I realise that. While I know the solution, I don't think some of the family would like it.'

'Maybe not, but it would solve most of the problems.'

'But I haven't said anything—'

'It's not necessary.' Vere leant forward. 'It's obvious to me and anyone with any sense: you return to the island, take over and let Ben and Noel do their own thing. You have the same temperament as Matthew, can handle staff and you know some of the older members, can cope with a crisis, while the locals and regular guests would be delighted.'

'You haven't mentioned Monique or what effect this would have on her marriage.'

'No.' Vere looked thoughtful. 'As you know, I'm very fond of Monique. I've spent the last two days thinking about her, what would be best for her, the future of the hotel and all of you. But it's none of my business.'

'That's not true, I really appreciate the time you're spending with me, your support and advice, and I know Dad valued your friendship. He told me that on numerous occasions. However, I don't think Noel would like Monique being at the hotel, and she wouldn't be very happy away from it; he'd resent her being there in the evenings and at the weekends.'

'Could Matthew's Will clarify the situation?' asked Vere.

'It's no good looking at me. I know Dad changed his Will after Maureen died. I don't expect anything. He looked after me financially a long time ago, but he could have changed it.'

Vere nodded and Peter resumed. 'You probably know Maureen left Monique and Ben substantial legacies; however I understand Ben is always short of money. He recently bought an expensive car and I wouldn't be surprised if, due to Cheryl's extravagant taste, he's spent most of the money Maureen left him.' Peter paused for a moment and then: 'I realise this sounds unkind but I feel that, with Cheryl's help, Ben would soon get through whatever Dad left him.'

'Yes, and that did worry Matthew. He often spoke about this, that he would like to see Ben married, with a family, someone to carry on the name.' Vere looked at Peter and sighed. 'You've had more than your share of sorrow without this happening. I wish there was something I could do, some way I could help the police.'

'You're here and Monique knows she can call on you at any time. As far as I'm concerned, that's the most important thing.'

*****

'Did you have a nice walk?' Noel glanced up from the Property Section of The Sunday Times as Monique leant back on the second sun-lounger.

'I don't know if you'd call it that. I wanted to see where…where Dad fell. It was a stupid idea. I could only go a little way up the path. I'd forgotten it was cordoned off.' Monique did not say that she had stood, gazing beyond the blue and white tape, amazed at the scene of activity until, her presence noted, Sergeant Batiste approached her.

'You know you shouldn't be here, Mrs Latimer. I suggest you turn back or take that little path which leads to some of the houses – forget that you've seen anyone in this area this afternoon.' Monique knew she had stared at him when he smiled. 'It's nothing for you to worry about.'

Monique shuddered as she recalled his parting words: 'There's no need for anyone to know we're here,' and said, 'I still can't believe that someone would do such a thing.'

His attention focused on the article, Noel muttered, 'Accidents do happen,' and was startled when Monique exclaimed sharply, 'But it wasn't an accident! You heard the Inspector say that some of the palings had been sawn through, and Owen's saw is missing.'

'He's probably mislaid it. He's always doing that.'

'No, he isn't. Owen's the best handyman and decorator Dad's had for years.'

Studying the hotel advertisements on the back page of the Travel Section, Monique was surprised when Noel suddenly asked: 'I suppose Peter is here for Liberation Day? Does he know about Matthew?'

'Of course, and like all of us he's devastated.'

'Will he be staying for the funeral? Is he coming to see us?'

Monique dropped her paper and stared at Noel. 'Why the sudden interest?' But curbing her rising anger, she said, 'Of course he'll be here for the funeral, whenever that is. But why should he come here? Neither you nor Ben have ever suggested it.'

'You or Matthew—'

'I wish you'd stop calling my father by his Christian name. I didn't like it when he was alive and it sounds worse now he's—' Monique faltered, '—dead.'

'I'm sorry, old girl. I didn't mean to upset you.'

'And that's another thing, stop calling me that! I do have a name.'

Noel was about to say, 'And it's a mouthful. Whose idea was it to call you that?' but quickly stopped and watching Monique turn to the front page, he silently admired her russet hair, refined features and slim — no, she was too thin for her height – figure; then she was saying: 'What do you think about asking people back here after the funeral?'

For a moment Noel stared at her. 'You mean a wake?' and when she nodded, 'What does Ben think?'

'I haven't asked him. The idea only just occurred to me.'

'It'll mean more work for the staff.'

'I realise that, and that a lot of people will probably attend the funeral but I'm sure, under the circumstances, the chefs and other staff won't mind.'

'Did Peter suggest this?'

'No, why should he?'

'So he can appear as the prodigal son?'

At this, Monique stood up, almost shaking with anger. 'Really, Noel! You'd take a first prize when it comes to saying something horrible and which I couldn't ever forget.'

From her tone and expression, Noel could see he'd gone too far. 'You shouldn't take me so seriously. Sit down and relax.'

'How can I when you talk like that and Ben rushes off to Cheryl? We need to be a team, especially at a time like this, and it's only the beginning of the season.'

The hotel, always the hotel, thought Noel. He'd been hoping to tell Monique about his plans to become an estate agent, and ask for a loan. Instead, and although he knew the minister from the Town Church had spoken to Monique, he asked, 'When do you think the funeral will be?'

'We can't make any arrangements until after the inquest; Reverend—' Monique hesitated, named the minister in charge of the church and resumed, 'he and the undertakers realise that and are being very cooperative. Obviously it will be at the Town Church, we were all christened and confirmed there, and we were married there.'

'Is it necessary for all of us to attend the inquest?'

'I'd certainly appreciate your support, and I'm sure Ben feels the same. Vere will be there as he found—' Monique faltered, '—and identified Dad. No doubt Inspector Le Tissier and Sergeant Batiste will be there.' Monique shivered, 'I'm dreading it,' and waited for Noel to comfort her, but when no response was made, she muttered under her breath: 'How am I going to cope?'

*****

Sergeant Batiste waited until Monique was out of sight then, moving into the centre of the grouped officers and looking at the young constable who had gone through the fence on Friday afternoon and was again securely roped, he asked, 'Are you ready?'

'Yes, sir,' and turning to a tall well-built sergeant he said, 'You remember the instructions Inspector Le Tissier gave you?'

'Of course.'

'Right, action!'

The roped constable walked the short distance, paused in the middle of the path and gave a start as the sergeant moved from the shade of the trees, gestured towards the fence and then the beach. The constable, the same height and build as Matthew Stenton, moved towards the fence, closely followed by the sergeant who pointed to the beach, at the same time moving behind the constable, pushing him. The constable swung round, the sergeant picked up a loose paling previously torn from the fence and struck out, again pushing; then, after the constable had disappeared, leant across the broken fence and again hit out.

Chapter 8

'What's the matter, why are you looking so worried?' Esme Levrier gazed at her husband, noting that although he was still holding the Financial Section of the Sunday Times he wasn't reading, and repeated the question.

'I've been thinking about Monique and what will eventually happen to the hotel.'

'Surely it will be left to Monique and Ben?' hazarded Esme, and then amended this to: 'But being Matthew's Advocate, you already know.' Esme leant forward to touch

Arnold's arm. 'I'm not expecting you to tell me any details but obviously you're very concerned, and I'm not surprised. Ben's attitude to work and his relationship with Cheryl Laval is general knowledge while Noel's friendship with Nevill de Garis is another source of gossip.'

'I know. Matthew was worried about Cheryl's influence and could have amended his Will without my knowledge but no one expected this! I hope the Chief is giving Le Tissier everyone he can spare and I'm sure Emile Girard, who was talking to Peter on Friday night, would like to be involved but he's dealing with the drugs problem.'

'They won't be able to do much tomorrow due to the Royal Visit and Liberation Day.'

Then with a sudden change of subject, Esme continued: 'I do hope my outfit for the service at Beau Sejour is suitable.'

Arnold smiled. 'It's very smart and you'll look lovely, as always. Now, if you don't mind, I'd like a cup of tea.'

However the Stenton family and Serena Beach Hotel were still uppermost in Esme's thoughts as she sat down again and sipped her tea. 'Is Peter aware of the situation at the hotel?'

'He saw Monique briefly yesterday and may have done so today. He was going to see Vere Hamilton again so Monique might go for a walk in that direction.'

Esme sighed. 'It's a pity Ben is so jealous of Peter and turned Noel against him. It's at a time like this they should all be together. Peter's had enough sadness in his life, his mother Iris dying when he was 14, then losing Melinda and Daniel in that awful accident. If he wasn't so involved in running his lovely hotel in the Cotswolds he might have remarried. He's still very handsome.'

'Esme!' The surprise in Arnold's voice made his wife laugh. 'That's what Roslyn says, and wonders why she's never met him before.' 'I thought she was a career woman.'

'She is, but these days they're after both. Anyhow, they're having dinner together tonight,' and at another gasp from Arnold, Esme continued: 'Roslyn's very interested in his hotel and she'll be good company.' Then, as the idea occurred to her, Esme rushed on: 'I'm sure Roslyn would love to meet Monique. Perhaps I could suggest something?'

'It's not going to be an easy week for Monique, especially if there's a funeral to arrange.'

'I'm only thinking of coffee, something to get her away from the hotel. Roslyn is always interviewing people for travel features or her own books.' Esme finished her tea and stood up. 'I won't be long.' Five minutes later she returned. 'Ros thinks it's a super idea and if Peter agrees will ring Monique tonight.'

Arnold shook his head in amazement. 'You do love organising people's lives.'

'Only if it's going to help someone.'

'That's all right as long as it doesn't have any unpleasant repercussions.'

*****

'Could I speak to Mrs Latimer, please? It's Roslyn Tempest calling.' The low but husky voice immediately aroused Monique's curiosity — she had read most of Roslyn's articles and two of her books but brushed this aside. She was relieving Pat for her supper break and said, 'Monique Latimer speaking. How can I help you?'

'I realise this is a busy and sad time for you, however I would like to meet you to discuss your views on tourism. Could you join me for coffee one morning?' And when Monique hesitated: 'I know my readers would be very interested to read about you – one of the most capable and successful hoteliers in the island.'

'I wouldn't claim to be that, however I'd be delighted to accept your invitation.' Monique suddenly realised it would be a change to meet someone new. 'Thank you.'

'That's fantastic. Would 11 o'clock Friday morning, here at my hotel be convenient?'

'Yes.' Monique hoped that the funeral could be arranged for Wednesday or Thursday, and the reading of the Will before the weekend. It was 10 minutes later, after talking to different residents who expressed their condolences, that Monique realised that Roslyn was staying at the same hotel as Peter and wondered if they had met. Peter had not mentioned her but, under the circumstances, that was understandable. As she moved, Monique tried to wriggle her toes and immediately knew that her new sandals were too tight and she would have to change into a more comfortable pair when Pat returned. As she regarded the practical low-heeled beige sandals, Monique wondered – and not for the first time – if she shouldn't be wearing a dark dress and shoes; then, seeing Pat, asked: 'Do you think I should be wearing a black dress or suit?'

'Oh no, I'm sure Mr Stenton wouldn't want you to do that.' Pat paused for a moment and then asked, 'Should I call you Mrs Latimer now you're in complete charge?'

'Good Heavens, no!' Monique smiled at Pat affectionately. She had worked for them for 15 years, and Monique regarded her more as a friend than an employee. Lowering her voice, she said: 'I'm not sure what's going to happen.'

Pat nodded, hesitated and then said, 'I know I shouldn't offer advice, but couldn't Ben do more?'

'I agree, but I don't think that's very likely. However I must go and change into another pair of sandals.' It was as she pushed a wad of tissue paper into the offending left sandal that, glancing out of the bedroom window, Monique noticed a wooden handle protruding from under the privet hedge. Curious, but aware that she probably shouldn't touch it, Monique ran into the lounge, unlocked and went out through the French window, across the tiny lawn and bent down. However, the dull glint of steel made her straighten and turn back towards the bungalow.

Five minutes later Monique sank into an easy chair and gave a sigh of relief. She had spoken to Detective Sergeant Batiste (Inspector Le Tissier being unavailable), who was on his way, phoned Vere who would inform Peter, and told Noel. His reaction had been:

'What is it? Who put it there?' whereas Vere had immediately enquired if she was all right and was there anyone lurking nearby? After assuring him that it hadn't been there that afternoon — she or possibly Noel would have noticed it when they sat in the garden, and there was no one about when she came across from the hotel — the residents were all dining.

'Yes, that's definitely it! ' exclaimed Owen Mahy a few minutes later as they stood on the patio and Batiste, wearing latex gloves, held the saw and queried, 'How can you tell?'

Owen pointed to some figures on the handle. 'Although there's a notebook where we enter whatever new tools are purchased, I always put the date on it.'

'That's very helpful, but we'll have to wait for the experts' opinion. They already have some of the sawn-off palings and will be able to tell us if this was the saw that did the damage.'

Monique was grateful that Owen had left his motorbike by the shed and that Sergeant Batiste and the two men who were now searching the ground beneath and the hedge itself had arrived in an unmarked car. The grounds and all their private gardens had already been searched, however the remainder of the small garden and surrounding area would later be scrutinised again. Batiste now slid the saw into a large clear plastic bag, at the same time thanking Owen for his cooperation, and added, 'This will also probably be used as evidence.'

'But I'll—' started Owen when Monique forestalled him: 'Don't worry, we'll buy you a new one.'

'Thanks,' and looking at Sergeant Batiste, Owen asked: 'Is that all? Can I go?'

'Yes, but we'll need your fingerprints, for elimination purposes.'

'Who could have put it there? How did this person get into the garden?' asked Monique.

'The front and back doors were locked.'

'It's possible the saw was pushed under the hedge from the outside.' Batiste nodded approvingly as the two boiler-suited men began their finger-tip search of the lawn, explained that although none were obvious they were feeling for any shoe imprints, and said that he was going to walk around the perimeter. 'However I'll make sure everything is secure and lock up here if you want.' Then, as the phone rang, Batiste indicated that she should answer it. 'It's probably for you. If it's Mr Hamilton or Peter you can bring them up to date.'

In spite of Batiste's presence and assurance, Monique still seemed apprehensive but a moment later her expression and voice changed as she exclaimed: 'Peter!' and then, 'Yes, I'm fine, thank you.'

*****

'It was only a brief conversation but it helped her,' said Sergeant Batiste later that evening.

'Peter and Vere Hamilton are certainly concerned about her,' commented Inspector Le Tissier. 'However, was it the missing saw?'

'Yes, it was probably pushed under the hedge from the other side. Owen Mahy was very helpful, while Monique and Noel were certain it wasn't there when they were sat outside this afternoon. The saw was obviously put there between them going across to the hotel and Monique returning to change her shoes.'

'Which was very opportune but we need a witness.'

*****

Noel waited until their main course had been served and then asked, 'What's going to happen to the saw now?'

'It will have to be checked for finger…'

'Why was it left under our hedge?' interrupted Noel, and without pausing for breath: 'Did you see anyone near our bungalow when we came across?'

Monique glanced around the dining room, noting there were only a few diners still eating, and continued: 'The residents were either in their rooms or in the bar having a drink before dinner.'

'We certainly don't want the police out here questioning anyone tomorrow.'

'That won't happen. They'll all be on duty in town.'

'Is everything satisfactory?' enquired Gerald, as he approached their table. Monique looked up at her cousin. 'Yes, it was very—' but before she could finish Gerald burst out:

'I saw Sergeant Batiste drive away in an unmarked car. Why was he here?' but before Monique could reply he was called away.

'I noticed you hesitated. What would you have told him?' asked Noel.

'Not the truth but he'll hear about it sooner or later. I don't want any of the staff upset or anything to go wrong tomorrow.'

Noel nodded. After his faux pas of that afternoon he had hoped to tell Monique about his opportunity to join Nevill de Garis in business but decided that, once again, this was not an opportune moment. However, he knew that Nevill was getting impatient, whilst he was anxious that Monique should agree to let him have the necessary capital…

Chapter 9

Peter stood at the bottom of St Julian's Avenue looking towards the 100ft mast recently erected on the roundabout as part of the Sea Guernsey 2005 celebrations. With the flags flying in the north-easterly wind it was an impressive sight but, once again, Peter's thoughts turned to Monique and the discovery of the saw.

He had been grateful to receive Vere's phone call about this and later, on learning that Roslyn had arranged to meet Monique, blurted out, 'That must have been before she found it.' Encouraged by Roslyn's spontaneous: 'What's happened now?' he had briefly explained and agreed that he was concerned about Monique.

'She must be a very special person. Esme, Arnold and this older gentleman, Vere Hamilton are also all concerned about her.'

'She is, but then I'm probably prejudiced. Dad was so thrilled when she was born and again, years later, when she was so interested in the hotel.'

Roslyn had nodded, saying that although she had visited the hotel on different occasions, noting and approving the improvements, she had never met Monique and looked forward to meeting her on Friday. As he crossed the road and looked over the careening hard wall, Peter considered that the high sand castle, which was more than 10 feet tall, was an amazing structure. Walking towards the Crown Pier and the marina Peter wondered where he, and possibly Roslyn, should stand to enjoy a good view of the Chevauchee and the cavalcade that would follow. The town side of the Esplanade would later be in the shade and, with the cool breeze, probably chilly. Although Arnold had booked a window table, thus ensuring a good view, Peter had already told him he would prefer to join the crowds while Roslyn, eager to absorb the atmosphere for the article she was writing, had done the same.

'It was a wonderful occasion, truly memorable for all those who attended the service,' said Arnold and seeing Peter's sombre expression added, 'Matthew was so looking forward to coming with us. He would really have enjoyed it. There'll obviously be a full report in The Press tomorrow so I won't bore you with the minutiae, however the theme was reconciliation — the Queen presented an honorary OBE to the Mayor of Biberach in recognition of his services for British-German relations.' Arnold, who had chosen to sit next to Peter rather than talk across the table, finished his first course and glanced at Esme, his wife, who was regaling Roslyn with what he considered frivolous chatter.

'We had to be in our places in Beau Sejour's Sir John Loveridge Hall quite early and saw people we hadn't seen for years.' Esme had already commented on the Queen's appearance and charm as she met the evacuees, deportees and those who had remained in the island during the Occupation; and on the numerous hats and elegant outfits.

Roslyn nodded. 'It must have been very emotional for the elderly people, however I'm looking forward to the procession and soaking up the atmosphere.' The main course had now been served and the conversation consisted mainly of comments about the delicious food when Esme suddenly asked, 'Are you going to watch the fireworks tonight?'

'I hope so but I'm not sure where the best viewing place is. The area around the harbour and marina will be very popular.'

'Yes.' Esme glanced at Peter, 'Are you seeing Monique today?'

'No. They'll all be very busy but did I hear you mention fireworks?'

'Yes, however I don't think Arnold and I will come into town for them. Parking would be difficult unless we went to the look-out near Les Cotils, or the Belvedere Field.' Then, as the plates were removed, Esme asked, 'Would you like a sweet, coffee or do you want to find yourselves a place amongst the crowds?'

'It seems awfully rude if we go now,' said Roslyn.

'Nonsense. We were delighted to have your company. I'll look forward to hearing your impressions.'

'Thank you.' Roslyn bent to kiss Esme's cheek. 'I'll see you for coffee tomorrow morning,' while Arnold said quietly, 'It's the inquest tomorrow, isn't it?'

'Yes. Vere and I are going together. I'm sure you'll hear the outcome. However I'll be in touch.'

As they emerged from the restaurant Peter noticed that people on the opposite side were moving about, hoping to gain a better viewing place. Taking Roslyn's arm he urged her across the road where they found ample space. Although Roslyn wore a warm but smart jacket he asked, 'Will you be warm enough?'

'Yes thanks,' and looking to the right she said, 'Oh look at those horses and the colourful uniforms.'

Peter nodded. 'It's a re-enactment of the 1813 La Chevauchee. Have you heard or read about them?'

'Yes. They used to inspect the hedges and roads.' Then, as they came closer, Roslyn said, 'I must say, John Bull's and all the other uniforms are very impressive.'

'Yes,' and indicating, Peter commented: 'They're two local politicians who have somehow acquired and are wearing clothes relating to the Regency period.'

Roslyn watched, fascinated, as a variety of vehicles — jeeps, trucks, bicycles and motorbikes slowly drove past. Heading this was a local man who had taken on the role of Churchill, complete with cigar and famous victory sign. Later, as a Bugatti and several Rolls Royces (which had been brought over especially to take part in this procession) drove past, Peter remarked, 'They're certainly in marvellous condition, aren't they?'

The cyclists on their bikes also earned cheers and encouraging comments from the crowds as did the bands and marching of the veterans. Later, after she watched the Red Arrows streak across the sky, Roslyn glanced at Peter, smiling her appreciation that he had suddenly spun her round to face the harbour and beyond. 'I understand they're here in September for Battle of Britain Week — that there's an air display over the harbour.'

'Yes. The highlight is when two of the Red Arrows, approaching from north and south, pass each other, then soar up over the cranes and Castle.'

'I'd like to see that. I must make a note in my diary, perhaps fly over for a few days.'

'A number of people return every year for the event. September is always a popular month.'

Roslyn turned to look up at Peter. 'Do you come back?'

'Not every year but I had intended to come this September, mainly to see my father.'

Peter's expression became grave. 'But at the moment I can't plan ahead. I may spend more time here this summer,' and when Roslyn looked curious, Peter continued: 'Unless the police find the culprit quickly, and although I don't live here, I may be able to help them with their enquiries. And while Monique is very capable of running the hotel, I am concerned about Ben and Noel.'

'What do you mean?' Then, on learning that neither were really interested in the hotel, Roslyn reflected that Monique, who she was meeting on Friday, might inadvertently impart something that was relevant.

Chapter 10

Detective Inspector Le Tissier pushed the post-mortem report aside and considered what progress had been made. The faint marks on the back of Matthew's jacket and the reconstruction on Sunday afternoon had established that he had been pushed, but had turned when he was hit by a length of paling.

Although this had only been mimed at the reconstruction, the young constable, suitably clothed, had gone through the fence and, wearing gloves and helmet, grabbed the rocks when the sergeant, still using the same weapon, aimed at his hands and head. The strength of the first blow, which had left marks on his jaw and neck, had sent Matthew through the weakened fence. He had obviously grabbed the nearby rocks, but the assailant had hit Matthew's hands and then his head until he relinquished his hold. The splinters extracted from Matthew's injuries matched those taken from the length of paling found in the undergrowth — this was now being tested for fingerprints.

One set of footprints was definitely Matthew's but the second set, which had been defined when the perpetrator stood under the trees, had become confused when standing near the fence and behind Matthew. These had yet to be identified as belonging to the same person. A button and fibre from a navy blue garment had also been found in the immediate vicinity while Monique had noticed, on Sunday evening, that a saw had been pushed under her hedge. This had been identified by Owen, the handyman and was now being tested for fingerprints. He knew that Owen, who locked the shed at six o'clock when he finished work, had not used the saw since Tuesday afternoon. He had been working in the hotel on Wednesday and Thursday, using other tools and had not noticed if the saw was in its usual place. The gardeners had been working in different parts of the grounds so did not know if anyone had been near or entered the shed. So it could have been taken at any time on either day, thought Le Tissier, then looked up as Sergeant Batiste entered. 'I've just read your report again. You certainly had a busy Sunday.'

'Yes, it was rather eventful.' Seeing another report on the desk, Batiste asked: 'Do you know how the saw got there?'

'Although the handle was close to the Latimers' garden it was probably pushed under the hedge from the other side.'

'Monique and Noel were both certain it wasn't there when they sat outside,' said Batiste, and after stating the time that they had left for the hotel, continued: 'It must have been put there between then and when Monique returned to change her shoes.'

'Which was unusual,' and in the same breath Le Tissier continued: 'Why did the perpetrator leave it there? Did he know the Latimers lived in that particular bungalow, or is there some special reason?' Then before Batiste could speak, 'Unfortunately there were no footprints in the grass between the path and the hedge, and while I can see you're bursting with a suggestion, I can't imagine anyone tiptoeing across that area carrying a saw.'

'Neither can I.'

'So you've had one of your bright ideas. What is it?'

'I've been wondering if a woman was responsible for Matthew's death. The idea occurred to me during the reconstruction.' Batiste noted that the Inspector looked doubtful but pressed on, 'Matthew was a healthy, good-looking man. There might be a number of disappointed widows or divorcees out there. I realise Monique and Vere haven't offered any information about female friends, but then they wouldn't. They're both too loyal.'

'What about local gossip? Do you know of anyone who—'

'My wife's Aunt Emily,' interrupted Batiste. 'Her daughter works for Monique. Pat is the head receptionist.'

'Ideal!' Le Tissier nodded. 'Perhaps your wife could invite Aunt Emily for coffee, or afternoon tea.'

Alone, Le Tissier's thoughts again turned to motive and possible suspects. He knew from Peter's phone call that the funeral had been arranged for Thursday afternoon but, as this would be followed by a wake at the hotel, the reading of the Will would now be on Friday afternoon.

He had noted and enquired about Peter's hesitancy when he learnt of Noel's intention to go into partnership with Nevill de Garis. Although he had already known that Ben had no real interest in the hotel, Le Tissier was amazed that Ben wanted to buy Cheryl Laval a new car as an engagement present. He had also learnt that Gerald, anticipating a bequest, had asked Monique for an advance of this, in order to repay an outstanding debt, and now wondered if either would take such drastic action in order to achieve their financial whims.

For a brief moment Le Tissier considered the contents of Matthew's pockets: a wallet containing driving licence, credit card, two £10 and two £5 notes. In handing a small bunch of keys over to Monique on Saturday morning he had learnt that one was the front door key for Matthew's bungalow, the smaller one for a private safe in the office.

He again wondered if she had yet checked their contents and doubted that there could be anything to help their enquiries.

*****

Although she had carried Matthew's keys in her handbag since Saturday, Monique decided to open his safe. Noel had volunteered to go to the bank, Ben had the morning off and was no doubt with Cheryl, so there would be no interruptions from either of them and, without any further hesitation, Monique opened the cupboard in which the small safe was installed, and inserted the key.

It only took a few moments for Monique to ascertain the contents of various envelopes and folders; letters from Peter were thrust in her handbag but as she picked up the package of photos she gazed, with a lump in her throat, at the one of Peter holding Daniel, a golden-haired three-year-old with a mischievous grin. A framed enlargement of this had sat on Matthew's desk until the day of the accident, when it was taken to his bungalow.

The thought of this reminded her that she would, at some time, have to go through all his personal belongings, and she bleakly wondered how she would get through the remainder of the week. As though sensing she was at a low ebb, there was a knock at the door and Pat appeared carrying a tray; but seeing the safe open and Monique's expression she said, 'I thought you might like some company other than family, but you're busy.'

'I'd rather have a few minutes with you.'

Pat watched as several photos of Daniel slid across the desk; setting the tray on an empty space, she reached across to touch Monique's arm. 'I wish there was something I could do. You've had so much sadness in a comparatively short time.'

Monique reached for a mug of coffee. 'It was seeing that particular photograph of Daniel, Dad's only grandchild, and remembering that tragic accident.'

Pat nodded. 'I only saw him once, when Mr Matthew took him down to the beach and they built a sandcastle. I thought he was adorable.'

But Ben was as jealous as hell, thought Monique and wondered, as she had on previous occasions, what his reaction would be if she and Noel had a family. Aloud she said: 'I know Mum was very ill, but for Dad to—' and shaking her head, 'Who hated him so much, to do such a thing?'

Again Pat commiserated: 'I'm sure Inspector Le Tissier will find the person responsible; however, any time you want to unwind, come round to the cottage. You know you're always welcome. Mother would love to see you.'

'Thanks.' Although she had still been at school at the time, Monique recalled her father's reaction on reading Pat's application for the position of head receptionist. 'She's local, aged 25, has all the necessary qualifications and apart from spending a year in France, has only worked at one other hotel.' That had been 15 years ago. Matthew had soon regarded her as the most valuable member of the staff. As soon as she started working in the hotel, Monique had felt the same, and she now said, 'I'd like that. I haven't seen her for a long while,' and knowing that Mrs Le Page had attended the service at Beau Sejour and seen the Queen: 'She'll be able to tell me about Liberation Day.'

'Good! Maybe one day next week. She'll probably want to make a gache for your tea.'

Alone, Monique quickly flicked through her father's personal bank statements noting that he had substantial balances on fixed deposit accounts at different banks whilst there was only a minimum amount on a current account. Placing these in their respective folders and back in the safe, which she locked, Monique considered that none of the contents would be of any help to Inspector Le Tissier. She would read Peter's letters and look through the photographs on another occasion but, as it was the inquest that afternoon, felt she should spend a few minutes quiet and alone.

*****

Inspector Le Tissier paused, looking at the group of people standing outside the coroner's court, pleased to see Noel shake hands and greet Peter. He noticed that Monique now looked less tense and managed a smile as Vere spoke to her; then he and Peter were on their way, when she turned and said, 'Good afternoon, Inspector.' Noel nodded and a second later asked, 'Do you know who left the saw in our garden?'

'Not yet. We were all otherwise occupied yesterday but we're looking into what little evidence we have.' Then, turning to Monique: 'You'll now be able to make the necessary funeral arrangements.' The inquest had been adjourned and Matthew's body released for burial.

'Yes,' and after a slight pause, Monique said: 'Dad was so well-known that Noel has suggested and invited Peter and Vere for dinner this evening when we can all discuss this.'

*****

'I'm sure, although his expression didn't change, that Peter was surprised at this unexpected invitation,' commented Le Tissier after he had recounted the proceedings of the inquest to Batiste.

'Knowing Ben's attitude I'd like to be there this evening,' said Batiste.

'Don't forget Cousin Gerald.'

'How could I, after this morning?' When asked for the shoes they had worn on Thursday evening, Noel had complained that they were his most comfortable pair of shoes, while Gerald had grumbled and sworn, also pointing out he had worn them every day since Thursday; and Ben had been downright rude.

*****

'You've invited Peter to dinner without consulting me!' Ben had reluctantly answered Monique's persistent knocking on his front door and now glared at her as she stood in the hall with Noel immediately behind her.

'Peter is family, the eldest son, and entitled to offer his opinion about the funeral,' said Monique.

'You should have—'

'And you could have come to the inquest but no, you have to rush off' and before Ben could speak, Monique continued: 'As Dad's best and most loyal friend, Vere is also coming.'

'Damn! That interfering old man.'

'Vere isn't old. He's younger than Dad, and is caring and considerate.' Monique was aware of Noel's fingers biting into her shoulder and was relieved to hear him say, 'We know you're shocked and upset about Dad but for everyone's sake, try to curb your temper.'

'Couldn't we just agree the day and time without all this fuss?'

'No.' Noel's voice was surprisingly firm. 'Haven't you any respect for your father? It's not just the service, which will be Thursday after—'

'Thursday,' interrupted Ben. 'Again, why didn't you ask me? I've arranged to take Cheryl—'

'I'm sure she'll understand,' said Monique, when Noel cut in: 'I must get over to the hotel,' and looking at Ben's casual shirt, 'And you should get changed.'

'Huh! You've suddenly changed your tune. I suppose you're hoping she'll finance your new idea,' muttered Ben, and when Noel glared at him, 'or haven't you told her yet?'

'You stupid fool,' hissed Noel before he turned away.

'Have you forgotten to tell me something?' asked Monique with a composure she did not feel and quickly followed this up with, 'Your partnership with Nevill de Garis?'

Noel stopped suddenly, aghast, and then hurried after Monique. 'How…how did you know about this?'

'I'm not blind or stupid. However we've a family dinner to arrange.' Monique stifled a sob: 'And Dad's funeral.'

'I wanted to tell—'

'I don't want to know, especially now.' Monique's voice was cold and almost unrecognizable. You'll have to wait.'

*****

Monique gave a sigh of relief as with a final wave Peter, with Vere in the front passenger seat, drove off. In spite of Ben's previous aggressiveness the evening had passed amicably, they had all agreed about the service and that those attending should be invited back to the hotel for refreshments. She had noticed the curious glances that Peter, who so resembled their father, had received from the remaining diners, and also Gerald's attitude.

As they left the dining room Peter had spoken to him but she was still puzzled by Peter's comment: 'Strange fellow, he's not very forthcoming, is he?' Reflecting that this comment would probably be explained the next time they met, Monique turned back towards Reception when Ben suddenly appeared, demanding: 'What's happening about Dad's Will?'

'What do you mean?'

'If people are coming back here after the funeral, Levrier won't be able to tell us what we—'

'Oh for Heaven's sake, don't be so mercenary. I'll be speaking to Mr Levrier tomorrow morning when I'll arrange an alternative appointment.'

'Can I have something in advance?'

'You'll have to ask Mr Levrier. Anyhow, what's the rush?'

'It's Cheryl's birthday soon. I want to get engaged — buy her a ring before she changes her mind.'

'Is that likely?'

'I know she hangs around Godfrey Reardon at The Sparrow's Nest in the evenings I'm not with her, and although she would prefer something more glamorous like a Sun Seeker, she goes out in his boat whenever he asks her. If I had a boat she wouldn't do that.'

Monique had seen Godfrey's Mitchell moored in the Albert Marina, also sleek Sun Seekers in the Q.E. 2 Marina and asked, 'Have you any idea how much they cost? Then there's the maintenance.'

Ben shrugged. 'At the moment I'm more concerned about an engagement ring. I've seen—'

'I'm sorry, there's nothing I can do,' interrupted Monique. 'Mr Levrier is Dad's Advocate and we'll all have to wait until the Will is read.'

Chapter 11

It was Wednesday morning and, frustrated at the lack of progress, Detective Inspector Le Tissier considered the positive and negative known facts, any possible clues.

The button found on the cliff path had been retained. It was possible someone might notice one missing from a garment worn by a member of staff or a visitor. An extremely short length of cotton (still through one of holes in the button) indicated that it had been cut by scissors while it was possible the navy blue fibre (wool and cashmere) came from either a pullover or cardigan; however why was the wearer standing so close to the trees?

It had been established that the broken-off twigs and tiny branches had been on the ground for some time but it was the second pair of footprints which were causing a problem.

The shoes which had been handed over, reluctantly, by Noel, Ben and Gerald were being examined and compared with the plaster casts which had been taken. Although Ben was the shortest, his shoes were only a fraction smaller than Noel's, whose were narrower than Gerald's. However the experts were dealing with these. The possibility of someone else actually standing in Gerald's footprints — and they didn't know yet that these were his — was quickly dismissed. There would have been a faint trace of a smaller shoe or, if this had been removed, an indication of a sock or even a bare foot. Le Tissier's thoughts turned to motive, and whilst he knew they each had a mercenary motive, he wondered how much Gerald really owed and to whom. Although he was family, very little was known about him. Le Tissier had learnt from a photocopy of the CV produced by Monique that Gerald had been a waiter on several cruise ships owned by the same company after which he had worked in Bournemouth. It was from there that he had come to the island. All his references were satisfactory but none referred to his temperament. When questioned, Noel said the guests complimented Gerald on the service and his team. Ben had said gruffly that he supposed Gerald was quite capable workwise but, whilst not making derogatory remarks, something unusual for him, remarked that there was something strange about Gerald's manner. Pat Le Page and Monique had said something similar. Hans, the head chef, had been unable to offer anything useful, while no one knew where or how he spent his days off, or of any friends of either sex.

'And now I come to Noel Latimer — peculiar man,' muttered Le Tissier. He knew that Noel had worked in various vineyards in different areas. Although he was now a member of the family, Monique had inadvertently taken a photocopy of his CV which had been included with others relating to senior members of the staff. Le Tissier, who had spent many holidays in France, now studied this, noting with interest that Noel had worked in the Bordeaux and Burgundy areas, and also spent time in the Garonne, Loire Valley before moving to Alsace. From there he had gone to south-west Germany where the grapes for Liebfraumilch were grown.

Vere Hamilton, who Le Tissier considered a kind and helpful gentleman, had offered further information. Matthew had first met Noel while on a wine-tasting tour in Bordeaux, and three years later, encountered him in Beaune. He was again impressed by Noel's wide knowledge of wines, fluent French and now German. Learning that Noel had no future plans, Matthew wondered if he would be interested in coming to the island; there would be a vacancy for a wine waiter at the end of the season. If he showed any aptitude for and interest in management, he could in due course become assistant manager to Monique, who would sooner or later take complete charge.

Le Tissier recalled Vere's conclusion: 'I'm sure you know the rest of the story, Inspector.

Noel came to the island seven years ago, met and fell in love with Monique, whom he married two years later; but he had no interest in acquiring any knowledge about the management side of the hotel, or taking on any further responsibility. Matthew was disappointed but his main concern was Monique's happiness. He was aware that for the last eighteen months Noel had become restless and often discussed a possible solution to the situation with me. Other than Pat Le Page, who has more experience than anyone else, and with the necessary training would be ideal as assistant manager, there was no one else on the staff suitable for promotion. I know Matthew was hoping to discuss this with Peter; but now Monique, on top of everything else, is faced with this problem. She, or maybe she and Peter, might decide to take this step and whilst it would no doubt be accepted by other members of the staff I doubt that Ben or Noel would approve.'

Le Tissier now considered that Monique and Pat would certainly present a very capable adversary to any other local hotel management team, but these thoughts were interrupted as Detective Sergeant Batiste knocked, entered, placed a cup of coffee on the desk, and asked: 'Can you spare Inspector Girard a few minutes, sir?'

Aware of Emile's friendship with Peter Stenton and hoping that this may be something relevant to Matthew's death, Le Tissier nodded. 'Of course.'

'Morning, Denis. I realise you're busy with the Stenton case but I thought you might be interested in my latest report from The Sparrow's Nest.'

Le Tissier glanced up at the older detective, a tall, powerfully built man who was still physically very fit and brilliant at his job, indicated a chair, offered coffee which was declined and enquired: 'Do you mind if Batiste stays? He's very much a part of this case.'

'Of course not.' Emile leant back, bracing his broad shoulders and began: 'I'm sure you're aware that young Stenton – in other words, Ben – frequents the place with his soon-to-be fiancée, Cheryl Laval, but she's there more often than him. Last night was another occasion and as usual when she's alone, she hangs around young Reardon.' Emile paused.

'You probably know this young woman,' and when Le Tissier shook his head, 'According to the neighbours, she behaves like a trollop when she's drunk or on drugs. As soon as he's out of the car she's tearing at his clothes, and has been known to—' Emile hesitated, and Le Tissier, who knew the Laval property, asked: 'How do the neighbours know about this? The place is surrounded by high hedges?' and in the same breath, 'Don't bother. Just tell me about last night.'

'She was pestering Godfrey repeatedly, asking him the same question, kept touching and grabbing his hand, almost throwing herself at him.' Emile chuckled. 'I'll spare Batiste's blushes, I won't use the expression used in the report. However, knowing about Ben's temper I'm sure he would've been furious if he'd seen Cheryl. I don't know what he sees in her; it's not as though she's pretty or attractive.'

'Apparently she takes after her mother,' volunteered Batiste, 'who also looks like a bag of bones, has a foul mouth and is man mad—'

'So, apart from the Laval woman's behaviour, what's your conclusion?' interrupted Le Tissier.

'Cheryl was heard to ask Godfrey, 'When are you expecting the next consignment?'

He muttered she would have to wait, like everyone else. There were a number of other youngsters who had earlier hung around the cashier, spoken to Godfrey and disgruntled, proceeded to get drunk.'

'Which means?' queried Le Tissier.

'The day trip from France was cancelled yesterday.'

'Do you think one of the day-trippers bring them in?' hazarded Batiste.

Emile shook his head. 'No, we think it's the regular courier and as they always have lunch at the Reardons' hotel, what could be simpler; but we haven't worked out exactly how it's done. One of my lads is friendly with the receptionist there. She can't stand Godfrey and is now watching every move that he or the courier make on days they come for lunch.'

Emile pushed back his chair. 'Sorry that took so long but as young Stenton is involved and there were occasions when he's been behaving very oddly, I thought you should know.'

'Thank you, Emile. It sounds as though you could soon be arresting the supplier, importer and/or distributor. Unfortunately I'm not making much headway.'

*****

Meanwhile, at the Valley View Hotel, Godfrey Reardon was in a bad mood, reluctant to admit that, due to his lack of interest, the chef was threatening to hand in his notice.

Godfrey knew that certain items, which included the slicer and dishwasher, should have been replaced but, adhering to his father's instructions that there was to be no capital expenditure, these items had, once again, been repaired. However both were still faulty and the kitchen staff were no longer prepared to use badly maintained equipment. On top of this, several guests who had come for the Liberation Day celebrations and had since departed, had complained about the bedrooms and that the corridor and stair carpets were a disgrace – worn and shabby. On hearing of the latter complaint, Godfrey glared at the receptionist. 'Tell the housekeeper to get them cleaned.'

'Yes, sir,' but Ailsa knew that this would have little effect. Similar complaints had been made by Easter guests and whilst she knew that redecoration and refurbishment of the second floor rooms was overdue, Ailsa doubted that Godfrey's father would commit himself to any capital expenditure. These thoughts were interrupted by Godfrey muttering,

'Damn the hotel, it's a constant worry and expense.'

'Not if you took a pride in your work, but you don't really do anything,' thought Ailsa.

She had stayed on when the Reardons bought the hotel eight years previously, and had become increasingly disappointed at Godfrey's lack of interest and his attitude to her and the rest of the staff. Ailsa recalled Godfrey's anger the previous morning when he learnt that, due to strong winds and rough sea, the luncheon for the French day-trippers had been cancelled. He had phoned and had a lengthy conversation with the regular courier and grumbled incessantly the whole morning.

As she had been on a split-shift and working in the evening, Ailsa had heard the argument between father and son and registered the former's annoyance when Godfrey announced, 'I don't care what you think, I'm going out.' And he was still in a bad temper. Ailsa sighed as she watched Godfrey storm past Reception, thought briefly of her new friend in the police and hoped that there would soon be a vacancy in Reception at the Serena Beach Hotel. Pat Le Page had assured her that she would be advised as soon as this occurred. While Ailsa dwelt briefly on a new and better job, Godfrey recalled the previous evening at The Sparrow's Nest and Cheryl Laval's peculiar behaviour. She had been a constant menace, adding to his frustration that there had been no ferry, and therefore no courier or goods.

Eventually, like most of the other youngsters, she had got hopelessly drunk and been sent home in a taxi. Godfrey wondered, as he had on previous occasions, if her parents were aware that, when drunk, she became vicious and offensive, and how Ben coped with her. If they did marry he doubted that Cheryl would be of any use in the hotel, and for a brief moment Godfrey considered what else he knew about Cheryl. To his knowledge she had never worked, while when drunk her manners and language were vulgar and obnoxious.

Other customers at The Sparrow's Nest withdrew whenever she approached, declining her offer to buy drinks, while the barmen, croupier and other staff disliked her ostentation. Had Monique ever met Cheryl, wondered Godfrey. What did she think of her and, in spite of his apparent obsession, would Ben really marry her?

By now Godfrey had reached the hedge that separated the hotel grounds from the now-deserted lane leading to the beach but glancing to the right he recognised the tall and awkward-looking figure of Gerald Stenton climbing the steep cliff path which led to the next bay. A good worker but a strange character, reflected Godfrey. His thoughts then reverted to his involvement with the importation of drugs, which was something his father would deplore if he ever found out. Godfrey then recalled that it was soon after their arrival in the island that he had been told about and found his way out to the popular nightclub, The Sparrow's Nest. This was owned by two brothers who had immediately befriended him. The younger had been a cashier in different casinos while Max had worked in several well-known London nightclubs.

Godfrey had soon learnt that both brothers were eager to increase the facilities and club membership while he had welcomed their suggestion that he should accommodate parties of French golfers at The Valley View. This had been a great success, especially as some of the golfers had a private pilot's licence and chartered small planes for their golfing weekends or longer stays.

It was also their idea that he should quote for lunches for the French day-trippers which had resulted in bookings for two, sometimes three lunches a week. It was only natural that he should meet the regular courier and before long he became personally involved. From the first luncheon, René had left his briefcase in the office, as agreed, and would leave with an identical briefcase provided by Max. The original would remain out of sight until the evening when Godfrey would take this out to The Sparrow's Nest and hand it over to Max.

He had never attempted to open the briefcase or query the contents but had realised that these were what was generally known as recreational drugs, and knew it was the younger brother who distributed them. There had been occasions when, accompanied by Max, he had taken his Mitchell to a point off the south coast to rendezvous with a French yacht. Godfrey had been walking along the cliff path in the opposite direction to Gerald but, seeing holidaymakers approaching, he stopped abruptly, and ignoring the fantastic view of the cliffs and beach below turned back towards the hotel. Gerald strode along the cliff path, shoulders hunched, hands thrust deep in his trouser pockets, deep in thought. How was he going to resolve his problem? Kevin McEnery was insistent in his demands for higher maintenance for his sister's children. Two boys, identical twins, had been born seven months after his arrival in Guernsey and Gerald still considered it was inconceivable that Kevin had found him. Regardless of his picturesque surroundings, he allowed his thoughts to wander. After working on different cruise ships for ten years he had become head waiter in a large Bournemouth hotel. During that time he had become friendly with and later had a relationship with the attractive housekeeper, Lilian McEnery, but this had ended amicably when she went home to Scotland. This had coincided with him leaving – without telling her or anyone else, he had flown to Guernsey. Three days later he had called on Matthew Stenton. Gerald recalled his uncle's surprise, their conversation when he introduced himself, and his own surprise that, at 70, Matthew was still good-looking, and very healthy. He had seen the advertisement in The Caterer and Hotelkeeper, but waited until he was about to leave when he casually asked whether there was likely to be a vacancy for a head waiter in the near future. Matthew had looked surprised, hesitated and said that the present head waiter would soon be retiring and asked if, having travelled for so long and worked in England, he would be prepared to live and work in the island?

That had been five and a half years ago and he was still amazed that Kevin had learnt of his presence in the island. He had later learnt that this information had been imparted by local people who were passengers on the cruise ship on which Kevin was barman. Kevin, six feet six inches and thick-set, had come ashore when the ship came to the island, told him about the twins who were three months old at that time, and insisted that he should pay maintenance. Gerald had not denied paternity, knowing that any tests would prove positive; but over the years Kevin, whom he saw every time his ship came to the island, had insisted on increased payments. Kevin always produced photographs of the boys and commented that they looked uncannily like Gerald. I was a fool, I should have insisted on having copies of each photo, and told Uncle about them, thought Gerald. He may not have approved, may even have suggested that I should marry Lilian, but he would probably have been interested to know that there was a younger generation of Stentons. Gerald then considered that his mother, wherever she was, would probably be delighted to learn she was a grandmother, but any further thoughts about her or the boys were dismissed as he turned the corner and was greeted by a party of walkers, and questioned about the view and the distance to the nearest bus stop.

It was as he set off again that Gerald wondered: should he tell Monique about the boys?

And, if so, when?

Chapter 12

Standing amongst the shoppers and holidaymakers, Inspector Le Tissier and Detective Sergeant Batiste watched as mourners paused to give their names before filing into the church. Neither were surprised at the number of dark-suited men and women, and as the last of these disappeared, the hearse turned the corner, more people gathered on the pavement outside, and Le Tissier said, 'Right, let's go.'

*****

'Good afternoon, Mr Levrier, how are you?' Le Tissier noticed that the Advocate looked rather uncomfortable in a tight-fitting suit.

'Hot and uncomfortable.' Arnold unbuttoned his jacket and glanced around. 'I noticed there were people standing outside the church and there's certainly a number here.'

Monique had suggested that both function rooms should be set up giving people ample space to circulate but even so there were small and large groups eating, drinking and chatting, many who had not seen each other for some time.

Le Tissier nodded. 'Matthew Stenton had been a hotelier for a long time and was a very popular man.'

'Yes, I see a number of other hoteliers are here,' Levrier was looking at a short, bald-headed man as he spoke, then transferred his gaze to the tall fair-haired younger man with a sulky expression, 'including the Reardons.'

Batiste followed the Advocate's gaze and said quietly, I believe Godfrey spends most of his evenings at The Sparrow's Nest.'

'Yes. It seems to be the 'in' place for the younger generation: cabaret, casino—'

'And other things,' interjected Le Tissier.

'I've heard rumours,' said Levrier, 'but you probably know more about it than I do. The unfortunate part as far as I'm concerned, not personally of course but on Monique's behalf, is that Ben and the Laval girl also frequent the place.'

'Emile Girard, one of our senior officers who should be retired, has someone out there observing but this is not the time or place to discuss such an important issue.'

'I agree, in any case we should circulate. I'll see you tomorrow afternoon, Inspector, and hope you acquire some information to help your enquiries.'

'I hope so but I'm not relying on it.' Then, as the Advocate moved away, Le Tissier told Batiste: 'I don't want to outstay our welcome. Move around, talk to people and meet me in the foyer in 15 minutes' time.'

Batiste, in a crisp white shirt, black tie and charcoal grey business suit, was immediately pounced on by two elderly ladies, the first of whom said: 'Such a lovely man. He always greeted us by name, didn't he, dear?'

'Yes. Absolutely charming and so good-looking. He'll be sadly missed.' And as her eyes misted over, 'I feel so sorry for Monique. If only Peter, who so resembles dear Matthew, still lived here.' Then looking directly at Batiste, 'We're regulars, you know, Sunday lunch every other week, family birthdays and Christmas. But somehow, although he's been here some time, we can't take to Gerald. He knows his job but he's so ungainly, all arms and legs, and as for the size of his feet, they're enormous.'

'You're observant, Miss Sebire, but I suppose that's part of being a successful author.'

Mildred Sebire, who wrote under a glamorous pseudonym, blushed. 'How do you know that, young man?'

'My wife reads all your books. She'll be thrilled to hear I've actually met and spoken to you.' As he bade them goodbye and moved away, Batiste heard the older sister say:

'Really, Millie, you shouldn't go on like that. People can't help the way they look.'

'It's not only Gerald's appearance, there's something about him that makes me suspicious; but then I'm always rambling on, it's to do with my writing.'

'And without that, where would we be? In a poky cottage, with little or no heating, no lovely meals out, or holidays. I'm sorry, Millie. I shouldn't be so critical and ungrateful.'

And in a whimsical voice: 'That was a nice young man. I wonder who he is?'

Struggling to keep a straight face Batiste found himself confronted by a tall, regal-looking woman in an elegant black long-sleeved frock adorned with a double rope of superb pearls, matching earrings, a stylish veiled toque set on curly white hair. He noted that despite the forlorn look in her eyes her make-up was unblemished, but her voice was husky as she asked, 'Was he a relative? Did you know him well?' Then before Batiste could reply: 'Matthew was such a dear, dear person. So many tragedies in his life. I knew Iris, his first wife; we were great friends since the day we started school, but I couldn't get near Matthew after her death – it was always work, work and more work.' Then, looking across the room, her eyes filled with tears and she clutched his arm. 'Oh my dear, I'm sorry to behave like this. It's seeing Peter, he's the image of his father at that age, very tall, distinguished, handsome and always so courteous to all his regular customers.'

'Would you like to speak to Peter?' Amazed at the sudden change of expression, her radiant smile, Batiste ventured: 'Shall I take you across the room to him?'

'Thank you,' and with her hand lightly on his arm Batiste elbowed a passage towards Peter at the same time saying, 'I'm sorry, I don't know your name.'

'Carol, Carol Cummings, a widow for a very long time.'

Peter, amazed at the warmth of all the local people and regular visitors who had greeted him, had noticed Sergeant Batiste leading a tall attractive white-haired woman in his direction, saw the sergeant shake his head indicating that he did not want his identity to be revealed, then Batiste was saying, 'Mrs Cummings was a great friend of your mother and, of course, your father.'

For a moment Peter was stunned then, on learning that this friendship had begun when they started school, exclaimed, 'That's amazing! I'm sure you could tell me so much about her that I never knew.'

'I did keep a diary, even as a school—' Carol stopped abruptly, and then, 'I'm so terribly sorry about what happened to Matthew. He was so charming, and in spite of all his other regulars, always remembered me.'

'So you've seen him over the years, since Mother died?' and when Carol nodded, despite and aware of curious glances, 'Would you be free to join me for dinner on Saturday?'

Another nod, Peter stated a time, named his hotel and in his normal voice said, 'Thank you for coming, Mrs Cummings.'

'Inspector, can I have a word?' Recognising the voice Le Tissier spun round. 'Certainly, Mr Hamilton, but if you're going to ask me what progress we've made with our enquiries, I can't help you.'

'No, it's not that.' For a moment Vere looked embarrassed and then said quietly, 'As you know, Mr Levrier is reading the Will tomorrow and for some obscure reason has asked me to attend. Do you know why?'

Le Tissier, who knew that Vere was a wealthy retired solicitor, was aware that it was normal for beneficiaries to be present and shook his head. 'I've no idea.'

'Perhaps he thinks I should be there, especially as Peter won't be, for Monique's sake, in case there's any unpleasantness.'

'I expect everything will be straightforward. However, should it be necessary, let me know.'

'Thank you, Inspector. I hope you soon find the...the bastard who did this. Anyhow, I've had enough. I'm going home.'

'Poor Vere, he and Matthew Stenton had become great friends, I think this afternoon has really upset him.'

Le Tissier and Batiste watched as Vere, slim, upright and smart in a dark suit, made his way towards Monique and kissed her on both cheeks when Peter suddenly appeared at his side and led him through the still-crowded room.

'That was a very interesting hour,' said Le Tissier as he fastened his seatbelt.

'What did you learn?' enquired Batiste.

'In spite of his help and advice when they first arrived in the island, Reardon senior was jealous of Matthew's success. He tried to poach some of Stenton's staff, encouraged Godfrey to marry Monique and was angry when Noel appeared on the scene and, in a comparatively short time, married her. He doesn't approve of Godfrey being constantly away from the hotel, either on his boat or out at that nightclub. However, what did you find out?'

Le Tissier listened, grinned and nodded as Batiste recounted meeting the Sebire sisters, and then Carol Cummings when he said, 'I saw you leading a very attractive woman across the room but at that distance didn't recognise her.'

'Did you speak to Monique?'

'Briefly. I was pleased to see the head receptionist, Pat Le Page was there keeping a motherly eye on her whilst Vere wasn't very far away.' Then, as Batiste turned right, in the direction of town, Le Tissier added, 'I noticed Ben and Noel, especially the former, looked furious at the attention Peter received.'

Batiste nodded. 'He, and I mean Peter, is a genuinely nice chap.'

'Yes and I'm pleased, for Monique's sake, that he's staying on for another week, at least.'

Meanwhile Monique stood in the spacious foyer watching the last guests depart and turned when Noel said, 'You're really amazing. I should think you spoke to everyone.'

'I didn't expect so many to come back after the service.'

'They certainly didn't leave much food, but why were the Inspector and his Sergeant here?' asked Ben, and took a step backwards when Monique said, 'Because I asked him.'

'Hoping he might learn something to help with his enquiries,' hazarded Ben, then without waiting for a reply: 'Obviously Cheryl didn't come this afternoon so I'm going to see her,' and in the same breath, 'Will I have the money to buy her that car?'

'I really don't know. We all have to wait until the reading of the Will.' Monique was aware that she sounded abrupt but didn't apologise and said, 'I'm going to change and go for a walk.'

Noel had just listened and now offered, 'Shall I come with you?'

'No thanks, I'd prefer to be alone.'

Noel noted Monique's forlorn expression and nodded. 'That's understandable. I'll see you later,' and as Monique stepped out into the sunshine and was out of earshot he turned to Ben: 'You certainly don't help the situation, do you? You're a selfish bastard.'

'I'm not the only one,' and his voice suddenly harsh and grating Ben asked, 'Do you really think she'll give you the cash you need to go into partnership with Nevill?'

Within minutes Monique, wearing trousers, tunic and trainers, was walking quickly towards the beach, then turned right towards the cliff path that led to the next bay.

Noel, standing outside the hotel, was not surprised Monique had taken that route. He was amazed that she had remained calm, her emotions under control during the service, interment and wake and he hoped that, alone, she would be able to give vent to her grief.

Noel wasn't the only one watching Monique's progress, Gerald had also seen her walk towards the beach and noted the direction she had taken but restrained himself from following her. He had been relieved to learn that his presence was required at the reading of the Will — that surely meant he had been left something, but how much and how long would he have to wait?

As she walked Monique tried to think of a positive solution to the problems that lay ahead of her. She was furious that, under the present circumstances, Noel should persist in his plans to become an estate agent while Ben had muttered that he didn't want to work in the bar — he had never liked it. In fact, he didn't want to be involved with the hotel.

'Families,' she muttered as she rounded a corner and then, at the sight of a dark-suited man bent forward on a bench, his head in his hands, she stopped abruptly when he looked up and directly at her, his face still damp and held out his hand. 'Come and sit down.'

Peter and Monique sat in silence for several minutes then he said, 'Matthew wasn't just my father, he was my best friend.'

Monique nodded, 'And mine. But I can't cry — cry properly.'

'You will. At the moment you've a lot to think about.' Peter grinned, 'I've a pair of broad shoulders if you want to talk.'

'Not today, perhaps after tomorrow afternoon. The reading of Dad's Will.'

Peter's expression changed, became serious. 'I'm sure whatever Dad did, was given long and careful thought and that Arnold Levrier will be only too pleased to help or advise you if there are any difficulties. I'm here for another week,' and seeing Monique's face brighten, 'or two. You can always phone me, day or night.'

Monique entered the foyer of the popular town hotel but before she could approach Reception a tall distinguished-looking woman came forward and greeted her. 'Monique! I'm so pleased you could spare the time to see me.'

The well-known travel writer and author had taken hold of Monique's hands, and kissed her on both cheeks. Monique stammered: 'How...how did you know who I was?'

'Peter described you.' Roslyn Tempest chatted effortlessly as she led the way towards the lounge. 'He's charming, isn't he? So well-known and popular, even though he doesn't live in the island.' Monique nodded, sat in the chair indicated, glanced around the high- ceilinged room noting the decor, tastefully chosen curtains and carpets. She had met the manager of the hotel on several occasions and knew him to be a very capable, astute and shrewd businessman, but her thoughts were interrupted as Roslyn asked, 'How do you like your coffee?'

'White, please.' As she poured, Roslyn said that she always enjoyed her annual visits and subtly questioned Monique about her views on the attractions of the island, and the future of tourism. Then: 'Is there anything you'd like to ask me, to discuss?' Monique was still amazed at Roslyn's friendly manner, not surprised that Peter enjoyed her company and found herself saying, 'I've read and enjoyed all your books however, when do you find time to write?'

It was some time later that Monique drove back to the hotel, feeling completely relaxed. She had enjoyed Roslyn's company, was surprised that she had also arranged to prolong her stay and agreed to meet Roslyn again the following week.

As she indicated and turned off the main road Monique wondered if Peter knew that Roslyn was staying on.

Chapter 13

'It would have been much simpler if we'd all come in one car,' complained Noel as he manoeuvred his Honda into the remaining parking space.

'I did suggest it but Ben is going on to Cheryl's and Gerald also needed his.' Monique straightened the jacket of her dove-grey suit as she stood up. 'I'm not looking forward to this.'

'It's to your advantage.' Noel reached into the back of the car for his jacket and put it on.

'Right, let's go.'

Five minutes later Arnold Levrier's gaze travelled from Monique's troubled countenance to Ben's and Gerald's, the former obviously expectant, the latter hopeful. Conscious of Ben's glowering disapproval, Arnold dealt with the bequests first, aware of Vere's surprise and Gerald's disappointment at the amount, and then the other legatees. These were for long-serving members of the staff and although the amounts were justifiable Ben was still scowling. The air was almost charged with electricity as Arnold reached the last clause and his voice was low as he read out, 'I hereby bequeath the shares in Serena Beach Hotel to Monique and Benedict,' but he was unprepared for Ben's outburst: 'Who inherits Dad's money?'

'Ben!' Everyone looked at Monique who, although embarrassed, continued: 'How could you?'

'He must have had some money—actual cash.'

'Your father was well aware of his assets when he made his Will,' interrupted Arnold, and before Ben could protest, 'and appointed Vere Hamilton as his Executor.'

'You!' Ben glowered at Vere. 'Why don't you mind your own business instead of being involved in our family affairs.'

'Ben!' Monique was so angry she couldn't restrain herself. 'Apologise at once.'

'Don't worry about it, my dear.' Vere spoke quietly. 'It's obviously a shock.'

'Too right. He should have told me—' Ben paused, glanced at Monique and amended this to: '—told us what he intended to do.'

'Perhaps he would have done,' Arnold Levrier looked at those seated around the table, 'but Matthew had no idea this was going to happen.' Then, in spite of Ben's still mutinous expression and Gerald's of dissatisfaction, Arnold looked at Monique and said quietly, 'If you have any queries, or there is anything you want to discuss, please let me know.'

As Monique stood up, Ben brushed past her muttering to himself, while Vere shook hands with the Advocate and taking the hint Noel and Gerald did the same. With Arnold's hand on her shoulder Monique turned towards the door and, aware that the others were out of earshot, Arnold murmured: 'You know where I am, my dear. Call me at any time.'

'Thank you.'

'What's going to happen now?' asked Noel as he drove out of town towards the hotel.

'I don't know. Ben certainly wasn't—'

'I'm not bothered about him,' and when there was no immediate response Noel persisted: 'You must have had some thoughts about Matthew's Will since last Friday.'

'I have had other things to think about.'

'But surely you realised that Matthew would die, one day,' insisted Noel.

'I suppose at the back of my mind, I did.'

'So you may have thought beyond—'

'That's enough. You can drop me here. I'll walk down the hill.'

Noel had just turned off the main road and slowed down. 'You can't walk home in those shoes—' but glancing down he saw that Monique was wearing smart walking shoes, and noting her determined expression Noel pulled into a lay-by and stopped. 'I'm sorry. I didn't mean to upset you.'

By now Monique stood outside, the passenger door still open. 'I need some fresh air and exercise. I'll see you later.'

Noel swore as he drove off. He knew he had not done himself any good by antagonising Monique and would again have to wait until he could approach her about his plans for the future.

Meanwhile, her arms around his neck, her pouting lips just inches from his, Cheryl was demanding, 'Well, how much did you inherit?' It was obvious from her behaviour and breath that Cheryl had been drinking and probably taken something. Although he had suggested and tried to dissuade her from taking what she described as recreational drugs Ben had never asked what these were, but he knew that when she was like this she rambled on and on.

'How much?' persisted Cheryl in between kissing him with increasing fervour. 'Can we go shopping for my ring?'

Ben knew she was going to be furious and took a deep breath. 'It's not cash. Dad's left me shares in the hotel.'

'What!' Cheryl looked and sounded aghast. 'What do you mean?'

'Monique and I previously owned some shares but now we've both inherited more. Monique has the larger proportion.'

That's not fair,' and her eyes glinting angrily Cheryl pouted, 'but his money – and there can't be a shortage of that – who gets it?'

Ben knew he dare not admit his ignorance about Mathew's bank accounts and muttered, 'There were various bequests, some to long-serving members of the—'

'Huh! They were, and probably still are, being well-paid for what they do.' Then she was pulling him close, tugging at his clothes and pushing him to the ground.

'No, not here on your front lawn. What will your parents think?' protested Ben.

'They're out but they'd probably wish they'd done the same. Anyhow we can't be overlooked, the hedges are over six feet high.'

'No!' With an extreme effort – although she was thin, Cheryl was strong – Ben pushed her off and stood up. 'Let's go up to your flat.'

'It's a mess.'

Ben knew this was probably an understatement. 'That doesn't matter,' and taking hold of her hand began to pull Cheryl towards the open front door.

'I've found it,' exclaimed Cheryl some time later.

'What?' Ben looked up as she leant over him, thinking that in spite of her behaviour she didn't really look provocative. Cheryl was so thin that in a few years she would be scrawny and, at times, that could be uncomfortable; then he repeated: 'What have you found?'

'I've thought of a solution. You could sell your shares. Monique would buy them. Then we'd have plenty of money.'

'It won't all be mine.'

'I realise that but there's so much there for the holidaymaker.' Cheryl enumerated the amenities which had been added over the years, 'and your private bungalows could be used for self-catering, or sold off as individual homes. The whole lot must be worth a fortune!'

With a blissful expression on her face Cheryl leant even closer. 'Aren't you going to congratulate me for being such a clever girl?'

'It's a good idea but I doubt Monique will agree.'

'You'll have to persuade her. Anyhow phone her, now!' Reaching across him Cheryl grabbed her mobile and thrust it into his hand insisting, 'Just tell her you want to discuss your father's Will when you get back to the hotel. That you're on the way,' and as he punched out the number she giggled. 'Don't forget to put your trousers on! '

*****

Monique strolled down the path, through the wooded valley, glad she was wearing comfortable shoes and a jacket. The path was uneven in places and with an easterly breeze it was quite cool under the trees. She had deliberately closed her mind to Ben's rude behaviour and Noel's persistent questioning, and was relieved that Vere had been present and would advise Peter of what had occurred; she was also grateful for Arnold Levrier's offer of help and advice. It was highly probable she would require both. Monique knew that Vere would deal with her father's estate according to his wishes but it was the recipients – Gerald whose disappointment at the stated amount was obvious and Ben with his outburst demanding cash – who could prove difficult.

Monique paused in what had always been her favourite spot, a small clearing with a view of the hotel, private bungalows, extensive grounds, beyond the beach and the sea. Over the years she had taken many photographs from here, in each season; some had been used for Christmas cards for the regular guests, and even postcards. Others had been enlarged, framed and hung in different rooms in the hotel. Monique sighed. It was only a 10-minute walk downhill to the bungalow she had regarded as her home ever since it was built, when she was 21. Another had been built for Ben when he reached that age.

She could hear the phone ringing before she opened the front door and hurried into the lounge noting that Noel, who was sat on the patio, had not moved. To her surprise it was Ben who sounded amazingly cheerful and astounded her by saying, 'Can I come round to see you? Now?'

'Yes.' Monique knew she sounded hesitant then heard him say, 'I've just had a marvellous idea.'

'I'll see you in a minute then.'

'It'll be longer than that,' and with the sound of laughter in the background, 'I'd better put my clothes on. I'm with Cheryl.'

It was as Monique replaced the receiver that Noel came in from the patio. 'Who was that?'

'Ben, he's on his way. He wants to have a chat about Dad's Will.'

*****

'Are you mad? Do you think I want to be burdened with a huge overdraft for the rest of my life? That's if the bank are even prepared to lend me the money.' Monique was still aghast at Ben's suggestion that she should buy him out, and her eyes widened as he resumed, 'There is another way – we could sell the hotel.' Ben looked at Noel as he spoke. 'Then we would all have the money to do whatever we wanted.'

'I don't think that's a good idea.' Noel's voice was quiet, and Ben carried on: 'If it was just a large amount of money in the bank it'd be simple, just halve it, but no, the old man had to invest everything in the hotel. Stupid old fool, what good did that do him? Work, work, work and now he's dead.'

'And you're insensitive, you've no real feeling. It's all money with you.' Monique was on her feet, glaring down at Ben, almost shaking with anger.

'You can't do much without it, and don't tell me about working in the hotel. I did, but now I want my share, in cash!'

Noel had been merely watching but now chimed in, 'It's not that simple, Ben. If Monique did agree to sell, the whole place would have to be valued, put in the hands of an estate agent, preferably one who specialises in hotels. I appreciate it's all in good condition but it may not be so easy to find a purchaser ready to invest in such a large property.'

Monique stared at Noel, surprised that he was not siding completely with Ben, who now snarled: 'I thought you'd agree with me. But don't worry, there are other ways,' and as he stood up and crossed the room Ben turned to look back at Monique. 'Don't forget, I am your next-of-kin. I should take care if I were you,' and then slammed the door.

Monique rushed to open it. 'Ben, come back,' but he was already out of sight.

'What did he mean by threatening 'if anything happened to you'?' asked Noel.

'He…he'd inherit.'

Noel swallowed – remembering the venom in Ben's voice and muttered – 'My God! How could he say that?' and decided this was not the moment to ask if Monique had made her Will. Instead he moved to sit beside her on the settee, his arm around her shoulders, and said gently, 'I'm sure he didn't mean it. He's still upset.'

'Ben's never satisfied,' said Monique. 'Look at the way he behaved when Mr Levrier read out the bequests Dad made to Vere and Gerald.'

Noel nodded; he had noticed that while the Advocate and Vere ignored Ben's outburst, Gerald had glared at the younger man, making no attempt to hide his dislike.

'I still feel so embarrassed at Ben's behaviour, his rude outburst when Mr Levrier stated that Vere was Dad's

Executor.' Monique sighed, 'I wonder if Cheryl is the reason for his obsession about money? It was to impress her that Ben bought that car, spent nearly all the money Mum left him.' Monique did not mention the bank statements and portfolio of investments she had found in her father's safe. She would hand these over to Vere whenever he required them, hopefully soon. Although there was only one key for the safe she would feel happier when these documents were no longer in the hotel.

*****

Detective Inspector Le Tissier shook hands with Arnold Levrier, 'It's very good of you to see me so quickly.'

The Advocate sighed. 'I'm sorry, there's not much to tell you. However, as anticipated, the hotel, or rather the shares, have been left to Monique and Ben. There were, of course, other bequests.' Arnold paused, recalling Ben's disapproval and Gerald's disappointment, but in his opinion not sufficient to justify a motive.

'Judging from your expression I should say there's something I should know,' said Le Tissier.

'Well, Vere Hamilton is the Executor which didn't please Ben; in fact he was extremely rude, and then wanted to know who inherited Matthew's money. I don't know anything about this, how much could be involved, but no doubt Monique has already found, or will find Matthew's bank statements and hand them over to Vere. I'm really glad Matthew appointed him as Executor, and whilst Vere is a very capable person I'll be only too pleased to help him.'

Le Tissier nodded. 'He's a nice man, very fond of Peter and Monique.' Then, as the thought occurred to him: 'I noticed Peter wasn't mentioned in the Will. Is there any special reason for that? Is it likely to cause any ill-feeling?'

'Not for Peter. Matthew gave him a substantial sum years ago, when Peter had the opportunity to buy the hotel he'd been renting. And although Peter is running a very successful business it's possible Matthew gave him a further cheque,' then as an afterthought, Arnold added, 'I expect Vere has been in touch with Peter regarding this afternoon. They were probably wondering how Ben would behave.'

Le Tissier nodded. 'I doubt this has anything to do with our enquiries but, as a personal friend of Matthew Stenton, can you tell me why Ben is so jealous of Peter?' and when Arnold hesitated: 'Peter has been out of the island for years.'

'That's the reason. You must have noticed yesterday afternoon the number of people who spoke to him, some at length, all really pleased to see him. It's been like that ever since he arrived last Friday. Everywhere he goes the locals are all delighted to see him.'

'The same goes for the older and more senior members of the force. In fact Emile Girard told me he's having dinner with Peter tonight.'

'Emile Girard,' repeated Arnold. 'He's due for retirement, isn't he?'

'Yes to both questions, but he's staying on until the end of the season.'

'I suppose he's keeping an eye on a particular nightspot.' Arnold had lowered his voice but noted the Inspector's expression remained serious and continued, 'Ben, and especially his soon-to-be fiancée, Cheryl spend a lot of time out there. So does young Reardon, much to his father's dismay.' Then, noting Le Tissier's raised eyebrows: 'Howard is a client who, on the rare occasions I see him, grumbles about Godfrey's nightly visits; also his boat trips in the most unsuitable weather. Although the Mitchell is very seaworthy Howard is always worried that Godfrey might have an accident. I noticed that they were both there yesterday, and that every time Godfrey tried to get near Monique someone local intervened.'

'I understand they have a regular twice-weekly booking of French day-trippers. Does Godfrey avoid those?'

'No, that was one good point Howard conceded in his favour.' Arnold paused for a moment and then resumed: 'Returning to Matthew's death, we both know the terms of his Will, the names of the beneficiaries; however is there anyone who could possibly benefit from his death in any other way?'

'What do you mean? Apart from financially, how could anyone benefit?' Le Tissier leant forward. 'Do you know something we don't?'

Arnold sighed. 'You know by now that Ben and Noel are unsettled, have been for some time. I wondered if Matthew's death might provide the opportunity for them to break away.'

'Are you suggesting that another hotelier, eager to acquire the Serena Beach, could be responsible?' Then before Arnold could comment, Le Tissier continued: 'I'm sure Monique would be loath to sell up, but if Ben wanted his share in cash she would need a substantial bank loan; the interest could be exorbitant. However, Monique's a very shrewd business-woman, while the hotel, extensive grounds and three bungalows would certainly provide sufficient collateral. I suppose if he moved out she could sell Ben's and Matthew's bungalows.'

Arnold hesitated and then volunteered, 'Ben asked who would inherit Matthew's money, but I haven't seen any bank statements yet so I've no idea how much is involved.'

'I'm sure Monique will let you have them as soon as she finds them.' Le Tissier thought she had probably already found them, but was uncertain as to what she should do with them, and continued, 'Whilst it may not be relevant, I have the necessary court orders which will enable me to question the respective bank managers.'

'Whose accounts are you interested in?'

'Ben's, Noel's and Gerald's,' and when Arnold looked shocked, Le Tissier concluded, 'It would all be very useful.'

Meanwhile in another part of the island Mary Batiste looked at her Aunt Emily and asked, 'Have you been anywhere or done anything special this week?' It was Friday afternoon and Mary knew her aunt either met a friend or went into town once or twice a week.

'I went into town yesterday, had an early lunch and then found a good vantage point to see all the people who were attending the funeral.'

'You mean Matthew Stenton's funeral?'

'Yes. He was a lovely man, very kind and understanding. It's not surprising there were so many people in the church and standing outside.' Emily nodded. 'He was clever, handsome and charming. Lost two wives, and there were probably those who thought he might remarry after Maureen died.'

Mary was immediately alert. 'Was there anyone?'

'Although he was still good-looking, upright and always smartly dressed, no.' Emily shook her head. 'He probably felt he'd had enough sadness in his life, he was very upset when Peter's wife and son died.' Emily's dark brown eyes twinkled. 'Now there's another lovely man.' Mary suppressed a grin at her aunt's description, and nodded as Emily continued, 'Peter's just like his Dad in looks and manner. I wonder if he'll come back and help Monique run the hotel?'

'I shouldn't think so. He has his own hotel in England,' then choosing her words carefully, Mary asked, 'Were there many women at the funeral? Anyone who you recognised, knew?'

Emily brightened. 'Little Esme Levrier was there with her husband. There were several women together, I think they were representing the WI and suchlike who used the hotel, and that rather elegant looking woman, I should call her a lady, Carol Cummings. She went to school with Iris.'

'That's right, Jimmy heard her tell Peter they'd been friends for a long time, when he invited her to dinner.'

'Did he? I wonder why?' Mary noticed the gleam in her aunt's eyes. 'Stop getting romantic ideas. You know perfectly well Carol's older than Peter.'

'Age doesn't matter. They'd make a lovely couple.'

'Really, Aunt!' Mary tried to look and sound cross. 'One of these days your imagination will get you into trouble.'

'Nonsense, my dear, I'm too old for that.'

Chapter 14

It was after the main course had been served and Emile had regaled Peter with his youngest grandchild's antics that Emile enquired, 'How's Monique and the situation at the hotel?'

'It was the reading of the Will this afternoon and I'm hoping to see her for a few minutes tomorrow morning. I understand from Vere Hamilton, whom you probably know, that his appointment as Executor hasn't been acceptable to everyone.'

Emile nodded, 'I'm sure he's very capable of doing whatever is necessary.' Emile finished his steak. 'That was really delicious,' and looking across at Peter, 'I can see you're worried. Is it Monique or the hotel? Do you want to talk about it?'

'It's Ben's attitude, which is really nothing new. He doesn't want anything to do with the hotel. He's suggested Monique should buy him out, or it's sold. He went straight to her after seeing Cheryl.' Peter paused, noting Emile's expression, and muttered, 'She sounds an avaricious young woman. He suggested this and even threatened her.'

'Monique actually told you that?'

'No. To my amazement Noel phoned me. I know they're going through a difficult patch but he sounded genuinely worried, and gave me the whole conversation verbatim.'

'What did Ben say?'

'I am your next-of-kin. I should take care if I were you.'

Emile nodded. 'If I remember correctly, they all have their own bungalow and garden in the hotel grounds, which are very extensive. Your Dad had been living in his, on his own, since Maureen died?'

It was Peter's turn to nod, 'Yes and you're brilliant, Emile.' Then, seeing his friend's puzzled expression, 'I realise you haven't said anything but we're both thinking the same thing: I move into Dad's place. I have a choice of excuses, the hotel can't keep me any longer or, as they're all so busy and it's an unpleasant task, I offer to sort out Dad's personal possessions.'

'Excellent! I always said we'd make a first-class team.'

'The alternative is that I ask Le Tissier to put someone out there—'

'No,' said Emile firmly. 'You can forget that idea. We're really short of men and it takes time to achieve results.'

'Why? What are you talking about?' Emile had already lowered his voice and Peter did the same. 'You've got someone watching a certain place?'

'Two. They take it in turns.' All of a sudden Emile wiped his mouth with the serviette. 'That was an excellent meal, I couldn't eat anything else.'

As the two men stood up the head waiter hurried across the room. 'Is anything wrong, Mr Stenton? Did you enjoy your dinner?'

'Yes, it was very good but we couldn't manage a sweet or even coffee. I think we both need some fresh air.'

'Of course, sir. It's very warm this evening – perhaps a stroll around the harbour?'

'Good idea. Thank you again.'

Neither hesitated as they left the hotel, turned left and within a few minutes had crossed the main road and were entering the lower part of Candie Gardens when Peter took a deep breath: 'Wise decision. We can enjoy the surroundings and continue our conversation.'

'In a moment. Let's head towards the top gate.'

From where we can see who's in this part of the Gardens, coming or going, thought Peter.

He knew better than to ask Emile why they were there, heading in that direction, and guessed that his friend might want to confide in him. Looking around, he commented on the shrubs, trees and carefully-tended flowerbeds then, as they reached the gate, Peter looked across the narrow road. 'This must be a very sought-after residential area. Secluded, quiet and not far from town.'

Emile looked concerned. 'Would you really be interested?'

'I'm sure my brother-in-law, in his future role as a property negotiator, would be only too happy to find me something around here, away from the hotel. However they're too close to each other; but that's not why we're here, is it?' and with a grin Peter added, 'There's no one lurking behind any of the trees or shrubs who can overhear what you're about to tell me.'

Emile hesitated but only for a moment. 'You know Ben frequents that place, don't you?'

'Yes, together with his girlfriend Cheryl, who I've yet to meet.'

'I don't know what he sees in her, a scraggy, money-minded bundle of bones. She's there more often than he is, flutters her eyelashes and pouts at Godfrey Reardon who seems to spend a lot of time there.'

'Do they, Cheryl and Ben, gamble?'

'Not seriously, a few minutes at the roulette.'

'What exactly does The Sparrow's Nest offer, and for what age group do they cater?'

'There's dancing, just a small area. They have a DJ on Friday and Saturday evenings. There's five fruit machines, a baccarat table which isn't very popular, and the roulette, of course.'

'Do you know what drugs are available out there?'

'The usual: cannabis, coke, some ecstasy. My lads soon picked out those who were users, noted the mood swings, full of energy then depressed, short-tempered. They both admit they're curious about Reardon's role; he stands back watching.'

'Has he got any money invested in the place? Is the owner or anyone else there a friend?'

'I doubt it but he knows the cashier – youngish chap, a peculiar type. He and his brother own the place. My lads have got their suspicions about Reardon.'

'Importing or distributing?'

'The former, but neither has seen anyone actually handling drugs there.'

Chapter 15

Once clear of the town and traffic, Monique's thoughts turned to Peter's suggestion that he should sort out and possibly dispose of some of their father's personal belongings.

Although she had agreed that he should do this, she wondered what Ben's reaction would be. Up to now, and it was 10 days since the tragedy, he had not been in Matthew's bungalow — he rarely went there when Matthew was alive, and had not volunteered any help in sorting out Maureen's personal possessions when she died. It was a well-appointed three-bedroomed bungalow in pleasant surroundings, and a lot of people would love to live there, reflected Monique as she turned off the main road and began the descent to the hotel.

She dropped to second gear, and kept her foot behind but not on the brake pedal. It wasn't until she was halfway down the tree-lined hill negotiating a treacherous corner that she put her foot on the brake but nothing happened. Monique gritted her teeth, dropped to first gear, wrestled with the steering wheel and applied the hand-brake. Somehow she got round the next bend, saw a wide uneven grass verge ahead and, pulling hard to the left, steered towards it. The impetus of hitting this slowed the Mini, which bumped up and down over the uneven ground, eventually stopping a couple of yards from a belt of trees.

Without moving her hands, she closed her eyes; then suddenly the sound of someone shouting roused her, and she looked up to see Peter running towards the car.

'Monique! Are you all right?'

'Yes. Yes, I think so,' but it seemed her voice was coming from a distance. 'Brakes, couldn't stop.'

'Are you hurt? Can you move?'

Monique moved her head from side to side, stretched her arms and touched her forehead.

'I'm all right.'

'We'll see about that,' muttered Peter. 'What about your legs?'

'They're fine.' Monique swung them out of the car, and was surprised when Peter steadied her and then lowered her gently to the ground.

'Don't worry, I'll just check you out. I have done a first aid course.'

Within minutes he was pulling up outside the hotel's main entrance where Pat was anxiously waiting. Noel hurried across the foyer. 'Peter! I've just had your message. What happened?'

'I'll tell you in a minute. Monique's in my car. Shall I carry her into the hotel or take her straight to your bungalow?'

'The bungalow. Come on, Pat, get in the back with me,' muttered Noel.

'Stop fussing,' muttered Monique.

'Sssh, do as you're told.'

*****

'What are you doing here, Dr Bryce?' Monique leant against the pillows, sipping a cup of hot strong tea, and stared at the tablets which lay in the palm of the doctor's hand, and protested: 'There's no need.'

'Yes there is. You've had a nasty shock, and you'll probably be rather stiff later.'

Dr Bryce, who knew and had looked after all the Stenton family, refrained from saying that she was extremely lucky to have escaped without any broken bones, or other injuries.

'It was the brakes, they didn't work.'

'I'm sure the mechanic will sort it out. Just you rest and relax.' As the doctor turned, Pat helped Monique into a more comfortable position and asked, 'Would you like me to stay with you?'

'No thanks. I'm already feeling drowsy.'

In the meantime, in the lounge, Noel and Peter were both pacing back and forth. 'Why were you there, driving behind her?' demanded Noel.

'I'm not sure, but after she left I remembered yesterday's phone call when you said she'd been threatened, and decided to follow her back to the hotel. It was as we were coming down the hill I could see she was having problems, the brakes on her Mini weren't working.'

'Thank God she's a capable and sensible driver, and that you were there. What do you think went wrong?'

They were both staring at each other when Dr Bryce entered, looked at them curiously and volunteered, 'Monique said the brakes weren't working.' 'I hope you don't think I'm interfering but I rang Bill Carre.' Peter paused. 'He always looked after Dad's car. I asked him to pick up the Mini. However, more important, how's Monique?'

'She'll be fine, probably still shocked, at the moment almost asleep. However, if she complains of any aches or pains, feeling unwell, let me know at once. I'll see myself out.'

'Thank you for coming so quickly.' Noel turned back to Peter. 'What are you going to do now? You said you were prepared to sort out Matthew's personal—'

'Something I should have done before,' interrupted Peter looking serious. 'Take a walk up to the place where it happened.'

Noel nodded. 'Monique wanted to do that earlier in the week but she couldn't get up there because of the police. She'll probably be up and about by the time you come back; perhaps we could all have some lunch together?'

Peter repressed his surprise. 'Thanks, I'd like that, but what about Ben? I don't want to upset him.'

'He's off until this evening. Probably with Cheryl.'

*****

Although still pale, Monique was assuring Noel and Peter that she did not have a headache, or any other aches and pains, when Pat approached their table.

'I'm sorry to disturb you, Mr Stenton. The owner of the garage, Mr Carre is on the phone for you.'

'My Mini's at the garage?' Monique looked from Noel to Peter. 'Who arranged that?'

'I did,' said Peter and turning to Pat, 'Where shall I take the call?'

'In the office, we're all coming. I want to know what's wrong with my car.' Monique sat in the large leather chair with Noel at her side, both watching Peter, and after a few seconds heard him exclaim, 'That's impossible,' and then immediately apologise. 'I'm sorry, Mr Carre, of course I'm not doubting your expertise, but was it really necessary to inform the police?' Then, a moment later: 'Yes, I suppose they will. I'll just ask Monique if she would prefer a hire car.'

'Yes I would. I'm not happy driving Dad's Volvo estate,' said Monique.

As soon as Peter replaced the receiver Noel asked, 'What was that all about?'

'I'm sorry. Mr Carre asked for me, probably because I—'

'We know all that,' interrupted Monique. 'What's wrong with my Mini? Why are the police involved?'

'There's no other way to tell you—'

'Oh, cut out the niceties,' said Noel.

'The brake cables had been cut.'

'Oh my God!' Peter watched as Monique closed her eyes, Noel reached for her hand and muttered, 'He didn't waste any time, did he?'

'Who? What are you saying?' demanded Monique, now staring at her husband, who reminded her, 'I'm thinking of what Ben said yesterday.'

Noel stopped abruptly as the phone rang and nodded that Peter should answer it, when Inspector Le Tissier said quietly, 'I'm glad you're still at the hotel, Mr Stenton. I understand you were driving behind Mrs Latimer, therefore I need to question you.' Then, without pausing, 'We're at the garage, have seen the car and will soon be on our way but, more important, how is Mrs Latimer? Will I be able to talk to her?'

'Yes.'

'Good. In the meantime will you, or her husband, ensure that the door to their garage, if it's open, is closed. Don't go inside, or touch anything. We'll come straight to the bungalow.'

'That was obviously the Inspector, what did he want?' asked Noel.

Peter glanced at Monique who nodded, told them Le Tissier's requirements and asked, 'Shall I go over and close the garage door?'

'No, we'll all go, then we'll be there when he arrives.' Noel looked at Monique. 'How are you feeling?'

'Much better but I don't like what's happening. Why can't we go into the garage, what's the Inspector looking for?'

*****

'I was very concerned to hear about your accident this morning, Mrs Latimer, and the cause. However I would like to ask you a few questions.'

'l don't understand why anyone would want to—'

'Cut the brake cables,' interrupted Noel.

'How, what did they use?' Monique was sat on the settee beside Noel, facing the Inspector and Sergeant Batiste while Peter, who she had insisted should remain, sat near the open French window.

'Pliers, secateurs,' suggested Le Tissier, 'but let's establish a few facts. When did you last use your car?'

'I took my Honda when we went to see Advocate Levrier yesterday afternoon,' volunteered Noel.

'And I used the Mini in the morning,' said Monique. 'It's been in the garage until I went into town today.'

'Was the garage door open all night?'

'No, I closed and locked it when I came back from the hotel,' said Noel.

'What time was that, sir?' asked Batiste, although he was still writing.

'About eleven-thirty.'

Le Tissier had already ascertained that Monique had returned to the bungalow at 10.30 and now asked, 'Did you go into the kitchen when you returned, and was the door leading from your kitchen to the garage locked before you went across to the hotel?'

Monique looked puzzled. 'No to your first question and yes to the second.'

'Did you unlock the garage door when you went to the hotel this morning?'

'I unlocked it, as usual, about eight o'clock.' It was Noel's turn to look perplexed as he continued, 'What are you inferring, Inspector?'

'So the times of your locking and unlocking the garage door were general knowledge?'

'I suppose so. I'd never really thought—'

'Who would benefit if anything happened to you, Mrs Latimer?' interjected Le Tissier.

'I haven't made a Will.' Monique turned her head and her eyes sought Peter's, but he waited a moment and then she resumed, 'Everything has changed since Dad died. I didn't have much money but now I've inherited a large proportion of the shares in the hotel.'

'Think before you say anything else,' whispered Noel and aloud he asked, 'Do you want to see the garage, Inspector?'

'Of course,' and standing up, Le Tissier looked directly at Monique. 'Who inherited the remaining shares in the hotel? Were they divided between your brother and your cousin?'

'Not Gerald. He was left—' Monique's voice faded and Noel asked, 'Are you insinuating it could be one of the family?' and looking at Peter, 'What do you think?'

'If a person is short of or desperate for money they might do anything,' and turning to the Inspector, 'If you want to know where I was, I spent the evening with one of your officers, Emile Girard. He left my hotel about midnight.'

'That was unnecessary, but thank you, Mr Stenton. Now, shall we make our way to the garage,' and with a slight grin, 'via the kitchen?'

'H'm, it was certainly done here.' Inspector Le Tissier indicated a large patch of oil on the concrete floor and after glancing at the few items on the shoulder-height shelf, asked Noel, 'Did you use your car this morning?'

'No.'

Batiste looked up from his notebook. 'Shall I ask the constable who's been checking outside to see if the pliers and secateurs are in their respective sheds?'

'Yes, perhaps the porter or even Owen Mahy could show him where they are.'

The Inspector looked at Monique who nodded, 'Tell him to go to Reception, in the meantime I'll ring Pat.' It was after she had done this that Monique glanced at her watch and suddenly exclaimed, 'I'll be late, especially as not having a car I'll have to walk,' then seeing puzzled expressions, she explained, 'I was going to have tea with Vere.'

'I could run you up there,' offered Peter when Le Tissier said, 'I haven't quite finished yet, Mrs Latimer. However, why don't you phone Mr Hamilton, but don't tell him what's happened, just that you had a slight accident?'

'Thank you. He tends to get rather anxious after what's been happening.' But before Monique could apologise Vere suggested, 'I'll come down to you and as I made a sponge, I'll bring it with me.'

'Well done,' said Le Tissier. 'I'd be glad if you don't tell anyone what really happened today.'

'What about Ben?'

'Tell him the same as you told Vere.' The Inspector's next question surprised Monique even more: 'I suppose Gerald Stenton is your cousin?'

'What?' and a second later she asked, 'What do you mean?'

'He isn't someone else claiming to be your cousin?'

'Of course not. The idea's preposterous.'

'Is it? No one, not even your father, had met or heard of him before.'

Monique turned to look at Peter, puzzled, and the latter offered, 'I've heard Dad talk about Uncle Roger, but that was years ago. He didn't hear from him after he left the island and I hadn't met Gerald until this trip.'

Le Tissier turned back to Monique. 'Would your father have had any family photographs of his brother?'

'It's possible. There were some in envelopes in the lower drawer of his desk. I brought one of them home but I haven't looked at the contents yet.'

Le Tissier glanced at Peter. 'Perhaps you could both do that later, after you've had your walk.'

'I could pick up the other photographs on my way back,' offered Peter when Monique reached for her handbag, extracted and handed over the keys and the Inspector asked, 'Are they always in there?'

Monique looked puzzled. 'Yes.'

'Not a good idea, especially if someone got hold of them.'

'I don't like the sound of that.' Noel stood up. 'I could cancel my haircut, but it is rather untidy and—'

'Oh stop fussing,' said Monique. 'You heard me arrange for Vere to come down so I won't be on my own for long.'

'That's fine, anyhow I'll come straight back,' and looking at Le Tissier, Noel continued, 'Obviously you don't trust anyone around here.'

'Keys are a great temptation to anyone,' and as Peter pocketed these, 'I'm sure you'll find a safe place for them when you return.'

Noel, who had already reached the door, now spun round and to everyone's surprise suggested, 'Why don't you move into Dad's bungalow for the time being? That way you can do what you have to do, and check that there aren't any strangers lurking around the other bungalows, hotel or grounds.'

'An excellent idea, Mr Latimer,' said the Inspector. 'One I was going to suggest myself. Thank you.'

'Good.' Noel glanced at Monique, amused that she was sat with her mouth half-open, still amazed. 'I'll tell Ben later and that it was my suggestion. I'll come straight back but you'll have Vere to keep you company. Coming, Peter?'

'Of course.' And with a 'See you later' to Monique and the Inspector, Peter followed Noel.

When they were alone, Le Tissier held Monique's gaze until she said, 'I don't know what's happened to make Noel so friendly towards Peter. I only hope it lasts. Anyhow, I'm going to make some tea. Would you like a cup, Inspector?'

'That's very kind of you, Mrs Latimer. Thank you.'

'Sir,' Batiste had suddenly appeared in the doorway. 'The constable's gone off with Cyril Maunder, one of the gardeners. If he finds anything he'll ring you direct, I lent him my mobile,' and in an undertone asked, 'what's happened? I saw Noel and Peter chatting quite amicably.'

'At the moment they're—' An unusual bleeping interrupted and a cheerful young voice exclaimed excitedly, 'Sir, Inspector Le Tissier, I've…I mean we – that's Cyril and I – have found his pliers but they're in rather a mess. Unfortunately I haven't a plastic bag that's large enough so I haven't touched them.'

'Good. Sergeant Batiste is on his way.' The next minute there was the sound of voices from the hall and Vere, holding a plastic cake container, appeared. 'Good afternoon, Inspector.'

'Hello, Mr Hamilton. I hope this sudden change of plan hasn't inconvenienced you?'

'Not at all. I'll just take my sponge through to the kitchen.'

Vere is certainly an unusual man, reflected Le Tissier. He had met the retired solicitor soon after his arrival in the island and found him to be a highly intelligent and charming person who he later learnt was an excellent cook.

'Are you really all right?' enquired Vere solicitously after he had greeted Monique.

'Yes, I'm fine now, thank you.'

Vere picked up the tray. 'I'll take this in for you. You can put the sponge on a plate and bring it in.'

Le Tissier accepted a cup of tea, complimented Vere on the lightness of his sponge, noted the rapport between Vere and Monique, and then stood up when the latter enquired, 'Am I allowed to ask if your constable has found what he's looking for?'

'You can, but I can't say more than that at the moment. However I must go. Thank you for the tea, Mrs Latimer.'

When they were alone Vere said, 'It wasn't an ordinary accident, this morning, was it? But if you prefer not to talk about it, I'll quite understand.'

Monique hesitated for a moment, and then burst out, 'My brakes didn't work when I came down the hill. And it was no accident – the brake cables had been cut.'

'My God!' Vere set down his cup and saucer with a clatter. 'How can you sit there and tell me that? Is that why Le Tissier was here?'

'Yes.'

'Does Peter know?'

Briefly Monique explained that he had been following her, brought her back to the hotel and arranged for her Mini to be picked up by their usual garage.

'And he phoned the police?'

'No, the owner of the garage did that, hence Le Tissier's visit.' Monique quickly related what had happened since the Inspector's arrival when Vere shook his head. 'I'm amazed you're talking about this so calmly.'

'Those who know have been very kind and supportive, and although it won't be general knowledge and he'll keep his room at the hotel in town, Peter's going to move into Dad's bungalow for a few days.'

'An excellent idea which I'm sure meets the Inspector's approval.'

'Yes, but Ben won't like it.'

Chapter 16

'What's going on, why is your garage closed and Noel's car parked outside?' Monique stared at Ben who had barely stepped into the hall and, aware of his growing irritation, said, 'Come in. It won't take a moment to tell you.'

'Oh, all right,' muttered Ben grudgingly, but on reaching the lounge refused to sit down. However his attitude did change when Monique told him, 'I had an accident when I was coming down the hill this morning. The brake cables of my Mini had been cut, but I—'

'My God!' interrupted Ben. 'You stand there and calmly tell me that. You could've been killed.' To Monique's surprise Ben hugged her tight. 'I know I have been and I am irresponsible and selfish, and say some stupid and unkind things, but I couldn't really bear it if anything happened to you. You're holding the place together, and all I can think of is myself and what I want.'

'There's no need for you to talk like that,' protested Monique.

'It's true – you're incredible. Most people would make a fuss. You should see the doctor—'

'I did. Dr Bryce came down and later Inspector Le Tissier.'

'Why?' Then after Monique had recounted that Peter had been driving down the hill behind her, pulled her from the Mini and brought her back to the hotel, Ben also learnt it was the garage owner (who had always looked after Matthew's car) who discovered the damaged brakes, advised Peter and also the police.

'What!' Then as he really understood the significance of what had happened, Ben asked, 'What did and what can they do?'

'After asking a lot of questions my Mini was taken to the police garage where they'll—'

'Someone did this deliberately?' interrupted Ben. 'And only 10 days after Dad was—' His voice faded. 'Who'd do this? Why?'

'Inspector Le Tissier wanted to know more about Gerald but although he's been here five years I couldn't tell him very much. They examined our garage but a more thorough examination will be carried out tomorrow.'

'What are they looking for?'

'I don't know and staying here, thinking about it, won't do me any good.'

'You're amazing! Where's Noel? Why isn't he here keeping you company?'

'He came back, looking much tidier but after a while got the fidgets and wanted to check the wine stock list.'

'Huh! That doesn't usually bother him. However if you change your mind about coming over, let me know.'

Alone, Monique wandered into the bedroom, and gazed at her reflection in the mirror. Yes, Ben was right, she did look pale. Monique then recalled that Dr Bryce had told her only that morning that she was too thin. She had noted the concern in Peter's gaze whenever they met but knew he was too polite to mention it, whilst Noel was currently concerned about what had happened and amicable towards Peter, she knew he was eager to begin a new career. But how would this affect her own future and the hotel?

Meanwhile Peter was slowly going from room to room in his father's bungalow without touching anything. He knew that Monique had put everything back in the right place after the break-in and, gazing around the lounge, wondered what the intruder had been looking for. Matthew had not owned anything of value but perhaps in due course, when he went through his father's personal belongings, he might find something of sentimental value. A few minutes later Peter drove up the hill recalling his walk on the cliff path. He had stood alone near the fence, the place from which his father had been eventually pushed, remembering the many happy occasions they had spent together and now wondered who was responsible for his father's unfortunate and untimely death, and causing Monique's accident.

*****

It was during Pat's dinner break that Ben found Monique in Reception and reluctantly accepted her explanation that she felt better if she was doing something. Still surprised at Ben's concern and thinking this was as good an opportunity as any, Monique said, 'I haven't had a chance to tell you that Peter's going to sleep in Dad's bungalow for a few nights. Inspector Le Tissier is concerned about what's happening out here but doesn't want to send any men down and was about to suggest it when Noel fore—'

'My God! ' interrupted Ben. 'Does the Inspector think you're in danger? Has he suggested you move out?'

'No, nothing as drastic as that. However it'll give Peter a chance to start sorting out Dad's clothes and personal belongings; but there's no reason why you shouldn't take whatever you want.'

'Thanks. I've got my key.'

Monique nodded. 'There are several ornaments which weren't broken that I'd like, but if you'd like them, I'm sure there'll be something else.'

'There's no hurry about that.' Ben stopped abruptly and still facing Monique, asked, 'Would you prefer to eat in your bungalow – have something sent over?' and when Monique shook her head, 'In that case I'll see you later.'

*****

On reaching his hotel Peter went directly to his room and quickly made some phone calls, informing Vere and Arnold Levrier that he would be sleeping in his father's bungalow and spending some time there for the next few days, but he was retaining his room here, at the town hotel. Vere admitted that he already knew about the accident, having had tea with Monique, but promised to keep this information to himself, while Arnold asked to be advised of any further developments or change of plans.

He then enquired, 'Will you see Roslyn before going back there tonight?'

'It's possible. Carol Cummings is joining me for dinner, so unless she's made other arrangements I might see Roslyn in the bar.'

'In which case you'll discover that she knows Carol. However, reverting to Roslyn, what are you going to tell her?'

'That I'll be spending time at the bungalow, and if she asks any questions, tell her that there was an accident.'

Changed and ready for his dinner guest, his overnight case packed, Peter was waiting in the hall when Carol, looking elegant in a sapphire blue dress and three-quarter length jacket, entered at the same time that Roslyn, wearing an emerald-green trouser suit, came downstairs. The two women greeted each other with cries of delight and both turning to Peter jointly exclaimed, 'How did you know we knew each other but haven't met this year?' This is unexpected, thought Peter and looking directly at Carol with raised eyebrows suggested, 'I'm sure you're both ready for a drink.' It was as he stood at the counter that Carol joined him and asked, 'Is my presence putting you in a difficult situation? Are you and Roslyn an item?'

'Good Heavens, no! I only met her a week ago and we have spent a little time together.'

Carol nodded. 'Why don't you ask her to join us for dinner? There'll be another opportunity, now that you're staying on, and after today's accident, for us to meet and talk about Matthew.'

'That's very thoughtful of you,' and as their drinks were placed on the counter, 'I'll ask Roslyn, and then speak to George.'

The white-haired head waiter greeted Carol with a welcoming smile. 'I'm delighted to see you, Mrs Cummings. I hope you have an enjoyable evening.'

'Thank you, George.'

As usual the meal was excellent, the conversation general and light-hearted. It was during Roslyn's absence, to take a phone call, that Peter asked, 'How did you know about the accident?'

'I was at the garage when you phoned about Monique's car. I hope she wasn't badly injured?'

'No, thank goodness. Dr Bryce came down and checked her over.'

Carol nodded, 'He's a good man, and also my doctor.'

But very discreet, thought Peter, standing up as Roslyn approached, smiling. 'Isn't it marvellous, everyone is so friendly. Esme has just invited me to spend tomorrow with them. She knows I enjoy a chat about our schooldays.' Later, having escorted Carol to her taxi, Peter returned to the hall to find Roslyn yawning. 'Oh excuse me. I'm so sleepy. It's all this lovely fresh air.'

Relieved that she would be spending the day with the Levriers', Peter agreed, wished her goodnight, watched as she headed for the lift then, using the stairs, quickly went up to his room. It only took a moment for him to change into a T-shirt, slacks and soft shoes, pick up his case and make for the back stairs, which it had been agreed he could use. Noel had suggested he should use the hotel car park where another hire car would not be noticed and that the night porter, a middle-aged local man, should be informed that Peter would be sleeping in Matthew's bungalow for the next four or five nights.

Peter let himself in and as he knew where everything was if he wanted a drink and without switching on any lights, went directly to the room that had been Ben's.

Chapter 17

When the phone rang on a Sunday afternoon it usually meant trouble and Detective Inspector Le Tissier glared at the offending instrument before picking up the receiver.

Detective Sergeant Batiste sounded apologetic as he said, 'There's more trouble at the Serena Beach Hotel, sir. It's Ben this time.'

'Has he been attacked?'

'No. Monique said there was glass in Ben's sweet. Dr Bryce had seen him and arranged for an immediate X-ray.'

'Could it have been an accident?'

'Monique, who sounded rather upset, said there were still slivers of glass in the apfelstrudel.'

'There's too many things happening out there. Matthew's death, Monique's accident and now this,' interrupted Le Tissier, and after swearing mildly: 'We'd better get down there. Can you pick me up, please, Batiste? My wife needs the car to take the children to a party.'

'Certainly, sir. I'm on my way.'

*****

Once again Le Tissier was impressed by Monique's composure as she led the way to the cold kitchen and indicated a foil-covered tray. Lifting this, the Inspector considered that the remaining slices looked delicious, heard

Batiste's stomach give a definite rumble and told Monique, 'We'll have to take these with us. However, where's the remains of Ben's sweet?'

'In the office.'

Batiste picked up the tray and exited by the back door while Le Tissier followed Monique through the large main kitchen and into the dining room, noting the crisp table-linen, gleaming silver and glasses set out for dinner, the gold and bronze patterned carpet and plain gold curtains. Beyond the large picture windows the grounds stretched to the beach and, beyond, the sea shimmered under a cloudless blue sky.

'It's quite amazing, isn't it?' Monique's voice came quietly from the doorway.

'Yes. One always hears such good reports of your hotel and its surroundings but as so often happens, we don't always visit our own beauty spots.'

'It was my father's life and now—' Monique faltered, and led the way to the office where, on a plate in the centre of the desk, was an unappetising mess of pastry and thin slices of cooked apples.

'Has anyone else touched this?' and when Monique shook her head, Le Tissier picked up a fork and moved it about, the fork clinking faintly in the silence as it struck a sliver of glass.

Eventually three splinters appeared at the edge of the plate when Monique, who was standing beside the Inspector, exclaimed, 'That's very fine glass, could be from one of our wine glasses.'

Then Noel appeared in the doorway, slightly breathless. 'What's happened? I passed an ambulance and Bryce's car at the top of the hill. Why are you here, Inspector?'

Monique glanced at Le Tissier and it was the latter who recounted the facts and asked, 'Where were you?'

'I took two of our regulars home, the Sebire sisters,' and when Monique nodded, 'Their taxi didn't turn up, they were rather agitated.'

On learning that Monique had eaten a salad before relieving Pat, that Noel was about to have the same, neither ate a sweet at lunchtime and that the three of them usually sat at a corner table (near the kitchen) in the dining room, Le Tissier asked, 'Do you always eat separately?'

'No, but Sunday lunch times are always busy so we all have a salad which we can eat at any time. Ben enjoys apfelstrudel and as an afterthought Noel asked, 'Did he swallow any glass?'

'I...I don't think so. Two of the waiters were still in the dining room, heard him make a peculiar noise, thought he was being sick and rushed over. Ben was holding his throat, and pointing to a smidgen of glass which he'd coughed up into his serviette. Gerald, who was also there, fetched me and I phoned the doctor who came immediately.'

'What happened to the serviette?'

'It's here.' At the same moment that Monique pointed to a crumpled serviette the phone rang, she answered it and a moment later her face brightened. 'So he didn't swallow any glass?' Then Le Tissier was reaching out, she relinquished the receiver and gave a sigh of relief while Noel said quietly, 'That was all very quick. There must have been a radiographer on duty.'

The Inspector had concluded his conversation with Dr Bryce and now said, 'Yes. There was a nasty car accident — three vehicles, this morning. Four people were badly injured. However I'm not happy about what's happening down here. I'll have to speak to the chef who made this, but I expect he's gone. Also the two waiters and of course Gerald. I need to know when the apfelstrudel was placed on the table, by whom and which members of staff were still on duty.'

'Of course. Gerald will be able—'. The gentle tap on the door from Reception had been ignored but this now opened and Pat, looking from Monique to the Inspector, said, 'I have Miss Laval on the line. She sounds—'

'I'll speak to her.' Le Tissier leant forward again but was unprepared for the shrill voice that demanded, 'What have you done to him? My poor darling Ben, rushed off to hospital. He can hardly speak! Why wasn't I told and why aren't you at his bedside? You can't be a very loving sister. You're just a greedy slave-driver, a workaholic who expects him to do the same for a pittance. Well he won't, I'll make sure of that. You're a—'

'Would you repeat that, Miss Laval?'

Monique and Noel stared at Le Tissier, whose voice was as grim as his expression, and watched him blink when the caller yelled, 'The conniving bitch! She's got you there taking her calls. How low can you get? It's no wonder there's talk about her having it off with that precious so-called half-brother—'

By now Le Tissier was on his feet, Batiste was standing in the open doorway from the foyer indicating that he had carried out certain instructions while Noel and Monique, pale and shaking, who had also heard every word, watched as Peter suddenly appeared behind Batiste. At that moment Cheryl's shrill voice could be heard, 'It's Ben I love and want, not Godfrey Reardon, although he can usually get the stuff I need.' Then, forgetting to whom she was talking and with a sudden whimper, 'And my God, I need some now. Get me some,' and in the same breath, 'I must go, there's someone at the front door. It could be someone with a supply, Godfrey knows I'm desperate.'

'They should be there,' said Batiste quietly while Peter took one look around and demanded, 'What the hell's going on?'

Within seconds Le Tissier recounted recent events, when Peter sought Monique's gaze. 'Are you all right?'

'Yes, but I can't really understand what Cheryl was talking about,' and turning to Batiste, 'I realise it's none of my business but, as she's involved with Ben, I would like to know why you were sending police to her house?'

Le Tissier, who was still standing, looked directly at Monique. 'This isn't my case but we do know that Cheryl is a frequent visitor to The Sparrow's Nest where drugs are available.'

And ignoring Monique's gasp, 'It sounds as though she's alone in the house and is obviously suffering from withdrawal symptoms, so Batiste arranged for a paramedic to accompany a policeman.'

Peter had manoeuvred his way round the office as the Inspector spoke and in spite of his previous conversation with Emile Girard, enquired, 'Is this your way of telling us that Ben's on drugs?'

'I really don't know, Mr Stenton. I'm still investigating the circumstances surrounding your father's death, but unfortunately, other unpleasant incidents have occurred down here.'

Le Tissier turned to Monique. 'Batiste and I will return later to question the chef, Gerald and the two waiters who were in the dining room. We would also like to speak to Ben while we're here.'

'He'll be home by then?' asked Noel.

'He won't be kept in hospital very long but he may have a sore throat,' and looking at Peter, Le Tissier continued, 'I'm sure, as far as you're concerned, the fewer people who know about this, the better.'

'Of course.' Peter looked at Noel. 'Did anything untoward occur in the dining room during lunch?'

'No. Everyone enjoyed their three course lunch. No complaints, as usual.'

'Did the staff have any apfelstrudel?'

'No. There was very little left, about four portions—'

'Which we've taken to check for any more glass. However we'll question the necessary staff this evening. About eight-thirty?'

'Yes. They like to finish early on a Sunday, if possible,' said Monique and as the door closed she sighed, 'What on earth is happening to this family?'

'And who would start such horrible rumours?' asked Noel.

'This Cheryl Laval sounds a most unpleasant person. Have you ever met her, has Ben brought her down here?' Peter looked from one to the other when they simultaneously exclaimed, 'No! ' and Monique asked, 'How did you know the Inspector was here?'

'I'd just returned from lunch with a friend and, although they were using an unmarked car, recognised it. Anyhow, I'm going back to the bungalow,' and lowering his voice: 'I've sorted Dad's clothes, and unless you have other ideas I thought those hardly worn could go to the Red Cross for their shop and everything else to the Salvation Army.'

Monique glanced at Noel who nodded, and with a catch in her throat, replied: 'That's fine. There are several suitcases, use them.'

'Good idea.'

*****

Monique woke with a start, blinked and suddenly realised she was lying on the sun-lounger on the patio, that Noel was standing beside her facing into the lounge, and it was the slamming of their front door which had woken her. Staring up at Noel she asked, 'What—' but he quickly put a finger to his lips and shook his head. Then a hoarse voice said, 'Ah, there you are!' Immediately Monique jumped to her feet. 'Ben! How are you? How did you get here?'

'Damn sore throat, ambulance car,' and without any bidding he stretched out on the lounger that Monique had just vacated and croaked, 'I need a drink. Something long and cool.'

'Of course,' but before she could move, Noel intervened. 'I'll get it,' and pushing her gently on to his lounger, 'You need a rest.' Glancing at Ben whose eyes were closed Noel mouthed, 'He's a selfish and inconsiderate brat who deserves a strong dose of castor oil.'

'Noel!' remonstrated Monique in a whisper, and a few minutes later watched as Ben swallowed the entire contents of a pint glass and closed his eyes again.

'Ungrateful b—' mouthed Noel who had brought out another lounger and sat down again.

It was half an hour later that Monique saw that Ben was lying in the same position, Noel had dropped off and realised that she had eventually dozed, but was now very thirsty.

Both men woke up with a start as she placed the tea tray on the table and Ben, his voice almost normal, asked, 'What's happened to Cheryl? What did you say to her?'

'Nothing. I didn't speak to her.'

'Neither did I, the second time I rang,' and Ben took the cup and saucer, drank some of his tea, gasped and glared at Monique. 'My God, that was hot! Put some more milk in it,' and resumed: 'A man answered, said she was sleeping and shouldn't be disturbed, that's why I came straight here. He eventually told me he was a paramedic but what was he doing there?' And, without pausing for breath, 'If neither of you spoke to Cheryl, who did?'

'Inspector Le Tissier,' said Noel and seeing Ben's bewilderment, 'The doctor called him and thought he should know—'

'Too true,' interrupted Ben. 'Someone tried to kill me.'

'Oh, don't be so dramatic. Those slivers wouldn't have done that,' said Monique.

'It must be one of the staff, any of those from the dining room or kitchen, they all had access to my sweet. What's the Inspector doing about it?'

'He's coming back later to question some of the staff and you.'

'I realise Cheryl is not to be disturbed, however I want to go and see her, so when, what time will he be here?'

'After dinner,' and wary of Ben's reaction, Monique suggested, 'Why don't you ring Cheryl's parents?'

'Huh! I'd be lucky if they were capable of answering.'

This time Monique couldn't help herself. 'Ben! That's not a very nice thing to say.'

'It's true. They both drink like a fish. I've only seen them sober once, and that was early afternoon. I doubt that they ever eat. She's painfully thin and even if they're expensive her clothes just hang on her, while her language…As for the old man, he's not that old but he's skinny, his face is a mess and he certainly doesn't care about his appearance.'

Ben's voice was now husky and Monique said, 'Go and have a rest yourself, then phone Cheryl. Find out if she feels well enough to see you.'

Ben swung his feet to the ground and stood up. 'I'm sure she'll be pleased to see me. Cheryl doesn't have any real friends,' and as he reached the French window: 'I'll be back before the Inspector arrives.'

'What a family!' exclaimed Noel as Ben disappeared. 'Have you ever heard anything about the Lavals?'

'No but I am concerned that at some time in the future Ben could be taking on the whole family.'

'You shouldn't worry about something that might never happen,' and unable to curb his curiosity, Noel continued, 'I wonder how Peter is getting on? If he's found anything that could help the Inspector with his enquiries.'

'He said he'd call in here, or the hotel, before he goes back to his hotel for dinner.'

'He could eat with us. It's rather ridiculous that he drives into town and then back out here later, to sleep.'

Monique nodded, hiding her surprise that Noel was now being so amiable towards Peter and suggested, 'Why don't you ask him?'

Monique was adjusting the waistband of her skirt, concerned that like other skirts, it was rather loose, when she heard Peter say, 'Thanks for suggesting it, but I've already made arrangements to meet an old school friend. Perhaps another evening?' and whilst he did not feel particularly fraternal towards his half—brother, Peter enquired, 'How's Ben? What time did he get back from the hospital?'

'They didn't keep him there very long. After a rest he went to see Cheryl but assured us that he'll be back to see Inspector Le Tissier.'

By now Monique was ready, emerged from the bedroom, greeted Peter and asked, 'How did you get on this afternoon?'

'I found and filled the cases which, if you agree, I'll leave at the respective charity shops tomorrow.' and when Monique nodded, 'As you know there was very little in the desk.'

Peter hesitated, 'It's a lovely old piece of furniture, been in the family for years — amazing it survived the Occupation, wasn't confiscated by the Germans. Dad was very fond of it.'

Peter paused. 'I don't want to be presumptuous but if Ben or you don't want it, I'll gladly buy it. However it's too early to think about such things, but I'll go through the drawers in the desk tomorrow morning.'

'There can't be much. They were all open and papers scattered on the floor. These are in a large envelope which I brought back here. I might look through them later.'

'There's no hurry, wait and see what I find.' Then, noting Noel's disapproval, Peter continued, 'Anyhow I must go. I'll see you both sometime tomorrow.'

*****

'I certainly saw Eduardo place Ben's salad and sweet, both covered in tinfoil, on the table, just before two o'clock. Ben usually comes in about five or ten minutes later.' Gerald had already told Inspector Le Tissier that Monique had eaten earlier, and continued, 'There was hardly anyone left in the dining room. It was a lovely day and most of the regulars prefer to eat early. I was on the far side of the room, checking the table for a dinner party but hurried over to Ben when he started coughing. The two waiters also ran over to his table, offering water and looking anxious.'

Le Tissier nodded; he already knew this, the two Filipinos had been very articulate, that no one had approached that table. Sonia, the plump Austrian patissier, her long blonde curls tied back, was tearful. Nothing like this had ever happened; she had no idea how any glass could be in her apfelstrudel. Hans, the head chef, was about to change when he heard coughing and reached the dining room to see Ben vomiting into his serviette and then clutching his throat.

Gerald resumed, 'Fortunately Dr Bryce was on call, came down immediately, and arranged for an ambulance. However, how is Ben?'

'Apart from a sore throat he's made a remarkable recovery and is now resting.'

Le Tissier looked from Hans to Sonia; they were all seated at one of the tables in the staff dining room, and he asked, 'Can either of you tell me firstly, how or when the glass was mixed in, and secondly, is there anyone in your department who dislikes Ben to such an extent?'

'No. As I told you this afternoon, there were no cracked or broken glasses in the kitchen.'

Hans glanced at Gerald who nodded. 'Wine glasses, in fact all glassware, are taken directly to the allocated area.' Le Tissier then learnt that no wine glasses had been broken, none were missing and although there was a special container for such breakages, the ordinary rubbish had been thoroughly searched but no fragments or particles of glass had been found.

Sonia continued to look puzzled, 'So where did it come from? Except for my ingredients, my working area was completely clean.'

'Were you called away or interrupted?' asked Batiste.

'No.'

*****

'So, who's responsible?' demanded Ben as Inspector Le Tissier, with Sergeant Batiste immediately behind him, appeared in the doorway.

'Unfortunately it's not as simple as that.' Le Tissier ignored Ben's lack of manners, noted his pallor, hoarse voice and that he was seated in the leather chair normally used by Monique. He had been pleased to see her in Reception and that the door leading into the office was ajar.

'What do you mean? Someone's responsible for the glass in my sweet.'

'No broken wineglasses have been found and none are missing from the dining room—'

'They're also used in the bar,' interrupted Ben rudely. 'It could have been taken from there, deliberately smashed and the fragments sprinkled in—'

'Now that's something we didn't take into consideration,' admitted Le Tissier, and promptly told Batiste, 'Go and check with the barman.' Then, turning back to Ben: 'It wouldn't be very easy for just anyone to walk into the kitchen and sprinkle—'

'It must be one of the staff,' interrupted Ben again. 'Someone who doesn't like me.'

'Have you any particular person in mind? Can other members of the staff walk through the kitchen while meals are being prepared?'

'No. Hans is very strict.'

'Which limits it to kitchen staff.' said Le Tissier.

'So what are you going to do now?' demanded Ben.

'The kitchen staff will have to be questioned tomorrow morning and the plates, already at the station, checked for fingerprints.' Le Tissier broke off as Batiste returned, followed by Noel, when the former said, 'The barman did a quick check – none missing.'

'That's ridiculous!' Ben's voice was so hoarse that Monique suddenly appeared in the doorway from Reception, and the Inspector, noting her concerned expression, said, 'We've almost finished. As you've probably heard, we're wondering about the wine glass which was used.'

Monique nodded, hesitated and then offered, 'We do have wine glasses in our De Luxe suites and although the occupants haven't asked for a replacement it could for some reason have come from there. Shall I ask the chambermaid on duty to check?'

'Tomorrow morning will do.' Le Tissier had already noted that Ben looked very tired and even paler. 'Perhaps you could phone me.'

'Of course.'

As he stood up Ben seemed to stumble. Noel jumped up and reached out to steady him, when Monique asked, 'Shall I come across to your bungalow with you?'

'Don't be so stupid, I'm quite capable of getting there. I just want to be alone.' As he reached the door, Ben turned and his gaze travelled from the two detectives to Monique where it lingered. 'After what happened yesterday and this afternoon I've a lot to think about.'

At a loss for words Monique stared after him and then called out, 'How was Cheryl?' and receiving no reply looked at Le Tissier, 'What do you think he meant? Is he worried about what happened to him, or Cheryl?'

'He'll probably tell you in good time. Excuse me a moment.' Le Tissier read the note which Batiste had thrust into his hand and then said, 'Can you spare me a few minutes, Mr Latimer?'

'Of course.' Noel glanced across the room at Monique who was now looking anxious. 'Do you want my wife to stay?'

'That won't be necessary. However, as it's such a lovely evening let's have a stroll in the grounds.'

Back in Reception, her thoughts confused, Monique watched as Noel led the way to the main entrance and outside, but was jerked back to reality by Pat saying, 'I've Ailsa Jehan on the line. She's enquiring if there's likely to be a vacancy in the near future.'

'I remember her. She's the receptionist at the Reardons' place and from what I've heard, extremely efficient. Ask her to come in and see you.'

'Me?'

'Why not? I suggest you offer Ailsa your position as head receptionist,' and when Pat gasped, 'I hope I'm not being too presumptuous, I haven't had an opportunity to discuss it with you, but I'd like you to take over most of my duties as assistant manager, and young Bryony isn't capable of doing your job. You would, of course, have a considerable wage increase.' And as Pat continued to stare at her, Monique resumed, 'You'll have to advertise the position in the local paper and interview anyone who applies but I'm sure Ailsa knows this is the usual procedure.' And when Pat nodded, 'This is something we should have done some time ago. Dad was always singing your praises, saying how capable and efficient you are.'

'Oh, how marvellous! ' Pat blinked back her tears and as she hugged Monique, 'This is the most wonderful thing that's ever happened to me. Thank you! '

Monique relaxed in her friend's embrace but the next moment remembered Ben's departing remark and Noel's restlessness; was the future of the hotel so assured that she could make such a hasty decision?

Chapter 18

'What's happened? Why do you want to talk to me on my own?' Noel stopped when they reached the slipway to the beach and glanced from Sergeant Batiste to Inspector Le Tissier.

'What were you wearing on the Thursday evening that Matthew died?' Le Tissier looked directly at Noel's left sleeve as he spoke, noting that the middle button was missing.

Noel frowned, obviously thinking and then said, 'This jacket, but why are you staring at my sleeve?'

'Do you know a button is missing?'

'Damn! That means Monique will have to buy a new set and change all the others.'

'I'm not concerned about that, Mr Latimer, but where the lost button was found.'

'What…what do you mean?' Noel stared at the Inspector uncomprehendingly.

'You omitted to tell us that you were on the cliff path that evening.'

'That's ridiculous! I don't have time to go for a walk in the evening.' Noel sounded resentful as he continued, 'After I've finished in the dining room, listed the wine I need for the next day, I change and go into the bar to socialise with the residents and any locals. The time varies, of course; if there's a dinner party or at weekends,' and without being asked, 'Gerald and I usually finish about the same time, half past nine. However, why are you so interested in my jacket?'

'Because the missing button, or one very similar, was found on the cliff path, close to where Matthew fell.'

'But I wasn't there. I told you my movements the first time you questioned me and now I've just repeated them.' Noel bent his arm to peer at the tiny space between the two remaining buttons when Le Tissier also lowered his head, noticed the ends of cotton protruding from the material and asked, 'Where do you hang your jacket when you're in the dining room?'

'I've always hung it in the staff dining room. I don't leave anything in the pockets and I've never had any problems.' Noel now looked puzzled. 'Why all these questions?'

'Because, as I've already told you, a button that could be from your jacket was found near the place where Matthew was pushed and fell. I need to take your jacket with me,' and, aware of Noel's expression: 'We'll give you a receipt.'

'I hope you don't have to keep it too long – it's my favourite jacket.' And as he handed this over, Noel resumed, 'Monique's bound to miss it, ask where it is. What do I tell her?'

'I'm sure you'll think of a suitable reply.'

*****

In the meantime Ben was deep in thought, worried about Cheryl. Although calmer she had clung to him, begging him to stay and in spite of his appointment with Inspector Le Tissier he had been reluctant to leave her.

They had heard the front door slam announcing her parents' return, their voices raised in yet another slanging match, when Ben realised it would be futile to tell them about Cheryl. The Lavals were really useless, reflected Ben. Their life, since they came to the island, was a constant round of drinks parties and it was obvious they neither knew nor cared how and where Cheryl spent her time. There had been occasions when Ben felt he should tell them that, through no fault of his (he had endeavoured to discourage her), Cheryl could easily become a drug addict. He had tried various substances which had resulted in daring and stupid behaviour but was not as outrageous as that of other habituees of The Sparrow's Nest. Although he knew many of them it was Godfrey Reardon who, for some strange reason, he distrusted.

*****

'Who do you think would benefit if Monique's and Ben's accidents had been fatal?'

Sergeant Batiste had waited until they reached the top of the hill before asking this question.

Inspector Le Tissier looked thoughtful. 'As far as Monique is concerned and unless she's made a new Will since her father died, which I rather doubt: Noel.'

'And Ben?' Batiste hesitated and then suggested, 'I suppose Peter, being a half-brother, would be next-of-kin?'

'Yes, but fortunately Monique and Ben are both all right. On the other hand we're even more involved.' Monique's Mini had been taken to the police garage, arrangements had been made for SOCO to check out the Latimers' garage, while the pliers had been sent to Forensic. 'Today's incident has been unfortunate but, apart from a sore throat and tiredness, Ben should be fine by the morning.' Le Tissier reflected that the Chief wouldn't be very happy about the time and manpower that was being spent in, or in the vicinity of, the hotel; then, as they approached the main road he dimly heard Batiste say, 'Do you think the button that was deliberately cut off is the same as those on the jacket?'

'It's possible. It's a four-hole button, there isn't any soil embedded in any of them so it was obviously planted there that evening.'

'By someone who wants to incriminate Noel. Could this be the same person who tampered with Monique's brakes and sprinkled glass in Ben's apfelstrudel?'

'It's obviously someone who could get into the Latimers' garage, uses the changing room and be able to walk through the kitchen without any comment from Hans, which means it's someone on the staff and the person most likely is—' Le Tissier paused and together they said, 'Gerald!'

'Who isn't very informative about how he spends his time,' said Batiste. Then, as an afterthought, 'Or anything else.'

'No one has mentioned a woman in his life, even in England,' said Le Tissier as Batiste drew up outside his house. 'Let's hope we learn something from their bank statements.'

*****

'I can't believe so much has happened in such a short time,' said Arnold Levrier.

'It is incredible,' agreed Vere. 'I'm just so glad that Peter is here and at present, spending some time in Matthew's bungalow.' Then, with his inevitable urbanity, Vere enquired,

'Is there anything I can do?'

'I'd be only too pleased to help with any personal papers,' offered Arnold.

'It's very kind of you both but really there's no need,' said Peter. 'Monique has a large envelope full of papers, could be letters or bills that were scattered on the floor after the break-in. She hasn't had an opportunity to look through them yet.'

'That's not surprising'. Vere's expression and voice were grim. 'It's a good thing I don't know who's responsible or I'd—'

'She certainly had a lucky escape,' interrupted Arnold and with bated breath, 'Does Le Tissier think the same person is behind all this?'

'He hasn't said but then he wouldn't.' Peter looked from one to the other. 'Would you like a sweet?'

Vere and Arnold exchanged glances and the latter said, 'Just coffee please, then I'll take Vere home. I don't want to be late and you've got to go back to the bungalow.'

Chapter 19

The manager of the first bank, a middle-aged Englishman who had been in the island for 10 years, known and admired Matthew's acumen and success, greeted Inspector Le Tissier in an affable manner. Although he had met the Inspector at the wake he again expressed his shock at Matthew's untimely death. He then asked, 'How can I help you, Inspector? Is this regarding Matthew's accounts?'

'No.' Le Tissier produced the necessary authority and a few minutes later learnt that Monique kept a minimum balance on her current account, her monthly salary being paid into a fixed deposit account.

'She's a remarkable young woman who inherited her father's flair and dedication. Unfortunately I can't say the same for her brother, nor can I offer any information about his financial affairs – he doesn't have a large balance on either account. I do know that his friendship, or whatever it is, with Cheryl Laval, worried Matthew. Obviously, as they don't bank with us, I can't tell you anything about Noel's or Gerald's finances. Monique's husband is a nice chap, doesn't seem to have made many friends in the time he's been here, while the cousin struck me as a rather indifferent character.'

Mr Chapman sighed, 'Although I attended his funeral I still can't believe this has happened. Matthew Stenton was such a likeable and popular person who will be missed by everyone who knew him.'

Then, as Le Tissier stood up, Chapman also rose to his feet and asked, 'What happened on Saturday morning? I heard

Monique was returning to the hotel when her car came off the road. Was she injured?'

'Fortunately, no. However I must continue with my enquiries. Thank you for your cooperation.'

The next bank manager was also cooperative and within minutes Le Tissier learnt that Noel had a reasonable balance on a fixed deposit and made very few withdrawals from his current account. Walking down the High Street to the next bank, Le Tissier considered that, apart from the time he spent in France and Germany, very little was known about Noel's background. He was an only child, born and educated in Bristol, and both parents had died in a multiple car crash whilst he was working in France.

The third manager expressed his concern that Matthew should have suffered such an untimely death. He also enquired about Monique, having heard about her accident and said that she was an extremely capable young woman. Le Tissier then learnt that Gerald had a current account, there were very few withdrawals but that regular monthly payments were made to a bank in Stirling, for an account in the name of Lilian McEnery.

These payments had begun five years ago and the amount increased annually.

'Obviously I can't tell you anything about this person, Inspector, whether she's an elderly relative or a young person but I must admit I'm curious.'

'So am I.'

Meanwhile, having opened all the windows, Peter noted that the only contents of the top drawer of the desk was plain white stationery. The second contained an address book which looked as though it had hurriedly been thrust back and he hazarded that Monique had probably checked if there was anyone in England who should be advised of Matthew's death. It was when he gathered up several hand-written but unsigned letters from the third and bottom drawer that Peter remembered the letter he had found in the inner pocket of the jacket of a light-weight suit. Reaching for his blazer he took a folded letter from an inner pocket and opening this, noted that there was no address at the top but that it was dated, and stared at the contents which were written in the same hand as those he had just found.

'My God!' he muttered, turning to the second page, and quickly sifted through the other letters, without success. They were all the same and unidentifiable. Noting that these had been written on the first of each month for a year, Peter asked himself 'Who is this person? Why didn't Dad tell me about these?' and in the same breath, 'Monique hasn't said anything so she probably doesn't know about them.' With the letters in chronological order in one hand, Peter reached for the phone and the next minute was asking Monique. 'Can you come over to Dad's bungalow? I've found something you should see.'

Peter was standing in the hall as Monique opened the front door. 'What is it? What have you found?' Then seeing the sheets of notepaper in his hand queried, 'Letters?'

'Come and sit down. I'm not suggesting you read them all, maybe the first and the last,' and when Monique looked up, 'That was in a jacket pocket.'

'And the others?'

'In the bottom drawer. Can you identify the handwriting?'

Monique wrinkled her nose as she bent her head, and said slowly, 'No, but I'm wondering if there's any more letters amongst the papers I picked up.'

'Where are they?'

'In my dressing table, in a large envelope. Shall I fetch it?'

'Yes. In the meantime I'll make some coffee,' A few minutes later Peter watched as Monique tipped the contents on the floor, then both kneeling, they quickly searched and simultaneously exclaimed, 'Here's one.' Comparing the dates, they had both been written the previous year; the handwriting was the same, the contents stronger in the second.

'Who is this woman and because of what's been written, it must be a woman.' Peter gazed at Monique over the rim of his mug, 'Was Dad involved with someone else? Seeing another woman, after Maureen died?'

'No, and I've no idea who this person could be, but she's certainly persistent.' Then seeing Peter's thoughtful expression, 'What is it?'

'I've just remembered.' Peter hesitated and then began again, 'It was after the funeral, back here at the hotel. Sergeant Batiste brought a most attractive woman across to meet me. She was a friend of my mother who spoke about Dad with affection and I invited her to dinner. As it happened, she knew Roslyn Tempest and I ended up with both of them for dinner.'

'What was her name, could she have written those letters?'

'Carol Cummings, but I doubt that she could be responsible.'

Monique nodded. 'I agree. Carol's a highly intelligent, very elegant lady,' and glancing at the letters on the coffee table beside Peter, 'Whereas she is obviously a very bitter woman. Shall I take them across to the office for shredding?'

'No. I think Le Tissier should see them,' and reaching for his mobile Peter continued, 'It could be my imagination but a person who writes such letters, each one stronger, could be capable of—' Then: 'Good morning, Inspector. I'm sorry to disturb you but we've found some letters which might be of interest.' Monique finished her coffee and stood up, still watching as Peter explained and then, 'I suppose you do. Obviously I don't know how many people have handled them, definitely Dad, Monique and myself but you may be able to find some fingerprints. I'll be coming back to town later this morning, would you—' but the conversation ended suddenly when Peter said, 'Very well. I'll wait for you.'

'Why is he coming out here?' asked Monique.

'I don't know. He didn't say. He's leaving now and is coming straight here.'

'Good. I must get back,' and after a slight pause, Monique resumed, 'You'll be surprised and I hope pleased to hear that I've promoted Pat to assistant manager, and she's arranged for Ailsa, the receptionist at Valley View – Reardon's place – to come for an interview.'

'That's fantastic, well done! '

'I haven't told Ben or Noel but I expect they'll complain and grumble that I didn't consult them.'

*****

'Have you any idea who wrote those letters? Do you recognise the handwriting?'

Wearing latex gloves, Inspector Le Tissier flicked through the letters and now looked from Monique to Peter.

'No,' they said in unison and Monique asked, 'Can I go back to the hotel? I'm sure Peter can answer any questions.' Le Tissier scrutinised the top letter again. 'You live in the island, so I must ask you: do you know of anyone who would write such letters to your father? This woman sounds as though she was jealous, resentful, especially in the last letter.'

'He obviously knew a number but didn't invite any here or take any out for a meal.'

Monique glanced at her watch, 'Could this woman have anything to do with Dad's death? Could a woman have sawn through those palings, inflicted those injuries?'

'It is possible. We're considering all eventualities.'

'Was the same person—' Monique glanced at Peter and then the Inspector. 'I really must go.'

As the front door closed Le Tissier asked, 'Am I correct in assuming Monique's intended question?'

I'm sure you are – was the same person responsible for her accident and possibly the incident regarding the glass in Ben's apfelstrudel?'

'The first is a possibility.' Le Tissier looked pensive and continued, 'Anyone who knew where to find the saw would have seen the pliers—'

'And even then, when Dad was still alive, could have planned Monique's—'

'This is someone who knows which is Monique's bungalow,' cut in Le Tissier, and added, 'and her car.'

'But why? What kind of person would plan Monique's accident only 9 days after—' Peter shook his head. 'I'm sorry. I'm finding it difficult to control my feelings. I don't know how Monique remains so composed.'

'She's a remarkable young woman and Noel Latimer is a very lucky man.' Le Tissier stood up as he spoke. 'Should either of you have any ideas about who could have written those letters, please let me know. I'll arrange for the handwriting to be sent to a graphologist. However I must be on my way. I've an appointment back at the station.'

At that moment the phone rang and answering it Peter glanced at the Inspector. 'Could you spare another minute, please? It's Monique – she has Hans and one of his young kitchen porters in her office.'

'Tell her I'm on my way but it'll have to be quick.'

Peter's reply floated after him. 'Ben's there.'

Ten minutes later Le Tissier gave a sigh of relief as he drove away from the hotel. He had been surprised to see Monique and Ben standing behind the desk, while a grim-faced Hans stood beside a lanky youngster who was unashamedly crying and hiccupping at the same time. In broken English he had said, 'I'm…I'm so sorry. I didn't mean to hurt Mr Ben. He was so angry with me on…on Friday, he called me nasty names, frightened me.'

It was at this point that Hans had intervened, explaining that Lars had been hopeless at work that morning, spilling food, dropping dishes and pans and, although scared, but not wanting Sonia to be blamed, had finally confessed. Hans had then looked from Ben to the Inspector, 'What's going to happen to him? Will he go to prison?'

Le Tissier had noticed that Monique had whispered to and restrained Ben on several occasions and remembering his previous outbursts had asked, and learnt that Ben did not intend to press charges.

*****

'How dare you go to the bank and question my finances.'

Inspector Le Tissier noted but ignored Gerald's anger and persisted, 'You told us that you returned to and spent the remainder of Thursday evening in your flat. Is there anyone who can substantiate this?'

Gerald glared at Le Tissier, taken aback at the sudden switch in questions, and snapped, 'You asked me that before, and I told you, no.'

'I find that difficult to believe.'

'I prefer my own company.'

'Or perhaps, due to certain commitments, you don't like spending your money on drink—'

'What do you mean, my commitments?' and then, 'My God! You've really been checking out my account.'

'I regret that it was necessary and now, due to those regular monthly payments, I'm rather concerned that you're being blackmailed.'

'Blackmailed!' echoed Gerald. 'I suppose you could call it that but although I haven't actually seen them—' then aware of the Inspector's puzzled expression, Gerald elucidated: 'My illegitimate twin sons, I was quite prepared to pay up.'

'Twins and you've never seen them,' whispered Batiste and unable to curb his curiosity, 'How old are they? Where do they live?'

'Five and they're in Scotland with their mother.' Then with a grim expression, 'Even at that age they're remarkably like me – there's no doubt that they're mine.'

'So there is another generation of Stentons! What did Matthew think about that?' asked Le Tissier.

'He didn't know. I never told him. I wasn't sure how he would react.'

'He was a family man, devastated when Peter's son died in that terrible accident. He would probably have been thrilled to know there was another generation.'

'I didn't want him telling me what to do – that I should marry Lilian,' muttered Gerald.

'He was a generous man, he would probably have helped you out financially,' offered Batiste.

'Everything could have been very different but it's too late now.'

'Why?' Le Tissier spoke quietly. 'I've a family myself. Do you want to tell us about it?'

Briefly, and without interruption, Gerald recounted his relationship with Lilian McEnery, housekeeper at the Bournemouth hotel. He knew that she would be returning to Scotland at the end of the season and it wasn't until he finished there himself that he decided to come to the island. He had been surprised and shocked to learn from Lilian's brother, Kevin, the following spring that she had had twins, and startled when Kevin insisted that he should pay maintenance. He realised it would be futile to deny paternity, he and Lilian had enjoyed a relationship, and any tests would confirm that he was the father.

'Gerald Stenton, the father of five-year-old twins,' said Inspector Le Tissier ten minutes later.

'It's amazing that he doesn't have a photograph, and no plans for seeing them.' Batiste looked sad. 'Two little boys who don't know and might never know their father.'

'At the moment Lilian is still single and satisfied with the monthly payments but Gerald could change his mind and decide to visit,' said Le Tissier.

'Is he still on your list of suspects?'

'Yes, but I'm not happy about his statement. One or more of the staff might have seen him going to or leaving his flat.'

'Heard the television or music?' suggested Batiste.

'That's no alibi. He could have turned on either and gone out. Get someone to check the statements of those who also live in the staff house and, if necessary, question them again.'

Batiste was immediately on his feet but on reaching the door he turned and asked, 'What about the letters?'

'I thought that would be your next question.' Le Tissier glanced at the letters, now in a plastic folder. 'They'll be sent off to a graphologist — a handwriting expert.' As the door closed Le Tissier considered it was amazing how much information could be obtained from the handwriting. He already knew that the letters were written by a woman but the experts would be able to tell him her age, if she was right or left-handed and other characteristics.

Le Tissier could see for himself, from the wording of the letters that the writer was an educated person, and not short of money. This was indicated by the quality of the stationery and the fact that a second piece of paper had been used instead of writing on the back of the first page. There were obviously four sets of fingerprints on each letter; fortunately they already had Matthew's, Peter's and Monique's, so it was merely a means of elimination. If these matched those on the saw, that would be a great step forward.

Le Tissier's thoughts turned to Monique's accident, and although the letters didn't refer to her, he wondered if the same woman could be responsible. It would be helpful to have the expert's opinion. The next moment he whacked the desk and swore softly. 'Damn it! Why didn't I think of that before?' His thoughts racing, Le Tissier briefly considered that this woman, the writer of these letters, could have been responsible for breaking into Matthew's bungalow, not to steal anything but to retrieve her letters. Fortunately she had not done so and the fact that they were still in the bottom drawer indicated that she had been interrupted or suddenly got cold feet. The French windows, desk and other furniture had been dusted for fingerprints, but were these the same as those on the letters?

In another flash of inspiration, Le Tissier exclaimed aloud, 'And the pliers! Where's Batiste?' and reached for the phone.

In another part of the island Ailsa sighed impatiently. It had been a frustrating and hectic morning. The French golfers knew their rooms should have been vacated at eleven o'clock and although these were ready for the new arrivals the chambermaids had offered to pack the remaining garments which were still hanging in the wardrobes but, knowing Godfrey's views about this, Ailsa had declined this suggestion. At chef's insistence, she had phoned the butcher, complained about the quality of the meat that had been delivered, asked that this be replaced by better quality and assured the supplier that she would speak to Mr Reardon about the outstanding account, and smiled at Howard Reardon as, holding a handful of monthly accounts, he approached Reception and asked, 'Have you seen Godfrey?'

'No, he went out but hasn't returned.'

'He's too fond of doing that. The only good thing he's done since we came was to keep you on in Reception.' But I won't be here much longer, thought Ailsa and heard Howard say, 'I hope he appreciates how much you do;' and then the golfers, talking excitedly burst into the hall, when Howard said, 'Tell Godfrey I've gone back to the cottage.'

'Certainly, sir.' Ailsa then turned to the group who were now heading in her direction and spoke to them in fluent French, when they all immediately left their golfing gear in an untidy heap and headed for the stairs.

Half an hour later, having found alternative accommodation for two couples who had been dissatisfied with their rooms, and she honestly but silently had to agree with them, Ailsa's thoughts on the future of Valley View were interrupted when Godfrey appeared and asked, 'Is everything in order?'

'Unfortunately, no. However there's something else I must tell you. Can we go into your office for a moment?' This was situated across the hall and leaving the door ajar Ailsa quietly said that she would like to give a fortnight's notice.

'You can't do that!' exploded Godfrey. 'You're the backbone of this place, everything will fall apart without you.'

'Nonsense. Verity is quite capable, and you're here.'

'But I don't want to be. I'm not really interested. Please reconsider your decision,' and then, 'Do you want more money?'

'No,' and thankful to make her escape, 'There's someone waiting at the desk.'

'Think about it,' pleaded Godfrey. 'I'll give you a bonus at the end of the season.'

'I'm sorry, I've made up my mind', said Ailsa as she headed back to Reception where an angry-looking holidaymaker was obviously waiting to complain.

Chapter 20

Monique glanced at Noel and then Ben. They were both enjoying their late lunch of lasagne and salad, deep in thought, but this was the best time to tell them the latest development. A gentle cough made them look up from their plates and she said quietly, 'Peter and I have found some letters that were written to Dad.'

'What's so special about them?' Ben sounded annoyed, while Noel asked: 'Who wrote them? Could they have anything to do with what's happened?'

'They're from a woman but unsigned.'

'How do you know it's a woman?' Although the dining room was almost empty Ben had lowered his voice. 'Because of what she's written.'

'Could she have anything to do with Dad's death?' asked Ben.

'What does Le Tissier think?' This came from Noel who continued, 'What's he going to do with them?'

'They'll be examined by an expert.' Although brief, Monique had been amazed at Le Tissier's explanation but did not offer this information.

'Could...could a woman have sawn through the fence, pushed Dad?' Then, as another idea occurred to him, Ben asked, 'Was this person having an affair with Dad, he jilted her and she turned nasty?'

'The answer to your first question is I suppose it's possible, and to your second, no. She was angry that Dad never paid her any attention. She could be a frustrated spinster, a widow, a divorcee, or even a married woman.'

'And you don't know or can't think of anyone?'

Monique looked at Noel as he asked this question. 'It's rather difficult when you think of the number of women who lunch or dine here, regularly.'

'Whoever it is, man or woman, knows their way around here to have taken the saw and later, hidden it under your hedge.' Ben stood up. 'I promised Cheryl—'

'Wait a minute,' interrupted Monique. 'Sit down again. There's something else I must tell you.'

Ben sat on the edge of his chair muttering, 'Well, get on with it,' while Noel, looking curious, asked, 'What have you done?'

'You might not like the idea, or approve, but—' Monique hesitated, and then rushed on: 'I've promoted Pat. She's going to take over from me. That way I can concentrate on all the many and different jobs that Dad did. He often spoke about promoting Pat so that I could relieve him of the more onerous—'

'But he never complained.'

'Dad enjoyed everything about the hotel and of course meeting the guests – so many are regulars who have been coming for years. Much as I also enjoy all of it I haven't got Dad's strength or stamina and the shock of what's happened-'

'And your own accident,' interrupted Ben. 'I think it's an excellent idea,' and turning to Noel, 'Don't you?'

'I suppose so.' This reply was so half-hearted that Monique suddenly snapped. 'You've never shown any interest in management. You surely didn't expect me to do my own and Dad's—' Monique faltered, and then resumed: 'Pat's loyal, efficient, has a pleasant personality and is very capable.'

'Mum always liked and approved of her,' said Ben and then asked, 'Have you anyone in mind for the position of head receptionist?'

'Yes. Bryony isn't really capable but Ailsa from the Valley View has asked to be considered if and when we have a vacancy.'

'Godfrey won't like that. I've heard he's rather awkward and can be unpleasant to his staff. His father will probably insist that he spends more time at the hotel and less at The Sparrow's Nest.' Ben was now standing. 'I know I haven't been very nice to you since Dad died but now I want to—'

'Oh for God's sake, don't be so soft and sentimental,' snapped Noel. 'Monique loves running the place, being in charge and telling everyone what to do.'

'How dare you talk to Monique like that!' exclaimed Ben. 'That's unkind, horrible and you're despicable.'

'While you've suddenly decided to become her adoring slave,' hissed Noel. They were now all standing around the table but somehow, glaring at Noel, Monique managed to keep her voice down. 'Stop this nonsense at once.'

'But I must talk to you,' persisted Noel.

'Not here and not now.' And as one of the waiters approached, 'Later, at home.'

'At last!' Noel threw the local paper aside as Monique entered the lounge and before she could sit down he said, 'Nevill phoned this morning. He wants to know when I can start and if I have the necessary capital available.' Monique was aware of Noel's air of expectancy, but shocked, sat down suddenly when he stated a six-figure amount and gasped, 'You expect me to lend you that amount?'

'Not quite all of it.'

'And where do you think I can find that amount?'

'Oh come on, you're not that short. You've the money your mother left you—'

'My God, you've got a bloody nerve!' exclaimed Monique, but Noel, whose voice had been getting louder, was now shouting. 'Your expectations from Matthew's estate and the hotel as collateral for any loan you wanted.'

'How dare you tell me what to do with what isn't even mine!' Her tiredness forgotten, Monique was on her feet again, standing over Noel, her grey eyes suddenly hard and glittering in a strangely pale face, her hands clenched and whole body shaking. 'How could you even suggest—'

'Matthew isn't here anymore. You can do whatever you like.' Noel looked at Monique, unperturbed by her pallor and expression but was unprepared when Ben, followed by Peter, burst into the room. To his utter amazement it was Ben who put his arms round Monique, hugged her and whispered, 'Don't listen to him. He's just a self-centred, selfish bastard.' Meanwhile Peter had reached and grabbed Noel's collar and yanked him to his feet. 'What do you mean by talking – no you were shouting – at Monique like that? Do you realise you could be heard not only in the car park but at the entrance to the hotel?'

Noel tried to shrug off Peter's grip. 'I didn't ask you to come barging in here, interrupting a private conversation.'

'Entertaining the residents would be a more apt description. Some of them were so aghast they were heading in this direction.'

'All hands to the rescue of the heiress,' sneered Noel and gave a grunt as Peter suddenly let go and he fell back on to the settee when he looked around and asked, 'where is she? We haven't finished our conversation.'

'I think you've said enough.'

Noel looked up at Peter, 'Where is she? I haven't had my cup of tea yet.'

'Oh, make it yourself! Then I suggest a cold shower and a long walk.'

'What happened? Did you hit him?' Monique set her cup in the saucer as Peter came into the room.

'No, I hardly touched him. However, more important, how are you?' and glancing at Ben who sat beside Monique, still looking anxious, 'Shall we phone the doctor?'

'Good Heavens, no! I was just so…so angry,' and looking from one to the other, 'As you were, both of you, when you rushed in.' Monique turned back to Ben, 'I never knew you made such a good cup of tea. Can I have another?'

'Of course. Would you like one, Peter?'

'Please.' Alone, and sitting in the armchair facing the two-seater settee Peter asked, 'Are you really all right?'

'Yes, but I don't want to go home tonight.'

'That's no problem. I wouldn't suggest you stay in the hotel, that would only cause comment, but there are three bedrooms here. I'm using what was Ben's room and I notice the bed in what was obviously your room is made up.'

'You could use my spare room,' offered Ben appearing in the doorway and as he placed the tray on a low table, 'I've just seen Noel heading towards the cliff path. Would you like me to pop into your place and pick up a few things?'

'Thanks.' Monique reached for her handbag, scribbled a few items in a small notebook and handed this to Ben. 'I'll need something different to wear this evening and tomorrow,' telling him where to find the necessary garments.

'It's not surprising you always look so smart and attractive. You're like Dad – well organised,' complimented Ben and with a cheeky grin, he ran off.

'I've never known Ben to be so thoughtful and caring,' said Monique as she reached for her cup and saucer.

'I must admit I was amazed at the sudden change in him.' Peter drank some of his tea.

'It was the sound of Noel's voice that startled us. We couldn't hear what he was saying but Ben, who's never said much to me, exclaimed, 'What's Noel doing to Monique?' and started running in this direction at the same time muttering, 'If he's laid a finger on her I'll—' and then we were here.' Peter hesitated. 'I probably shouldn't have told you, I'm still amazed that in spite of his rudeness and aggressiveness Ben is really a caring and protective person.'

'I agree but that doesn't solve my problem – what am I going to do about Noel? He really wants to go into partnership with Nevill and I doubt that he'll even turn up for work this evening. If he had a place to sell or even mortgage I might consider lending him part of that figure but to expect—'

'Wait a minute,' interrupted Peter and looking thoughtful, asked, 'When did his parents die? What do you know about them?'

'Not much. I do know that they died while Noel was working in France, otherwise he seldom talks about them.'

'Noel probably sold the house so the proceeds from that, and any contents, must be somewhere.' Monique shook her head, 'I don't know anything about his finances except that he doesn't spend much money.'

'And he certainly doesn't have any household expenses,' muttered Peter.

*****

'You should have heard Monique. She really lost her temper and I don't blame her. He was almost shouting at her so Peter and I rushed over from the hotel.'

'Who's 'he'?' asked Cheryl.

'Noel,' muttered Ben and continued to pace back and forwards when Cheryl told him to sit down, and stared when he asked, 'Can I make some tea first? Monique says I make a good cup of tea.'

'Oh, all right. I'll have one as well, I'm still thirsty, but don't be long.' Although Cheryl had known that Noel was dissatisfied, and being unsettled, her cup rattled in the saucer and she gasped in amazement on hearing the amount Noel wanted. 'What does he know about properties in the island, the complexities of local and open market? Anyhow, what's Monique going to do, is she going to lend him the money?'

'I doubt it. I left her in Dad's bungalow. She's going to stay there for a couple of days. Noel went off in a huff and she wondered whether he'd come in this evening.' Ben drank the rest of his tea. 'That was good, even if I say so myself.'

'I agree. Mum's never bothered about tea. It's usually coffee or, more often than not, something stronger. Anyhow, what's going to happen now?'

'I don't know,' and as he suddenly remembered, Ben said, 'The police have some letters that were written to Dad. We're hoping they'll help with their enquiries.' Cheryl had left her living room door open and at that moment the front door banged, there was the sound of someone running upstairs, swearing and then falling. This was followed by a scream when Cheryl sprang to her feet. 'I suppose one of them is drunk again.'

Ben followed Cheryl to the landing and looking down saw the crumpled figure of Mrs Laval and asked, 'What are you going to do?'

Cheryl shrugged. 'She'll probably—' but just then her mother groaned and kneeling, slowly rose to her feet; clutching one piece of furniture and then another, she made her way to one of the ground floor rooms, muttering to herself . It was as she reached the hall table that the front door opened again and Mr Laval, swaying on his feet, gazed around, saw her and bellowed, 'You stupid woman! I can't take you anywhere. You're always getting drunk!' Without speaking, Ben grabbed Cheryl's arm and pulled her back into the living room, and although he knew it to be a regular occurrence, hissed, 'Does this happen very often?'

'Yes, but Mother's getting worse. I know I don't eat regularly but they eat even less.'

Cheryl's eyes were huge in her pale face. 'I'm scared, Ben. They've spent nearly all their money on drink, either or both of them could have an accident. How would I cope?'

*****

'Is this where it happened, where Matthew Stenton fell?' A quiet voice interrupted Gerald's thoughts and he turned to see a tall, silver-haired woman who he recognised as Julia Mostyn, one of the hotel's regular clients.

'Yes, but he didn't just fall. The fence was sabotaged and he was pushed.' The woman nodded; Gerald had indicated the new palings and she now asked, 'Are the police making any headway with their enquiries?'

Gerald shrugged. 'I don't know.'

'But you're worried about something,' and when Gerald turned to look at her Julia continued, 'possibly the future of the hotel, or your own future,' and when there was no immediate reply, 'Let's go home and have a cup of tea. If you want to talk I'll be pleased to listen.' Ten minutes later, sitting in a large comfortable armchair, glancing around at the pale cream walls, paintings of local landscapes and granite cottages, Gerald felt totally relaxed. Julia had placed a cup of tea and a plate with a slice of home-made fruit cake on a small table then, sitting opposite, looked at him with concern and said, 'You can tell me to mind my own business.'

'No, certainly not. You're very kind and I do need to talk to someone.' Leaning forward, his hands clasped between his knees, Gerald recounted the facts in the same manner as when he told Batiste and Le Tissier.

'What did Matthew say?' asked Julia. 'Was he pleased there's another generation?'

'I didn't tell him. I haven't told anyone; that is until I told the Inspector and now you.'

'He would probably have been delighted, especially as he lost his own grandson.

'Two 5-year-old sons whom you've never seen,' Julia refilled their cups as she spoke. Then sitting down again asked, 'Has Lilian ever suggested that you should visit them?'

'I haven't actually heard from her. It was her brother Kevin who found and told me about the boys in the first place. Since then I see him when his cruise ship visits the island and he's off duty.'

'Lilian must be a very capable person to be bringing up two little boys on her own.'

Gerald nodded. 'She was very efficient and hardworking when I knew her.'

'Is there—' Julia was about to ask 'another man in her life' but stopped abruptly and a moment later asked, 'Although it hasn't been suggested, have you ever thought of going up to Scotland to see them?'

'Yes, but if they don't know about me, I'm not wanted.' Gerald looked desolate but his expression changed when Julia chided him, 'You've told me they both look like you, aren't you curious to see them? They're your sons, you pay regular maintenance, you're entitled to regular visits.' Then, without pausing for breath, Julia asked, 'Are you going to tell Monique about them?'

'Inspector Le Tissier knows, has suggested that I should. She'll probably think I'm a fool and I can't blame her. I always knew that Lilian would return to Scotland – we never discussed a future together.' Gerald glanced at his watch and jumped to his feet. 'I'm sorry, I've taken up so much of your time. Thank you for the tea, and especially for listening to me.'

'I've enjoyed your company. If you're free next Monday, come again'

A few minutes later Gerald paused before turning left on to the cliff path which led to the beach and the hotel. Julia's bungalow was one of several set in a lane which ran parallel to the cliff path. As he walked, Gerald found himself thinking about Julia Mostyn, a caring and thoughtful woman, probably about the same age as his mother. For a brief moment he remembered his father – a dour, uncommunicative and selfish man who had died in his early fifties.

Gerald had not heard about this until several weeks later; he had recently joined his first cruise ship and had been in the Mediterranean at the time. He was not surprised when his mother told him, in the same letter, that she had sold the house, small and inconvenient at the end of a terrace, and taken a position as live-in housekeeper to an elderly gentleman.

However she had not given him her new address or written since. He knew she was considerably younger than his father and had been unhappy, but that had been a long time ago and Gerald now wondered what had happened to her. If she was still alive, why hadn't she tried to find him?

Chapter 21

'You're looking very thoughtful.' Owen Mahy stopped and looked down into the weather-beaten face of Bert Duport who had been the senior gardener at the hotel for many years and continued, 'Has something else happened?'

'No, but like you I'm concerned about what—' Bert stopped abruptly, then a moment later resumed: 'Terrible about Mr Matthew, and then Miss Monique's accident. Good thing she wasn't hurt and that Mr Peter was there.' The old man's face crinkled as he smiled, 'It's good to see Mr Peter – known him since he was a youngster. He looks and talks just like his Dad.' Bert blinked, wiped his eyes and shook his head. 'No one's been arrested yet, obviously the police haven't found out who did it,' and gazing at Owen, 'You heard anything?'

'No, but I've been thinking about Sergeant Batiste's question – do I know the names of any of the people who stroll around the grounds before going in for lunch or dinner.'

And when Bert looked puzzled, Owen jerked his head in the direction of the cliff paths, 'You know who I mean, those who live in the posh houses up there.'

Bert nodded, 'Some comment on the flowers and shrubs whilst other ask questions, and sometimes you find them in the most unexpected places.' Owen was suddenly alert, 'What do you mean? Where have you seen them, and who?'

Bert removed his cap and scratched his nearly-bald head. 'There's a little bloke, keen gardener who often disappears behind some of the taller shrubs and bushes.' Bert paused and as Owen nodded knowingly, 'Oh, I hadn't thought of that. And then there's that tall silver-haired woman, quite smart—'

'I know who you mean,' interrupted Owen. 'She usually wears a trouser suit,' and when Bert agreed, Owen asked, 'Where did you see her?'

'Wandering around by our shed, and I've also seen her near your shed, where you keep all your tools. I suppose she could have been interested in some of the unusual herbs which we grow, maybe wants to grow some herself, but she never asked about them.'

Bert shrugged. 'I can't see her doing anything with delicate plants – not with hands like hers. They're unusually large for a woman.'

'You're very observant' said Owen.

'Habit,' acknowledged Bert. 'Anyhow I'd best get on but if I think of anyone else, I'll tell you.'

'Thanks.' Owen watched Bert bend to inspect his parsley bed and then turned to look at the sea, calm and shimmering, but still thinking of what he'd just learnt. He knew that the woman in question lived in a large bungalow accessible from the cliff path but for the moment could not remember her name.

*****

'Owen, Owen who?' queried Sergeant Batiste late on Monday afternoon, and on learning the surname said, 'Yes. Of course I'll speak to him.' Nodding and grinning with anticipation, Batiste furiously made notes of what Owen told him and eventually thanked him profusely, then reached for his copy of the house owners in that area.

'What's happened?' Inspector Le Tissier looked up from his ever-growing pile of paperwork and continued, 'Why are you grinning like a Cheshire cat?'

'I've just had a phone call from Owen Mahy,' and as the Inspector raised his eyebrows and nodded, Batiste, with hardly any reference to his notes, recounted the conversation between the handyman and the old gardener.

'So this woman was seen near the shed, the door was open and she probably saw all the tools. What else did you find out about her?'

'She's a regular at the hotel that is she lunches and dines there regularly. And, as I said before, according to Owen, she lives in a bungalow in the lane that runs parallel to the cliff path, but he doesn't know her name.' Batiste watched as Le Tissier reached for the phone and a moment later said, 'I wonder if you can help me, Mr Hamilton?'

Batiste listened to the one-sided conversation; it was obvious that Vere's replies were concise, and then the Inspector was saying, 'Thank you very much, Mr Hamilton. You've been most helpful' Then, before Batiste could speak, Le Tissier continued, 'We already know from the details supplied by the house-to-house team that the owner of the third bungalow is Julia Mostyn. Vere has just confirmed she's a widow. Her husband, who was much older, was Quentin Mostyn, a well-known artist. He died three years ago. Vere has confirmed her description – tall, slim, silver-grey hair – but can't remember seeing her at the funeral or wake. He does know more about her but is going to collate this and pass it on.'

Meanwhile Vere was pacing to and fro on his secluded back lawn wondering why the Inspector was so curious about Julia Mostyn. He had met them both at a drinks party given by neighbours soon after they arrived. Quentin had been unwell then but after accepting other invitations they had given a small party themselves. Neither Julia nor Quentin had offered much information about themselves, but somehow minor details had been gleaned by curious neighbours. Time to amass what he did know, thought Vere, and returned to the house.

Vere had just started writing, a cup of tea within reach, when his phone rang. Peter immediately apologised that he had not phoned earlier in the day.

'It's very thoughtful of you to do so and whilst I'm always pleased to hear from you, there's no need to phone me every day.' Vere hesitated; did the Inspector's request for information have anything to do with his current enquiries? Then Peter was asking, 'Did Dad ever tell you about the monthly letters he received?'

'Letters? What letters? Who wrote them?' and without pausing for breath, Vere asked, 'Was he being blackmailed?'

'No. Judging from the content they're from a woman. Unfortunately they're not signed.'

'Have you any idea who this woman is? How long has this been going on?'

'No, and in answer to your second question, they date back to last year. As you can guess, having found and read them, we're both puzzled, whilst they weren't actually threatening, advised Le Tissier.'

Hence his phone call, thought Vere and asked, 'Is there anything I can do? How's Monique?'

'Thanks for the offer but no. Obviously Monique is busy but with Pat's help, coping.'

Then, after arranging to meet Vere later, Peter stood in the open French windows gazing at the small but neat garden. He had suggested that Monique should have a rest but wasn't surprised when she told him she needed some exercise and fresh air. He guessed she was probably enjoying the solitude and shade of the tiny paths that led up the hill behind the hotel and which few visitors ever found. He had been amazed at Ben's unexpected defence of Monique and knew that he had gone to see Cheryl, but where was Noel?

As she followed the path that wound round the back of the hotel Monique noticed Gerald, who had been approaching the staff house, suddenly turn in her direction. As he drew nearer she noticed his worried expression and asked, 'What's the matter?'

'It's—' Gerald hesitated. 'I must talk to you. There's something I have to tell you, but not now.'

Monique felt a flicker of apprehension and then Gerald continued, 'Can you spare me a few minutes after dinner?'

'Of course. Shall we say half-past nine and come across to Dad's bungalow?'

'Thanks.'

'I wonder why he's so worried,' said Monique a few minutes later, after she had recounted their brief conversation to Peter and when there was no immediate reply, 'Is he going to tell me he's leaving or that he's going to claim against Dad's estate?' Then, staring at Peter she asked, 'He can't be another brother or half-brother, can he?'

'Of course not! Now sit down, have a cup of tea and tell me about your walk.' It was some time later, after she had described the different wild flowers and well-kept paths that Peter asked, 'Would you like me to be around when Gerald comes over, not necessarily in the same room? I'm meeting Vere for an early evening meal so I can be back before Gerald arrives.'

'That's a good idea, yes please'. Monique glanced at her watch. 'Do you mind if I have a shower before I change?'

'Of course not. Make yourself at home.'

'Thanks.' Monique stopped abruptly as there was a knock at the front door, when Peter also stood up; then Ben was standing in the doorway and, looking anxiously at Monique, said: 'I've just seen Noel going into your place. He looks a bit calmer, however I was thinking that if he doesn't turn up Manuel could do the wine this evening.'

'Good idea. Anyhow I'll be over presently.'

*****

'I'm surprised Vere Hamilton hasn't told us more,' and before Sergeant Batiste could speak, Inspector Le Tissier elaborated: 'Julia Mostyn is involved with several different charities, helps at the Red Cross shop and spends time at the hospice. We need to know why she spends so much time in the hotel grounds.'

'Perhaps she was checking to see who lived in which bungalow,' interrupted Batiste. 'It's possible, if she wrote those letters, that she wanted to retrieve them.'

'If she wrote them,' echoed Le Tissier and in the same breath: 'We know the name and description of this woman, that she lunched or dined regularly at the hotel; however the letters were only found this morning so we'll have to wait until we hear from the graphologist.'

'It's doubtful that anyone would have seen her break in. Owen Mahy and the gardeners don't work on a Saturday.' Batiste looked thoughtful and continued, 'The surrounding hedge is quite high. It was one of the lower panes of glass that was broken so, if it was Julia, she could have bent down, got her hand in and reached up for the key.'

As Batiste paused, Le Tissier took over. 'Once inside she smashed ornaments, overturned some of the furniture so it looked like a break-in but she didn't find the letters. Something must have stopped her, the desk drawers were left open; but we do know from the contents that the author of those letters was a very frustrated woman. If the fingerprints on the notepaper match any found in the bungalow – she may have removed the gloves for some reason or other – then we'll have her for the letters—' Le Tissier stopped abruptly.

'Why didn't I think of it before?' And reaching for the phone: 'I'll ask Monique if and what she knows about Julia Mostyn before we go and find out for ourselves.'

'Nothing new,' grumbled Le Tissier a few minutes later, and reaching for his jacket: 'Let's go.'

Meanwhile Julia was pacing to and fro in her lounge and muttering to herself. 'I can't believe it – Gerald, the father of five year-old twin boys and he's never seen them. But they're my grandchildren and I want to see them! What's the matter with Gerald; he's paying maintenance but doesn't attempt to get in touch with their mother, or arrange to see them?' However, in spite of asking herself these questions Julia knew why Gerald did not want to accept any parental responsibility, and that she and Roger were to blame.

At first, and until they had been married six months, she had thought Roger was considerate, caring and attentive, but had been shocked when he announced they were moving to England. Her protests had been ignored and she had been disappointed at the terrace house and area in which they would be living. She then discovered that Roger was really selfish and unsociable, remembered her parents' remarks and her own surprise that Roger had not been interested in the family hotel or working there. Although a fully-qualified shorthand typist with other secretarial skills and excellent references, she had suggested it would be sensible if she applied for a job in the same department store when Roger lost his temper and said there was no need for her to work, he was quite capable of providing for the two of them.

Ten months later Gerald had been born and although he had reluctantly agreed that she could tell her parents, Roger had adamantly stated that he had no intention of informing his father or brother. The marriage had not been a happy one and whilst she had enjoyed a happy childhood, her friends were always welcomed by her parents, Roger didn't encourage Gerald or herself to invite anyone to the house. She had soon learnt it wasn't wise to remonstrate with Roger – he had hit and punched her on several occasions and, in spite of her height, Julia knew better than to retaliate. Then, as though he could read her thoughts, Roger said that if she thought of taking Gerald back to Guernsey or anywhere else, he would find them – their place was with him. The neighbours, a friendly middle-aged couple had been taken aback when Roger refused their offer to baby-sit, telling them to mind their own business. In spite of this they had still been kind to her; had been amongst the few who attended Roger's funeral, and genuinely sad when she sold the house.

Julia felt there was no point in dwelling on the past and her thoughts turned to her first meeting with Quentin Mostyn, a successful artist, in his home in the New Forest – that was when her life changed. Within weeks she was amazed to discover that Quentin was a thoughtful, appreciative employer who was eager to show her the neighbouring villages and countryside. Julia's thoughts of Quentin's proposal and the happy years that followed were interrupted by the squeaking of her neighbours' gate when, glancing through the open window she saw two men turn right – they were probably police, but plain-clothed this time. Why were they calling again – what did they want?

Chapter 22

'Why are you so interested in those letters?' Batiste had waited until they were clear of town, on the road to the south of the island. 'The contents provide the writer with a motive. She, whoever she is, wanted more than conversation with Matthew.'

'An affair? Something more serious?' And when Inspector Le Tissier shrugged, Batiste continued, 'Do you really think a woman was responsible for Matthew's death?'

'It is possible. It was obviously premeditated: the fence was sabotaged, and the perpetrator eventually hit him again to make sure he fell.' Le Tissier had been studying the houses on his left and now said, 'Down here,' but Batiste had already turned and was driving down a narrow lane between two large properties then a moment later he turned to the right and stopped outside the first bungalow. Although the house-to-house team had learnt that the residents in that area had not seen any suspicious characters behaving in a strange manner on the Thursday evening of the murder, Le Tissier had suggested that they call on Julia's neighbours again. The two couples on the left confirmed their previous statement, again expressed their concern that such a terrible thing should happen when the two detectives left for their next call; but before Le Tissier could reach for the bell the front door opened and he was looking into a pair of clear grey eyes on a level with his arm.

Although she had been described as tall he had not expected Julia to be his height and considered that she was an attractive and obviously wealthy woman, but quickly introduced himself and Batiste, stepped into a wide hall when, in a low but pleasant voice she explained, 'I saw you leave next door and guessed you were coming here.'

Seated in the spacious and tastefully furnished lounge, Le Tissier noted that Julia's replies were the same as those previously given. She had not seen any suspicious characters on the cliff paths or loitering in the lanes. She also told them she often lunched or dined at the hotel (which they already knew) and sometimes spent hours strolling around and enjoying the vast grounds. He had learnt from Vere that Quentin had been a prolific artist and spent several summers, before his marriage, in the island, painting. He had also enjoyed the slower pace of life and meeting local people. These were two of the reasons he decided to move to the island and Julia had obviously agreed with his decision. Le Tissier now considered it was strange that, in spite of his request, Vere had been so informative about Quentin but really said very little about Julia.

It was later, after Batiste had negotiated the narrow lanes and they were back on the main road that Le Tissier voiced his earlier thoughts, nodded when Batiste commented that there were no photographs, and Le Tissier continued, 'Where was Julia and what did she do before she met and married Quentin? Although she was considerably younger than him she could have been married before, and whilst they haven't visited her here, there might be children and/or other relatives.'

'So you'd like me or a WPC to make discreet enquiries?' And then Batiste asked, 'Do you think Julia could have killed Matthew?'

'It's possible. She uses the hotel, must be aware of his regular evening walks, while she's tall and strong enough, but why? As for other suspects, who do we really have?

The barman and customers all said that Noel was in the bar until midnight. The brown button found on the path didn't match those on his jacket – it was smaller and a lighter shade.

We know Ben's fed up working in the hotel, but again the barman and customers said he was working in the bar until midnight. The only person without an alibi is Gerald, who has a motive – he needs the—'

'He should have told Matthew and Monique,' interrupted Batiste. 'They would probably have helped him, he is family.'

'I know, we've been over this before,' then with a gleam of anticipation in his eye, Le Tissier said, 'We also have the writer of those letters, whoever she is.'

Meanwhile Julia was gazing at Quentin's self-portrait and asking, 'Why didn't I tell Gerald the truth: that I'm his mother? I promised you that I would, and that was three years ago, just before you died. He was here, I had the opportunity to tell him but, like a fool, I didn't.' As she continued to berate herself, Julia moved to the bookcase, pulled out and opened a copy of The Book of Ebenezer Le Page and studied the photograph of a five-year-old Gerald, one of the few she had kept. The thought of the two little boys in Scotland made her even more angry. She could and wanted to do so much for them, to be their grandmother, able to visit and spend time with them, but first she had to tell Gerald.

'I'm sure you're worrying unnecessarily,' said Peter as Monique gazed anxiously out of the window which faced the hotel.

'It's not knowing what he's going to say,' and then as Gerald left the hotel, 'He's on his way.'

'So am I, but remember I'm not far, in the kitchen.'

'Thanks.'

'I didn't want to bother you about this but I was advised to tell you.' Gerald glanced around the comfortably-furnished lounge as he sat down.

'What is it? Are you ill?' Monique noticed that Gerald had changed into an open-necked shirt and smart navy blue trousers.

'No, thank God!' Gerald spread out his large hands. 'I should've told Uncle Matthew when I first knew, and now I don't really know how to tell you.'

'Oh, for Heaven's sake get on with it,' said Monique, exasperated.

'I've...I've two little boys, five years old, but I've never seen them.'

'Two little boys – twins,' echoed Monique, her expression changing from one of concern to utter amazement, and with a sudden smile, 'Where are they?'

'In Scotland, with their mother.' It was Monique's smile and genuine interest that encouraged Gerald, when he quickly recounted Kevin's visit and the resultant payments.

It was then, unaware she was raising her voice, Monique declared, 'You must see the children, they're growing and changing all the time,' that Peter suddenly appeared in the doorway, greeted Gerald and asked, 'Would you like a coffee, or something stronger?'

'A coffee would be great, thanks,' said Gerald and a few minutes later as they all sat with mugs of coffee he resumed, 'I suppose you heard what I had to tell Monique, what I should have told Uncle Matthew years ago.'

Peter nodded, remembering that Mathew had been devastated when Daniel and Melinda were killed in a multiple car crash but managed to say, 'I'm sure he would have been delighted that there's another generation, as would your parents.'

'I doubt that Dad would have approved. Life wasn't very easy for my mother, who was quite a lot younger. Dad wasn't a very nice person, unkind, insensitive, even—' Gerald's face darkened and he stopped abruptly. Then: 'I was pleased to get away. I was at sea when Dad died and didn't know about it until a few weeks later. Mother wrote and told me she'd sold the house and taken a job as a live-in housekeeper. I don't suppose she got much for the house or contents. Mother told me she wanted to get a job when I started school. She had been a secretary but Dad refused, and in spite of her pleading I wasn't allowed to bring any friends home.' Gerald paused to drink his coffee. 'Although all the staff, crew on the different cruise ships were friendly, and the manager of the Bournemouth hotel was pleasant to the senior staff, I've never known anyone so well-liked and respected by guests, staff and local people as Uncle Matthew. In spite of my personal and financial problems I've been happier here than anywhere else. However whilst I have no doubts about Lilian's capabilities as a mother, I would like my children to have a better and happier childhood than I did.'

As he said this, Monique thought about her father's bequest to Gerald. At the time he had probably considered £10,000 was generous, however it was obvious Gerald had not inherited anything from his father, or mother if she was dead, and Monique quickly decided to discuss with Peter what she now considered could be a solution before she saw Arnold Levrier the following morning.

*****

'Where were you last night, why didn't you come home?' demanded Noel angrily as he approached Reception.

'I slept in Dad's bungalow.' Monique had noticed Noel's expression but her gaze and attention were focused on an e-mail enquiry for a party of 20 walkers in October.

'That's ridiculous – there was no need for you to be so stupid. Our conversation yesterday afternoon was inconclusive.'

'Not as far as I'm concerned. However, as you can see, I'm standing in while Pat has her breakfast.'

'And the bloody hotel always comes before everything else.' Noel's voice was rising. 'As I told you yesterday, Nevill is waiting for my input, so I need a cheque for—'

'I've already told you I can't.'

'You can,' Noel reached over the counter and grabbed Monique's wrist, 'and you will or…Ouch, bloody hell!' Noel almost crumpled with pain as a sudden and sharp blow was delivered to his right forearm, the collar of his shirt and jacket were grabbed and he was spun round to face a furious Ben who hissed, 'Are you threatening my sister again?'

'Oh, don't be so melodramatic. I was just—'

Still holding Noel with his left hand but his right raised, Ben said, 'I heard what you were saying. However this isn't the time or place for such an important discussion.'

'Oh, so you now want to play the protective brother, do you? But my requirements are none of your business. This is between my wife and I.'

'Not any more. I know Monique is quite capable of dealing with this situation but I don't like your manner. We'll talk about it later,' and suddenly, without any warning, Ben released Noel who almost stumbled, then straightened himself and grunted, 'You two-faced bastard! ' At that moment the porter, a thickset Latvian appeared. 'Do you need me, Mrs Latimer, Mr Ben?'

'No thank you,' said Monique while Noel glared at her and Ben, 'You're both pathetic! I'll get that money one way or the other! '

Chapter 23

'Good morning, my dear.' As usual Arnold Levrier was courteous as he greeted Monique and once she was seated he enquired, 'How are you? How can I help you?'

'Can I tell you about Gerald, first?'

'Of course. What's happened?'

Monique hesitated, then gradually recounted the previous evening's conversation and concluded, 'I suppose I should have spoken to Vere about this, however Peter and I would like to help him financially.'

'Two little boys! ' exclaimed Arnold and then, in a brisker tone, 'They're definitely his?'

'He's seen photographs and whilst he doesn't have a copy says there's a remarkable resemblance.'

'H'm.' Arnold was still looking thoughtful when there was a knock at the door; his secretary entered, placed the coffee-tray on the table, and glanced at the Advocate who nodded his thanks. Indicating the coffee pot and that he preferred black coffee, Arnold asked, 'Does Gerald intend to visit the children and possibly, at a later date, marry their mother? Then there's the alternative that he could take the money and disappear.'

'I may be trusting but I'm not stupid.' Monique placed a cup and saucer in front of Arnold. 'Peter and I would open an account in our joint names and arrange for a specific amount to be transferred, monthly, to Gerald's account. We would be prepared to consider any unusual or necessary expenses.'

'That makes sense but his attitude doesn't. Why is he depriving his sons of a normal family life? Is he selfish like his father, unprepared to accept the responsibility or does he have someone,' Arnold paused, 'male or female, here? What do you know about his personal life? His preferences?'

Monique had been looking at Arnold over the rim of her cup and as she set this down she said, 'He and Lilian, that's her name, were together for five years but neither were prepared to make a permanent commitment. He knew she was going back to Scotland; it was when she left that he decided to come to Guernsey. He's lived in the flat allocated for a head waiter in the staff house ever since he's been here. No one has seen him with a girl, older woman or anyone else. He's always alone, which has been noted and commented on.'

Arnold nodded. 'I don't see any reason why you shouldn't go ahead. After all, the account will be in Peter's and your name, for the benefit of the children.'

It was after Monique had replenished their cups that Arnold said, 'Forgive me for asking; do you know if there's likely to be an arrest in the near future?'

'I don't know.' Monique hesitated, and then burst out, 'I'm not sure if I should be telling you this, but you and Dad were good friends – did he ever tell you about the letters he was receiving every month?'

'My God! ' Arnold leaned forward, 'Are you trying to tell me he was being blackmailed?'

'No.' Again Monique hesitated, 'Not in the usual sense. These were from a woman who was very angry and frustrated that he didn't pay her sufficient attention.'

'Who is she? Where did you find the letters?' And after Monique had explained, Arnold asked: 'Apart from checking the handwriting, what is Le Tissier doing about them?'

'He obviously wants to find this person.' Monique sighed. 'So much happened yesterday, I was really glad that Ben was there as well, and so helpful.'

'That sounds unusual. Is there something else I should know?'

Monique nodded. 'Peter told me to bring you up to date,' and quickly recounted her contretemps with Noel the previous afternoon and that morning.

'My dear girl!' exclaimed Arnold, leaning forward again and taking her hand. 'You can't carry on with all this happening. Couldn't Peter take over running the hotel?'

'That's no problem. I can cope with that, especially as I've promoted Pat to be my assistant manager. Although we're advertising for another head receptionist, Ailsa from Reardon's place has been waiting for a vacancy to occur.'

Arnold nodded. 'That's another good move, although Godfrey won't be very happy. One doesn't hear very good reports about The Valley View; the old man doesn't like spending any money on the place, unlike your father. However, coming back to you and your personal problems, is there anything I can do, any way in which I can help?'

Monique looked doubtful. 'Thank you for offering, but no. As you already know, Noel is determined to go in with Nevill de Garis; however I don't intend to give or lend him the amount he's asking.'

'It's a very large amount. Has he any money of his own? Did he inherit anything from his parents?' but before Monique could reply, Arnold continued, 'You're probably worrying how this is going to affect your marriage.'

'Yes I am. He always resents the hotel being so busy, the fact that I enjoy being so involved and his attitude certainly won't change when he has his evenings and weekends free.' Monique sighed. 'I'm sure Pat will be happy to share these duties with me but I've been asking myself: do I want to spend all that free time with Noel?'

'All marriages go through a sticky patch,' said Arnold. 'When did you last have a holiday?'

'Last October/November and that wasn't a success. We went to Cyprus but the only thing Noel enjoyed was visiting the different archaeological sites. It's an interesting and lovely island, I'd be happy to go back and explore the area around Kyrenia, however Noel wouldn't agree to a holiday at the moment. He wants to start working for, or with, Nevill.'

'Then let him, and see how things work out.'

Monique nodded. 'You're right. If I hold him back he'll become more frustrated and whilst I don't want to question his finances I'll suggest I lend him an equal amount.'

'Good idea.' It was as they both stood up that Arnold asked, 'How does Ben feel about owning 40% of the shares in the hotel, being a co-owner?'

'He hasn't mentioned it. I'm still amazed that he's become so protective towards me.'

'That's good. However, don't hesitate if either of you want to see me.'

'Thank you.' Monique slowly made her way down several flights of stairs, deep in thought. She knew that Noel's parents had lived in Bristol and died whilst he was in France, but nothing else. As she reached the street and began down the hill Monique remembered that it was on his return from a wine-tasting tour of the Beaune area that Matthew, impressed by Noel's fluent French and German, and wide knowledge of wines, told him there would be a vacancy for a wine waiter at the end of the season. He had then learnt that Noel had no wish or reason to return to England, his parents had died in a multiple car crash and he had no close relatives. Strange, thought Monique as she turned left at the bottom of the hill, Noel seldom spoke of his parents, or even any school friends.

After five years of marriage she really knew very little about him; but any further thoughts were immediately dismissed as Monique was greeted by Carol Cummings, who said, 'How lovely to see you. Have you time to join me for a coffee?'

'I'm sorry, I must get back. My appointment took longer than expected.'

'That's often the case.' Carol hesitated, then placing her hand on Monique's arm she said, 'You're a very brave young woman. Matthew was very fortunate to have such a lovely, intelligent and capable daughter. I'm sure he would be very proud of you.'

'Thank you.' Monique blinked back threatening tears and dimly heard Carol continue, 'If there's anything I can do, even if it's just listening, please let me know,' and before Monique could reply, Carol was walking quickly down the narrow street.

*****

'Why didn't you tell me you were going out? Where have you been?' Monique had seen Noel pacing outside the main entrance but now, as she approached the hotel, was unprepared for his aggressive expression and tone of voice and told him, 'I had—'

'I'm not interested in that,' and then, as the idea occurred to him, 'Unless you've got my cheque.'

Monique had phoned before she left town, knew that Ben and Peter were already in the office and feeling more optimistic said, 'I think the office is the best place to discuss this,' and briskly led the way across the foyer.

'What are they doing here?' demanded Noel as Monique opened the door and he saw Ben and Peter sat on either side of Matthew's leather chair.

'This is a family affair,' said Monique sitting down, glad she had briefed them of the Advocate's suggestion with which they had both agreed.

'So, let's get on with it,' and seeing a completely clear surface, Noel asked, 'Where's the cheque book?'

'It's not as simple as that.' Monique was aware it was now crunch time and continued, 'The best arrangement would be if we lend you the same amount as you're invest—'

'What are you talking about?' interrupted Noel. 'I haven't got that sort of money.'

'I'm not suggesting you have, however the sale of your parents' house and the contents must have realised a substantial amount which would attract a good rate of interest.'

'How...how do you know about that? The bank aren't allowed to disclose—' Noel stopped abruptly and pushed back his chair, when Monique said quickly, 'Properties in certain areas of Bristol usually fetch a good price.'

'I need to see the bank manager, find out what's going on.'

'And give notice for the withdrawal of a large amount. We'll have to do the same when we know how much you're investing.' Monique glanced at Ben and then Peter. 'We'll need some sort of agreement, however I'm sure Mr Levrier can deal with that.'

Noel had reached the door and now glanced over his shoulder, 'I won't be long. I must let Nevill know what's happening and phone the bank. We can finalise this later,' but his expression changed when reminded that he would probably have to wait for an appointment and any further discussion would have to wait until he had seen his bank manager. Noel glared at Monique. 'I never realised you could be such a mercenary bitch!'

And slammed the door.

'My God, sis, you were fantastic!' Monique was overwhelmed as Ben hugged her and then Peter was saying, 'You didn't really need us.'

'Oh yes I did. But was it the right solution? At the time I thought Levrier's suggestion was brilliant but now I'm wondering if, as a result of this, I'm going to create a financial disaster.'

'There's only one way to find out; where did Dad keep his bank statements?' This came from Ben, when Monique and Peter looked at each other, surprised; then she produced a small bunch of keys and selected one. Within minutes they were each studying the statements of three different accounts. Neither Monique nor Peter were surprised at the balances on these but Ben gasped at the final balance on the statement in front of him then, glancing at the other two statements asked, 'Why did Dad keep so much money in the different banks?'

Monique glanced at Peter and explained: 'Dad had an arrangement that, at the end of each month, he would inform them of the amount to be transferred to the current account to meet the monthly wages, which are quite considerable in a hotel of this size, and the monthly trading accounts.'

'Although I have a smaller hotel, I do the same,' volunteered Peter.

Monique nodded. 'Dad's been doing it this way for years and as I'm a signatory for the hotel accounts there won't be any difficulties with the banks; however we should make the necessary arrangements so that you can sign any cheques.'

Monique noticed Ben frown as though he was worried that he might be asked to take on more responsibility and said lightly, 'Only in case of emergency. However, returning to current expenditure, the final accounts for the carpets, soft furnishings and new furniture still have to be paid.'

'It was a busy winter programme,' agreed Ben. 'All the regulars on the second floor are thrilled.' The rooms and three suites had been redecorated and completely refurbished, while the bathrooms had been updated to a high standard. Then, with a sudden burst of pride, Ben continued: 'Dad was already working on next winter's programme, doing all the first floor rooms-' but stopped abruptly, and after a moment resumed, 'If we're lending Noel a huge amount will we be able to afford it?' and his gaze travelling from Monique to Peter: 'Who's going to mastermind it?'

'We don't have to do all the rooms, or we could use the same scheme as that—' Monique hesitated and looked at Ben, 'But we don't need to do that when we have someone who worked for a prestigious company in England.'

'You'd...you'd give Cheryl the chance to—' Ben almost choked on his words.

'Why not?' Monique and Peter exchanged amused glances and the former continued, 'Talk to Cheryl about it. Tell her what's involved.'

'This could be just what she needs – thanks!' Ben knew that Cheryl had wanted to continue her career as an interior designer when they moved to the island, wanting to join a local company but her mother had decried this suggestion, saying that Cheryl should meet other young people and enjoy herself before she started work. 'I'll see her this afternoon, but in the meantime I must see what the barman needs from the store.'

It was only a short distance from the office to the bar, nevertheless there was time for Ben to recall Cheryl's horror and disgust at her parents' behaviour the previous afternoon.

He knew it was at their suggestion that Cheryl had met and become involved with the offspring of those who spent most days and evenings in different bars, hotels and one another's houses, forever drinking. The younger set had invited her to The Sparrow's Nest and it was there she had met Godfrey Reardon who had encouraged her to sample some of the drugs; and it was on one of those evenings that he'd met her. That was two years ago, soon after her arrival in the island. Ben shivered, aware that Monique and his father had been worried and concerned about him. It was seeing others become addicted, realising this could happen to Cheryl that brought him to his senses, when he tried to discourage her from visiting the popular Sparrow's Nest so often. He knew that Godfrey spent most of his evenings there and often wondered if he was responsible for supplying the drugs.

Ben realised there must have been other frustrated habitués of the nightclub, and now hoped that if Cheryl was gradually recovering, would be interested in Monique's proposition, there was a good chance of their future together, with Monique's and even Peter's approval.

Scrutinising the shelves and the list the barman had given him, Ben unlocked the storeroom and, at the same time wondered if Noel had seen the bank manager, and how the outcome would affect the future of the hotel and Monique.

Chapter 24

It was almost midday when Inspector Le Tissier received a phone call from the Registry Office in Southampton. Earlier that morning Sergeant Batiste had learnt and informed the Inspector that Julia had been Quentin's housekeeper/companion before he married her; however that was really irrelevant, and Le Tissier now heard a female voice query, 'You were asking for details about Quentin Mostyn's wife?'

'That's correct.'

'I was on duty the day they were married and with such an unusual name I certainly remember him. He was a charming man. The information on the Marriage Certificate states that Mrs Mostyn was a widow, her previous surname was Stenton, nee Domaille.'

'Good Heavens!' exclaimed Le Tissier and then, lowering his voice, 'Would you mind repeating that?'

'Certainly, Inspector. It is rather unusual. Would you like a copy of the Marriage Certificate?'

'Yes please. You've been most helpful. As he replaced the receiver the door opened, Batiste entered, and taking one look at the Inspector's expression asked, 'You've heard?'

'Yes, and I'm still recovering from the shock.'

'What do you mean? Who is Julia? Is she someone we should know?'

'You could say that.' Le Tissier knew he was grinning, 'There's certainly a local connection,' and briefly recounted the knowledge he had just acquired.

'What!' Batiste stared at the Inspector, his mouth agape, and then the questions began, 'Does this mean...If she's Roger Stenton's widow, surely Matthew and Gerald would have recognised her, or any other friends,' and when reminded that she had been out of the island a long time and had possibly changed, Batiste agreed but persisted that Gerald, who had seen her regularly at the hotel, would surely have known her.

'Unless she's had cosmetic surgery,' suggested Le Tissier. 'However, it's certainly going to be a shock for him and the rest of the family. I wonder if Quentin knew that Julia was local, and also of Gerald's existence. If they ate at the hotel while he was alive he would have met Gerald.' Le Tissier paused. 'Do you think there's any resemblance?'

Batiste looked doubtful. 'Not facial, but Julia's very tall for a woman and they both have large hands and feet.'

While Batiste was offering this, Le Tissier was muttering, 'There's a number of Domailles in the island but we do know that the Julia who married Roger Stenton was an only child, so the closest relatives would be cousins. Arnold Levrier is always very knowledgeable,' and ignoring Batiste's: 'But he's considerably younger than Julia, and with a name like Domaille, there could be another Julia Domaille,' Le Tissier said, 'I'll ask him.'

Once again Batiste watched and listened to a one-sided conversation with interest and curiosity then at last Le Tissier was saying, 'Thank you very much, Mr Levrier. As always you've been most helpful.' Then, aware of Batiste's intent gaze, 'You won't believe this: obviously Levrier didn't know her personally, but a Julia Domaille worked for one of the other Advocates.'

'So what happens now?' asked Batiste.

'Mr Levrier is arranging for us to see Mr Naftel this after—' Le Tissier picked up the receiver on the first ring and after a moment asked, 'Why are you telling me about an accident, Sergeant?' and then, 'Noel Latimer and the Lavals!'

Silently mouthing: 'What's happened?' Batiste edged forward on his chair while Le Tissier was asking, 'Is anyone seriously injured? Have Mrs Latimer and Cheryl been advised?'

Then, after a slight pause: 'I'll send Sergeant Batiste out to the hotel. Ben might prefer to tell Cheryl himself.'

'Why am I going out to the hotel? What's happened?' repeated Batiste as he stood up.

'The Lavals were standing on the edge of the pavement outside the Town Church, waiting to use the pedestrian crossing. They were very drunk, unsteady on their feet and quarrelling. One pushed the other but they both fell into the road and were struck by a car being driven rather fast. The driver, who was Noel Latimer, swerved to avoid them, then swerved again because of a lorry, when he possibly hit the Lavals. They've all been taken to hospital.

'Is he...do you know the extent of their injuries?'

'No. I'm sorry, you'll have the unpleasant task of breaking the news to Monique. At least she knows you. However I'm going to phone Peter; it might be a good idea if he's around when you arrive. Hopefully he'll be in his father's bungalow. Anyhow, off you go.'

Batiste was just driving into the hotel car park when his mobile rang. Le Tissier said, 'I've just been in touch with the hospital but obviously they won't tell me anything. However I have spoken to Peter.'

'He's here, walking towards me.' Batiste noticed Peter's anxious expression and asked, 'Have you spoken to Monique or Ben yet?'

'No.' Peter paused as they approached the hotel when, on learning there was no news from the hospital, he said, 'It's incredible that it was Noel's car that went into the Lavals. Do you know how it happened?'

'Statements are being taken from pedestrians on either side of the road who were waiting to use the crossing. Fortunately those standing on the church side scattered as the car swerved to the left, on to the pavement. Two ambulances were on the scene within minutes but only Monique and Cheryl will be advised of any injuries.' They were now crossing the foyer. Pat Le Page recognised Sergeant Batiste and quietly asked, 'Not more bad news?'

Batiste nodded, ascertained that Monique was in the office and asked, 'Could you ask Ben to join us, please?'

'Oh my God! Is Noel, are the Lavals badly injured?' Monique's gaze travelled from Ben to Batiste. 'Does Cheryl know?'

'No, Inspector Le Tissier thought it would be better if Ben told her,' and, as Ben stood up, Batiste asked, 'Would you like a WPC to accompany you?'

'No thanks.' Ben shuddered then, as though searching for words, 'I don't want to sound disloyal to Cheryl, or her parents, whom I don't really know, but she has been rather concerned about them.' Ben then asked the same question that Monique had asked about Noel earlier, and received the same reply. 'No information is given on the phone, only face to face, in private, after your identity is validated by myself, or someone else from the force.'

At that moment there was a knock at the door; a waiter appeared with a tray which he placed in front of Monique, and withdrew.

'Good! Hot strong tea,' said Batiste. 'Can I have a cup, please?'

'Of course.'

'Was it Noel's morning off?' Batiste noticed that Monique glanced at Peter but before either could reply, he continued, 'I'm sure he's a very capable driver, however could there have been something wrong with his car?'

'No.' Monique shook her head. 'Noel's always very fussy about it,' and looking at Peter who nodded, 'but there is something you should know.

'It may be irrelevant—' Pushing his cup and saucer aside, Peter recounted the discussion that had taken place earlier that morning. As he concluded, Batiste, who looked very thoughtful, said, 'It's possible the bank manager wasn't very helpful and Noel was still annoyed.' Then, aware of the anxious expressions: 'Obviously we'll have to question him.'

'And the Lavals?' Ben hesitated and resumed, 'If yesterday's drunken behaviour is anything to go by, you may have to wait some time before one of them is sufficiently sober to answer any questions.'

Batiste nodded. He had heard about the Lavals and the daily drinking sessions and now said, 'Let's hope that neither of them are seriously injured.' His gaze lingered on Monique. 'Would you like to go to the hospital now, Mrs Latimer?'

'We've a W.I. luncheon, I must tell Gerald—'

'I know,' interrupted Peter. 'I took the liberty of asking Pat to tell Gerald that Noel won't be here.'

'But I must tell Gerald the truth.' Monique glanced at her watch and dialled the dining room extension.

'What's the matter? Are you ill?' asked Gerald as he gazed at Monique's pale face and Peter's solemn expression.

'No, I'm all right but I thought – we thought you should know why—'

Monique faltered and Peter took over. 'There's been an accident. Noel's been taken to hospital.'

'Peter and I are going there now with Sergeant Batiste when we...' Monique faltered. 'We hope to learn if he's badly injured.'

Gerald nodded. 'As though you haven't enough worries. If there's anything I can do when this lunch is over, and when you have any news, just let me know.'

As the door closed, Monique asked, 'Should we tell Vere? I wouldn't like him to hear about this from someone else.'

'Not until you've spoken to someone at the hospital.' Ben had already departed, having arranged that he would tell Cheryl and then proceed, with her, to the hospital where they would meet Sergeant Batiste and the necessary formalities could be carried out.

Peter took one look at Monique's ashen face and holding her in his arms quietly asked, 'How is Noel?'

'Not good. I couldn't see him. When the para—' Monique swayed, and as Peter led her towards a chair, Sergeant Batiste who was looking at her anxiously hurried off to get some tea and returned in time to hear Monique say, 'When the paramedic assessed Noel at the scene, his blood pressure was dropping, and he was very breathless.' Monique accepted the container, drank some of the tea and, her gaze travelling from Batiste to Peter, said, 'It's my fault. I should have lent him the amount he wanted.'

'That's nonsense,' protested Peter.

'If he hadn't gone to the bank this wouldn't have happened.' Then, blinking back threatening tears, 'He hadn't fastened his seat belt, must have hit his head. He's lapsing in and out of consciousness.'

'Noel's young and strong. He'll soon recover.' Batiste noticed that Peter spoke with forced cheerfulness then, her voice still dull, Monique resumed, 'He'll be going for X-rays to check on internal injuries.'

'Your husband is in good hands. The consultants, specialists, doctors and nurses are all excellent.' Batiste stood up, at the same time asking, 'Is there anything I can do for you? Phone anyone?' They both shook their heads and Peter said, 'We'll wait here until there's some definite news.'

Batiste nodded. 'I'll be around if you need me. In the meantime I'll go and wait for Ben and Cheryl.'

'Should we tell Vere? And what about Nevill? He'll be waiting to hear from Noel.'

Peter looked at Monique who, although still pale, was less tense; 'We could just tell them that Noel's in hospital,' and when she nodded he asked, 'Will you be all right if I go and make the necessary calls?'

'Of course.' But alone Monique muttered, 'Is Noel going to recover? When will I be able to see him?' Then, clasping her hands together, she bent her head, her lips scarcely moving, and prayed.

Chapter 25

Although Ben had explained about the accident to her parents and the necessary formality that Sergeant Batiste would be waiting for them at the hospital, Cheryl repeated, 'How did it happen?' but before Ben could reply she continued, 'I'm surprised this hasn't happened before. They're always drunk, completely irresponsible.' Ben knew this was true; nevertheless he said, 'Hopefully they're not badly injured.'

Cheryl had been gripping Ben's left arm with both hands but now relaxed her hold. 'I gave up a good job. I was doing well and enjoying it, to come here with them, and look at me! I've been a fool, drinking and taking drugs. You're the only good thing that's happened. It's thanks to you and the doctor who came to see me on Sunday – he gave me a good talking to – that I'm beginning to think clearly.'

'That's good. You need to look after yourself – eat properly. You've lost a lot of weight since I first met you.'

'I realise that. I used to cook an evening meal for the three of us before we came here; I enjoy cooking. Unfortunately, even though they're so thin, my parents aren't interested in food.' Then, as it occurred to her: 'Is Noel badly injured, and how is Monique coping?'

'I don't know but I expect by now she's been told.' Ben paused. 'Monique's so brave and resourceful while I've been selfish and ungrateful, taking everything Dad and Monique did for granted. It was her accident, when the brake cable of her Mini had been cut, that really shook me, made me realise and appreciate how much she did, and how well she was coping without Dad.'

'I didn't know, you didn't tell me.' Cheryl glanced at Ben, wide-eyed. 'That's…that's attempted murder.'

'Exactly, which is why the police didn't want it to be general knowledge.'

'And Peter?' asked Cheryl.

'Apart from being a dedicated hotelier, which he inherited from Dad, he's a genuinely nice bloke – thoughtful and understanding. There's no reason why I should've been so jealous.'

Cheryl knew that Peter's wife and seven-year-old son had died in a car accident and now asked, 'Peter's never remarried?'

'No. However, before this accident happened, Monique had a marvellous idea and we all hope you'll agree.' Cheryl continued to stare at Ben as he recounted Monique's idea and she repeated, 'Monique would like me to do a colour scheme for all the bedrooms on the first floor of the hotel.'

'Yes.' Ben hesitated. 'But there's something else I should have told you. Monique and Peter suggested that I bring you back to stay in one of the bungalows.'

'That's a fantastic idea! I'd like that,' but no sooner had she said that than Cheryl's face clouded over. 'But it all depends on what the doctor tells me.'

Ben nodded, and seeing an empty space turned into the car park.

A few minutes later Cheryl found herself gradually relaxing as the doctor – a kindly-faced, middle-aged man told her, 'There's no need for you to look so terrified, Miss Laval.

I'm happy to tell you that neither of your parents are badly injured. Mainly cuts and bruises, no broken bones.' And as she gazed at him, open-mouthed, 'Yes, it is remarkable but, on the other hand, when an inebriated person falls they rarely hurt themselves.'

Cheryl nodded. 'Mother's always falling over; she must be covered with bruises.'

'She'll have some more now; but we'll keep them both in overnight.'

'It's incredible, neither of them are badly injured. They can come home tomorrow morning.'

'That's good.' Ben was pleased to see that Cheryl was so cheerful, and nodded when she said she would like to fetch their toiletries, nightwear and a change of clothing for the morning. It was when Cheryl mentioned her conversation with the doctor that Ben began to pay more attention. 'I told him that I would soon be moving out but that I'm concerned about their drinking habits – he's going to have a long talk with them tomorrow morning. He also suggested that arrangements should be made for the domestic help – a homely middle-aged woman – to come on a daily basis.' Cheryl hesitated. 'Suddenly I feel full of confidence but I do think we should talk about our future.'

What is she talking about, thought Ben and the next minute he asked, 'You are going to marry me?'

'Of course, but coming back to the present, will I be moving into your bungalow?'

'I think that was the general idea. There are two bedrooms if that's what you want and I'm sure Monique—' it was as he mentioned her name that Ben suddenly realised he still didn't know the extent of Noel's injuries and said, 'I wonder where Monique and Peter are?'

'You didn't look for them while I—' Cheryl stopped abruptly. 'Of course you didn't or you wouldn't have said that. I'm being a selfish bitch again.'

At that moment there was a gentle knock at the door which opened, Sergeant Batiste appeared, and seeing their expressions asked, 'Any serious injuries?'

'Fortunately, no. Just cuts and bruises,' replied Cheryl, 'but more important, what's the news about—'

'Where can I find Monique?' interrupted Ben.

'Two doors down.' Batiste had just seen Peter talking on his mobile. 'Monique's on her own – there's no news about Noel yet.'

Ben glanced at Cheryl. 'I'll look in and see her before I take you home.'

Monique turned expectantly as the door opened; she had been pacing to and fro but her expression changed when she saw Ben and said dully, 'Oh, it's you.

'I'm sorry I'm not the doctor.' Ben gazed at Monique's ashen face and putting his arm around her led her towards the chairs that were lined up against the wall. His arm still around her shoulders as they sat down, he said, 'I saw Peter at the end of the corridor. Is there anything I can do?' and when Monique shook her head, 'Would you like me to stay with you now, or I can come back after I've taken Cheryl home?' and before Monique could ask, 'Her parents are fine. Only cuts and bruises, but they're being kept in overnight.'

'That's good. I was concerned they might have been seriously injured.'

Ben then noticed the empty plastic container. 'Can I get you some tea?'

'No thanks,' and aware of Ben's intent gaze, 'There's no need for you to come back. Peter's here and hopefully someone will let us know what's happening.'

'What did the doctor say? Have you any idea?'

'Noel hadn't fastened his seat-belt so his injuries could be—' Monique faltered and had just buried her face in Ben's shoulder when the door opened, Peter appeared and hurried forward. 'What's happened? I didn't see the doctor or anyone else come in.'

'They haven't.' Monique sat up, fumbled for a tissue and dabbed her eyes, 'I'm probably being silly.'

'No you're not. You're worried, that's understandable, but you're also very brave.'

Ben scribbled a number on a scrap of paper and gave it to Peter. 'That's my mobile number. I'm taking Cheryl home, then I'm going back to my bungalow. Call me if you need me, if you want me to come back here.'

It was half an hour later that Monique and Peter sprang to their feet as the doctor entered, when they asked simultaneously, 'How is Noel?'

'I'm sorry, Mrs Latimer. It's not good news. Unfortunately, due to his condition, we're unable to fly your husband to Jersey, therefore I'm unable to tell you the full extent of his internal or head injuries.'

'It's my fault,' said Monique. 'I shouldn't have—'

'Stop blaming yourself,' interrupted Peter while the doctor said, 'It's a pity your husband didn't fasten his seat-belt. However, he's now being taken to Intensive Care.'

'Can I see him?'

'Just for a moment. He's lapsing in and out of consciousness.'

Although the doctor had explained that she could only stand in the doorway, that Noel was on a ventilator, Monique looked towards the unrecognisable figure in the bed, swayed and clutched Peter, while the nurse who was in attendance enquired, 'Would you like a glass of water? To sit down?'

'No thanks,' then turning back to Peter, Monique said, 'Perhaps in spite of what the doctor said, I should stay,' but before he could reply the nurse intervened. 'I don't think that's advisable at this stage, Mrs Latimer. If and when your husband regains consciousness it would only be for a few seconds.'

Chapter 26

'Julia Domaille?' echoed Henri Naftel and nodding, continued, 'Yes, although it's a long time ago, I do remember her. She was tall, quite attractive and a very efficient secretary. I was sorry to lose her.' The elderly Advocate, white-haired, still bright-eyed, reminisced.

'Julia married Roger Stenton and went to England but she wasn't very happy about that.'

Le Tissier and Batiste exchanged glances and the former asked, 'Why? Roger didn't even consult her. He merely told her he'd got a job and found a house.'

'How do you know all this?'

'Julia was very friendly with and confided in Rosemarie who later became my secretary. Rosemarie told me that Julia, although much younger, had been in love with Matthew Stenton and heart-broken when he married Iris. Apparently she and Roger had a son and although Mrs Domaille told me, I can't remember his name.'

'You kept in touch with the Domaille family?'

'Yes. Mrs Domaille was a pleasant, homely person, upset that she never saw her grandson, that Julia didn't return to the island for a holiday. I haven't had any news about Julia since her mother died.' Mr Naftel sighed. 'It's a pity. I often think about Julia and wonder what happened to her after Roger died.'

'Would you recognise her if you saw her?'

'Is that possible? Is Julia back in the island?'

The information received from the Southampton Registry Office and whether Henri Naftel should be advised of this had been discussed on the drive out to the Advocate's house, and Le Tissier now recounted what they knew about Julia.

'So Julia remarried and has been living in the island for seven years while Gerald has been working for his uncle for five?' Henri looked thoughtful and then asked, 'Why do you want me to identify Julia? Is this connected with Matthew's death?' and before Le Tissier could reply: 'How are you going to arrange that we're at the same place, at the same time?'

'I suggest that you and Mrs Naftel are enjoying a mid-morning coffee in town,' Le Tissier named a well-known patisserie, 'where Carol Cummings will be entertaining Julia.'

'Carol! Now there's an attractive and very charming woman,' and in the same breath, 'Is she also helping you with your enquiries?'

'I'm sure she'll be only too pleased to help. She was very fond of Matthew Stenton.'

Henri nodded. 'I'm going to enjoy this. However, tell me: if I do recognise Julia, what exactly do you want me to do?'

'Speak to Carol who will probably introduce you, when you can try the usual ploy: 'You remind me of my most efficient secretary.' Le Tissier grinned. 'There's no need for me to tell you what to do or say, you've had plenty of experience appearing with GADOC, you're more than capable.'

A pair of bright blue eyes sought Le Tissier's. 'Thank you. However, returning to Matthew Stenton's death: that was no accident. Are you likely to make an arrest soon?'

And without pausing for breath: 'I heard that Monique had a narrow escape when her brakes failed and now, today, that her husband was involved in a car accident. Do you know what happened? Is he badly injured?'

My God! News travels fast, thought Le Tissier. Batiste had phoned Peter who was still at the hospital before they left but there had been no news about Noel. Ben had already told them the Lavals were only bruised but being kept in overnight. Then Henri Naftel elucidated: 'My grand-daughter was waiting to cross the road when it happened. She heard another bystander, who obviously recognised Noel, call him by name.'

Henri looked at Batiste and then Le Tissier, who said, 'We don't know yet.'

'And what about the couple who were so disgustingly drunk?'

Is there anything the old boy doesn't know, wondered Le Tissier only to hear Henri say, 'My grand-daughter's a reporter on an English paper, currently here on holiday. She's a clever girl, very observant. Although they'd been arguing the couple lay huddled together, crumpled and very bloody. "Pathetic" was her description.'

*****

'Henri Naftel is an amazing old man and very cooperative' said Batiste as he drove back to the station.

'Yes, so is Carol Cummings.' Le Tissier had spoken to her and made the necessary arrangements for the following morning before they left Henri. Le Tissier now sighed;

'I can't help thinking about Monique Latimer, she's really had more than her share of trouble.'

'Yes.' Batiste's reply was so half-hearted that Le Tissier glanced at him and asked, 'What's the matter?'

'I was thinking about our visit to Julia Mostyn yesterday. Did you notice what was draped across the back of one of the chairs?'

'A dark jum—' Le Tissier stopped abruptly. 'Was it black or— ?'

'Navy blue,' interrupted Batiste. 'I also noticed her shoes: low-heeled, moccasin-style.'

Le Tissier nodded. 'We have commented on the size of her feet and I'm sure you, like me, have wondered if she could be responsible for the second set of footprints.'

'At the moment we've no good reason to ask for those shoes or the navy blue garment.'

Looking thoughtful, Le Tissier slowly enumerated what they knew about Julia Mostyn.

As a young woman she had been in love with Matthew, but married his brother Roger and moved to England. After his death she had remarried, returned to the island but her second husband had died three years ago. She had been seen in the hotel grounds by the handyman and head gardener on numerous occasions – both had commented on her height, large hands and feet; and she was obviously known to some of the hotel staff. Le Tissier recalled Monique's remarks about Julia Mostyn: that, even after her husband's death, she was a regular at the hotel, i.e. she lunched or dined two or three times a week, and always enjoyed her food. Monique also said that Julia spent a lot of time walking in the grounds where she often met and chatted to the residents. However he now had to wait for Henri Naftel's confirmation that Julia Mostyn was the same Julia he had employed as his secretary.

Once again Le Tissier's thoughts turned to the Latimers, and he sighed with frustration, when Batiste said, 'If you feel like that, how do you think Monique feels?'

'Worse, but we can't just sit here.' At that moment the phone rang; they both leant forward but it was Le Tissier who queried, 'Who?' And after a slight pause, 'Oh, that's a different matter. Put him through,' and nodding at Batiste, the Inspector mouthed, 'It's Noel's bank manager,' then he was saying, 'Good afternoon, sir. How can I help you?'

As usual Batiste noted Le Tissier's changing expressions then finally he said, 'That was all very interesting; however I'm unable to give you any information about Mr Latimer's condition. As you already know, Mrs Latimer is still at the hospital.'

'What was that all about?' asked Batiste.

'Noel's bank manager has just heard about the accident, and rather than worry Monique, thought we should know that Noel was extremely rude and in a foul temper when he left the bank; which probably accounts for his erratic driving, and the fact that he didn't fasten his seat-belt.'

'Are you going to tell Monique?'

'No. I'm sure she's already realised that Noel's injuries are due to the fact that he hadn't used his seat-belt; but I would like to know if they've seen him and are still at the hospital.'

'I've Peter's number,' but as Batiste reached into his pocket the phone on the desk rang and Le Tissier was saying, 'Good afternoon, Mr Stenton, Peter, how is Mr Latimer? Have you any news?'

Batiste watched as the inspector's expression became grim and he eventually said, 'That's understandable. We can only hope and pray that Noel will make a complete recovery. I'm sure Ben and Vere are relieved that you're taking care of Monique.'

Then, after a slight, pause: 'I think you should know I've just had a call from Noel's bank manager. He'd heard about the accident, enquired if he was badly injured and told me that Noel had been very rude and left in a temper. However, I hope that by the morning there's an improvement in his condition.' Then, before Batiste could speak, and as he replaced the receiver, Le Tissier continued, 'They were only allowed to stand in the doorway. Noel's on a ventilator and is still unconscious. Peter took Monique, who's obviously very distressed, back to the hotel; but they'll be seeing Noel this evening. Peter will let me know if there's any change but I don't expect to hear anything tonight.'

'Do they know – did Peter say what the injuries were?'

'No, and I wouldn't expect him to do that. Although she's a very brave person it wouldn't do Monique any good to hear them being listed. She's fortunate that Peter and Ben are there for her, that Vere is equally supportive, while there's a very loyal staff headed by Pat Le Page. However we still have to find the person responsible for Matthew Stenton's death, tampered with Monique's Mini and—'

'And writing those letters,' interrupted Batiste.

*****

Monique replaced the receiver, re-tied the belt of her dressing gown and looked at Peter. 'There's no improvement or change.'

'Has the doctor seen Noel?'

'Not yet. It is rather early.' Peter had just placed two cups of tea on the low table between the armchair where Monique sat and the settee where he now seated himself. Concerned at her pallor, the fact that she had hardly eaten anything the previous evening and had had a restless night, Peter said, 'I realise you're worried but you must think of yourself. It's still quite early,' it had just turned half-past seven, 'so I suggest you go back to bed for a couple of hours, and then I'll make you some breakfast.'

'I can't do that—' Monique faltered, and then started as the front door opened and closed, and Ben wearing jeans and a T-shirt appeared, and rushed across to her: 'Are you all right?' then, turning to Peter, 'What's happened?'

'Monique hardly slept so I'm suggesting she should go back to bed.'

'I should be at the hospital with Noel,' insisted Monique.

'Not yet.' Ben reached for and gripped her hands. 'You need to rest – relax or you'll make yourself ill.' Peter and Ben watched as she freed her hands, drank some tea and nibbled a digestive biscuit, then setting her cup down with a clatter said, 'I should shower, dress and go over to the hotel.'

'There's no need. I was on my way there when Pat arrived,' and as Monique gave a sigh of relief Ben continued, 'Now please go back to bed. As you've said yourself, Pat is very capable, knows Peter is here if she needs his advice, and that I'm around.'

Monique shook her head in amazement, 'I'm so surprised. You're suddenly very protective.'

'You are my sister and I'd prefer not to call the doctor—'

'I don't need the doctor. I'm not ill, just worried about Noel.'

'Who is in good hands.'

Monique looked from one to the other, noting their concern. 'Oh, very well. I'll go back to bed, just for a little while.'

As she closed her eyes Monique's thoughts turned to Noel and once again she doubted that, when she did visit, he would be aware of her presence, or hear her.

It was eleven o'clock when, feeling better, Monique walked across to the hotel where she was greeted with a welcoming smile and hug from Pat who immediately asked, 'How's Noel this morning?'

'He regained consciousness but only for a few seconds. However Peter and I are going up to the hospital now.'

Pat nodded. Peter and Ben, both with grim expressions, had told her the extent of Noel's injuries and she now said, 'Please give him my best wishes.'

Chapter 27

Henri and Ruth Naftel looked around the terrace, admiring the many and colourful flowers and plants whilst noting that locals and holidaymakers were enjoying delicious gateaux with their coffee. For a moment Henri's gaze lingered on the latest arrivals who seated themselves at a table near the entrance to the patisserie. The cappuccinos which had been brought to their table were still untouched as they enjoyed their surroundings; then Ruth broke into his thoughts.

'Isn't that Carol Cummings over there? Doesn't she look stunning? I think she's one of the most attractive and elegant women in the island.'

'I agree.' Henri picked up his cup; he had already approved the azure blue suit, the superb pearls at her throat and matching earrings, the flawless complexion and hairstyle.

'It's really lovely here, we should come more often, especially on a day like this,' said Ruth.

'Yes, my dear.' Henri was now deliberately scanning the occupants of the other tables. Blessed with good eyesight he had noted that Carol's companion was a very tall, silver-haired woman wearing a turquoise trouser suit and was aware they were now studying a menu. Seated in the middle of the terrace it would be necessary for them to pass the two ladies; however Henri turned to look at his wife, once again grateful for his good fortune. They both enjoyed good health, annual visits from their children and grandchildren, and took a three-week cruise either in the spring or autumn.

It was half an hour later that Henri paused at Carol Cummings' table and said, 'Good morning, my dear. How are you this lovely morning?'

'Very well, thank you, Henri.' Carol smiled. 'Surely you're not on your own?' and before he could reply, 'Do you know Julia Mostyn?'

Aware that a pair of clear grey eyes were looking up at him, Henri hesitated, then in a voice that was now low and husky she said, 'It's been such a long time since I worked for you, I don't expect you to remember me, Mr Naftel. I was Julia Domaille.'

'And the best secretary I had. Of course I remember you.' Henri feigned surprise and continued, 'Are you here on holiday?'

Carol's laughter was always infectious. 'I know you live in the country but the island isn't that big. I'm surprised you haven't seen Julia before. She came back seven years ago with her late husband, Quentin Mostyn.'

Immediately Henri was profuse in his apologies and looking at Julia again said, 'I'm sorry. We don't socialise very much these days.' And then, to his relief Ruth was at his side smiling at Carol and saying, 'Oh, there you are!'

'And look who's here, after all these years – Julia, who was my most efficient secretary.'

'Good Heavens!' Ruth's surprise was genuine and when Julia's large hand gripped hers, 'I didn't go into the office very often but I remember you were always so polite when I phoned.'

Julia smiled at this unexpected compliment, revealing large but even white teeth, when Ruth said, 'Unfortunately we have an appointment, but maybe we could meet here for a coffee. Perhaps you could give us your phone number.'

'Of course.' Immediately Julia took a small notebook and pen from her handbag, wrote the required information and handed this to Ruth who now tugged at Henri's sleeve.

'Come along, dear, or we'll be late.'

'Where are we going?' asked Henri a few minutes later as they climbed the wide street leading to the War Memorial.

'I thought you'd want to see the gentleman who called on you yesterday afternoon, and that it was better to come this way rather than go directly from the hotel.' Then, as Henri paused to glance sideways, Ruth continued, 'Obviously I don't know what it was all about but for you to receive a phone call from Arnold Levrier and then a visit from Inspector Le Tissier and his sergeant, I guessed it must be something important, and after this morning's encounter, to do with Julia.'

Henri nodded. 'Congratulations, my dear. You're very perceptive.'

*****

'I certainly didn't expect this!' exclaimed Inspector Le Tissier some 15 minutes later as he again studied the piece of paper on which Julia had written her name and phone number. Not only had Henri recognised his ex-secretary, his wife had obtained a sample of her handwriting which would now be sent off to the experts. Le Tissier had congratulated Ruth Naftel for the information that she had, only held this slip of paper by the lower right-hand corner and, once out of sight, slipped this into an old envelope and then into her handbag. He and Batiste had been amused at Henri's bewilderment at Ruth's behaviour but he had conceded, 'I suppose it's not surprising. Ruth is always reading P.D. James., Ruth Rendell or some other well-known crime writer. However, and please excuse me for asking, obviously I don't want to phone Monique – is there any news about Noel Latimer?'

'I haven't heard anything since early this morning and like yourself I don't want to trouble her or Peter. They both went back to the hospital last night and stayed for an hour.'

'Is Noel badly injured?' enquired Ruth Naftel, and when the Inspector nodded, she persisted: 'Any brain damage?'

'Really, my dear,' scolded Henri. 'You mustn't pester the Inspector with all these questions.'

*****

'Noel's not going to recover, is he?' Monique and Peter had walked from the ICU in silence but now, as they reached the main entrance and before Peter could reply, she continued, 'It's not just his internal injuries, he could be in a coma—' Monique stopped abruptly when Peter suggested, 'Would you like a drive out to the west coast or perhaps the south coast? We could have a walk along the cliffs.'

'That sounds nice, thank you.'

It was some time later, as they stood looking across to the Hanois lighthouse, that Peter asked, 'What did you think of Cheryl?'

Hoping it would distract Monique, Ben had arranged that Cheryl should come and look at his bungalow and, at the same time, meet Monique and Peter. 'She's painfully thin but that could be due to drugs and not eating properly. Although she's no longer a child or teenager her parents haven't noticed or bothered about her – apart from Ben, she hasn't met anyone who cares. At the moment she needs someone who's prepared to spend time with her, share her interests.' Peter relaxed, Ben's suggestion was certainly helping. Monique continued: 'Cheryl kept apologising that her parents were the cause of Noel's accident, and wanting to hug me. She's really keen to move into the spare bedroom in Ben's bungalow and wants to know if she can help, in any way, in the hotel, or even in the garden.'

'It's obvious she wants to do something, be occupied. Will you be able to find something?'

'I'm sure between Pat, the housekeeper and old Bert they'll be able to keep her busy.

She's fetching her parents this afternoon.'

*****

'This is silly,' said Monique as she carried a skirt and two blouses on hangers into the bedroom she was occupying. 'I should move back to my own bungalow.'

'I think you're better here,' and before Monique could protest, Peter appeared in the hall and resumed: 'Vere has just asked which would you prefer: to go up to him for a cup of tea or should he come down here?' At the mention of Vere's name Monique felt guilty; she hadn't seen or spoken to him for several days, and although she had enjoyed being on the cliffs that morning, the idea of a walk through the lanes up to his bungalow was suddenly appealing. 'We'll go and see him.'

As they turned right at the top of the steps and followed the path that led to the lanes in which the ten bungalows had been built in recent years, Peter was glad they would not be passing the vantage point from which their father had been pushed. Although he knew it was partially due to the exertion of climbing the steps, Peter was also pleased to see some colour in Monique's cheeks and listen to her comments on their delightful surroundings.

They had just turned the corner and reached the first bungalow; while Monique admired the manicured lawns and colourful flower beds, Peter turned to appreciate the sea view.

Trees and shrubs had been cleverly chosen and planted in the 18-foot area between the lane and cliff path to ensure that while the residents retained their privacy they also enjoyed a sea view.

'It's certainly a lovely area – did all this land belong to one family?' enquired Monique.

'Yes.' Peter mentioned a well-known local name, wondered why Monique was suddenly walking very fast, and then learnt that the attractive pale pink bungalow they had just passed belonged to Julia Mostyn.

'How do you know that?'

'I was admiring her garden, then saw and recognised her – she's one of our regulars. When Inspector Le Tissier asked about her, I could only tell him that she used to come with her husband, who was Quentin Mostyn – a well-known artist.'

'Why did the Inspector want to know about her?' asked Peter as they approached Vere's bungalow.

'I don't know.'

*****

'That was a really enjoyable afternoon' said Monique two hours later as she and Peter walked back through the lanes. Apart from the initial enquiry, Vere had not spoken about Noel, but entertained them with various amusing incidents and interesting characters he had met during his career as a solicitor.

'We're very fortunate to have such a kind and caring friend,' said Peter.

'Yes. He must miss Dad. Not only did they meet every morning on their walk, they often met later in the day.'

Meanwhile Gerald, who had been walking along the cliffs on the other side of the valley, was now retracing his steps back to the hotel. He had received a phone call from Julia Mostyn earlier that afternoon, inviting him to tea on Friday afternoon. She had sounded quite agitated when she said, 'There's something I must tell you,' which had immediately aroused his curiosity and now, as he reached the top of the steps, he reflected that she was an unusual woman.

This really is a lovely island and the hotel is ideally situated, thought Gerald as his gaze travelled from the calm sea – the incoming tide gradually covering the golden sand – to the opposite side of the valley, where he saw Monique and Peter approaching the steps.

For a moment he wondered if they had been to visit Julia Mostyn but quickly dismissed this idea — neither of them really knew her. Gerald's thoughts then turned to Noel. Monique had told him, at lunch time, that there was no change or improvement in his condition; he had not recovered consciousness, and that she would be returning to the hospital that evening. He, Gerald, had also noticed and been pleased about the complete turnaround of Ben's attitude towards Monique and the hotel but now, still gazing out to sea, Gerald wondered what would happen if, due to his head injuries, Noel became permanently immobile. It was general knowledge that Peter would remain in the island until Matthew's estate was settled and everything in the hotel was running smoothly.

The sound of an angry voice suddenly penetrated Gerald's thoughts, when he saw a short, overweight man shouting as he approached Monique and Peter. 'Why didn't you speak to me yourself, tell me the truth yesterday? Is Noel badly injured? I've a right to know, we were going to be partners. I phoned the hospital again this morning but they still won't tell me how he is, or allow me to visit. Noel always said you were a hard, calculating bitch—'

'Excuse me, Mr de Garis.' Peter's voice was very calm and his expression grim. 'I'd advise you not to speak to my sister in that tone or manner.'

'I've only heard about Ben, so who are you?' Nevill glared at Peter, and as Gerald, having heard the shouting and resultant altercation, joined them, 'And who's he?'

'Our cousin,' said Monique and Peter in unison as Gerald also towered over Nevill.

'Huh! ' The estate agent turned back to Monique. 'Are you going to tell me what's wrong with Noel and that I can visit him?'

Monique sighed, 'Oh, very well,' but aware that guests returning to the hotel were looking at them curiously and glancing from Peter to Gerald, Monique suggested, 'Why don't we go over to my father's bungalow?'

'Do you really want me to come along?' Gerald looked at Monique and then Peter. 'I was going to check if there were any more bookings for tonight.'

Monique nodded. 'You carry on. This shouldn't take long.'

Nevill's eyes widened as he gazed around the large tastefully-furnished lounge, sank into one of the comfortable armchairs indicated and asked, 'Why are you deliberately keeping us apart? I'm sure Noel is wondering why I haven't been to see him.'

'He—' Monique faltered. 'He doesn't know. He's still unconscious.'

'Since yesterday?' Nevill suddenly looked aghast. 'I heard about the accident before and—' jerking his head in Peter's direction, '—you phoned. And then there were several versions of what happened – you know what this island's like.' Then turning to Monique who was sat on the settee beside Peter he said, 'Is he badly injured?'

'Yes. Talking to him hasn't done any good, or playing his favourite tunes. No response whatsoever. And his internal injuries—'

'Don't, I can't bear it,' interrupted Nevill. He had been fiddling with his cuff-links and running his fingers through his thinning hair since he sat down and his face, which had been flushed from running, was now ashen. 'Although we hadn't known each other very long, two…nearly three years, I'd become very fond of Noel.'

'What—' started Monique and then glanced at Peter who shook his head, while Nevill, trying to control his emotions, struggled to his feet and said, 'I appreciate what you said. However can I see Noel? I won't speak to or upset him. I'll only stay a second.'

Again Monique glanced at Peter before she said, 'I think it's you who'll be shocked. His face, what you can see of it, is bruised and almost covered with plasters.'

'Can I go now?' Nevill looked from Monique to Peter, when the latter said, 'I'll just phone the nurse who's monitoring Noel and, if she agrees, give her your name.'

'Thank you.' Nevill stood up, unaware that his suit was now badly creased and his general appearance untidy, and repeated, 'Thank you very much.' As Peter picked up his mobile and went into the hall, Nevill glanced around again and couldn't help himself: 'I had no idea your father lived here, that it was privately-owned.'

'So are the other two bungalows which my father had built for Ben and myself.'

'I've seen them from a distance, of course, but didn't realise they were so... ' Nevill waved his hand, 'so spacious, so luxurious. I wondered if they were time-share or even belonged to a wealthy English couple or family.'

'No, it's all family property. Ben and I were very fortunate to have such a thoughtful, caring and generous father.' At that moment Peter reappeared, 'You can see Noel just for a moment. But as Monique warned you, you won't see much of him, he's all bandages, tubes, etc.'

'But I can see him,' and as he followed Monique to the front door Nevill whispered, 'Oh my poor boy, what has happened to you?'

'He's rather a strange character,' commented Peter a few minutes later. 'Have you met him before? What do you know about him?'

'Not much. There are two other partners, one is retiring. That's one reason he's so keen for Noel to join them. He's divorced – his wife went off with a younger man.'

'How do you know all this?'

'Mrs Le Page, Pat's mum is a mine of information.'

'What did you make of Nevill's remark that he had become very fond of Noel – is he gay?'

'I don't know! Anyhow I'm going back to my place to change,' but as she picked up her handbag Monique suddenly said, 'I wonder if Inspector Le Tissier has had any results about the handwriting.'

'It's too soon and, as far as we know, he hasn't any samples for comparison.'

Chapter 28

Monique stood up, walked to the end of the bed and gazed back at Noel's inert body. She had seen the doctor on arrival at the hospital earlier that evening when he had told them it was unlikely that Noel would last the night. That was three hours ago, the nurse had brought her sandwiches and coffee, it was now 11 o'clock and as she moved back towards the chair the nurse reappeared and said gently, 'Why don't you go home, Mrs Latimer? Try and get some sleep. Your husband doesn't know you're here and you must think of yourself. The doctor certainly didn't expect you to stay all night, or for so long, and I'm sure your brother didn't.'

There was a slight movement in the doorway as the nurse spoke, when she turned and nodded, 'Ah, you're here, Mr Stenton. I was just talking about you.'

Peter moved into the small but highly equipped room and when she shook her head he said, 'You must come home and rest, Monique.'

'No, I want to stay.'

'You can't do anything, only make yourself ill and we don't want you to do that. The doctor was adamant that you should rest.'

Although tired and finding it difficult to keep her eyes open, Monique asked, 'When did he say that?'

'As I left. He suggested that I come and fetch you.'

'I don't believe you,' protested Monique but again the nurse nodded. 'He did. I'd just come on duty and I heard him.'

Still protesting, Monique allowed Peter to lead her along the now dimly-lit and silent corridor towards the main entrance and his car, which was parked immediately outside.

Within minutes they were back at the hotel where Ben was waiting, the front door of Matthew's bungalow open and welcoming. Hugging her gently he said, 'Don't talk, you must be exhausted. Once you're in bed I'll bring you in some soup – one of chef's specials.' Monique blinked back tears, she was unaccustomed to so much affection and attention from Ben and whispered, 'Thank you. Although I'm tired I doubt that I'll sleep.'

*****

'Peter! How long have you been standing there?' Monique opened her eyes to see her half-brother standing at her bedside.

'You looked so peaceful I didn't want to disturb you but—' It was the last word he uttered that immediately registered with Monique and she quickly said, 'What's happened? Is it Noel?'

Peter nodded, his expression grave. 'Noel died at 3 o'clock—'

'I should have been there.' Monique's voice was quiet and again her face very pale. 'I know it was inevitable…so many injuries,' and biting her lip she shook her head, 'I still can't believe it. Why didn't you wake me, tell me?'

'I only knew myself half an hour ago,' and as Monique was about to throw back the bedclothes, Peter continued, 'Stay there,' and indicating the cup and saucer, 'drink your tea. Pat's on duty this morning. Ben can—'

'What can I do?' Ben stood in the doorway, glanced at Peter and then moved towards Monique, sat on the edge of the bed and held her tight. Both men waited for her to burst into tears, but she just gripped the top sheet, closed her eyes and began to take deep breaths; then, after a few minutes: 'I'll have my tea and get up.'

'But—' said Ben and Peter together when she continued, 'I'm not ill, and staying here won't do me or anyone else any good. I'll have to go up to the hospital and—' Monique faltered, '—and there'll be arrangements to make.'

'I could do—' started Peter but, looking from one to the other, Monique interrupted, 'I'll be pleased to have your help.' Reaching for her tea, 'The staff will have to be told. Gerald and Hans can tell their respective teams.' Ben was now standing, and she continued, 'While Pat can tell the porters and ask the housekeeper to do the same for the chambermaids.'

'What about Nevill, would you like me to phone him?' asked Peter.

'No.' Monique reached for her dressing-gown, 'I'll do that before I have my shower.'

'How can she remain so calm?' whispered Ben, and without pausing for breath, 'Cheryl is supposed to be moving in today but I'll ring from the hotel and suggest she waits until tomorrow. No doubt you'll ring Vere.'

'I hadn't thought of him,' admitted Peter. 'He'll probably want to come and comfort Monique, so I'll wait until she says she wants to see anyone. And I suppose I should phone Arnold Levrier.'

'Would you like me to make the necessary arrangements for Noel's funeral?' asked Peter as they walked towards his car. Monique had remained silent as they stood and regarded Noel's peaceful body and Peter had noticed that the doctor, whom they had met on previous occasions, had looked at her with concern.

'No, but I would like you and/or Ben to be there when the funeral director comes, I'll ring him when we get back to the hotel.' Monique lapsed into silence, her hands clenched in her lap, until they were halfway down the hill at the exact spot where her brakes had failed when she suddenly exclaimed, 'It's my fault Noel's dead. If I'd agreed to let him have the amount he needed he wouldn't have gone to the bank and this accident wouldn't have happened.'

'Nonsense, that's not true.' Peter had gently turned towards and parked on the grass verge.

'It was during his interview with the bank manager that he lost his temper.'

'He'd already done that,' interrupted Monique.

'Well, whatever he said annoyed Noel so stop blaming yourself, but have a good cry.'

'I...I can't cry. Even when Dad—' Then, to her own surprise, Monique burst into tears and her words were muffled: 'I really do miss him. Dad was always there, loving and kind.'

His seat-belt quickly unfastened, Peter leant towards and put his arms around Monique, and with a hint of humour: 'I don't mind a damp shirt.'

Meanwhile back at the hotel Ben and Pat were dealing with numerous phone calls about Noel. Le Tissier's call was the first that Ben received and he was not surprised when the Inspector enquired, 'How's your sister? Is there any way, in a personal capacity, in which Batiste and I can help?' The door between the office and Reception was open and during a lull Ben asked, 'How do all these people already know?'

'It only needs a few to spread the news. Your family are well-known and respected,' then, as the phones rang, 'Here we go again.'

At the station Sergeant Batiste was also being inundated with calls from different people. The first call had been from Peter who told him that Vere Hamilton, Arnold Levrier and Nevill de Garis had already been informed. Le Tissier was still wondering how Henri Naftel had heard the news when he found himself talking to Noel's bank manager, who exclaimed, 'It's terrible news! I feel personally responsible. I should have explained more fully but he was in such a hurry, didn't or wouldn't understand that he couldn't withdraw such a huge amount without giving the necessary six months' notice.' The man would have rambled on but, with his usual diplomacy Le Tissier assured him that Noel had been angry when he left the hotel; then, in reply to the query about the couple who had fallen into the road, said, 'They weren't really hurt — went home yesterday.'

Back at the hotel Ben and Pat, who had been shocked and concerned about Monique, had agreed to wait until after breakfast had been served before they told the heads of departments. Gerald, being family, was told first when, aghast, he immediately asked, 'When did this happen? How's Monique?'

'Upset, naturally but she'll be coming over to the hotel later.'

'The phone hasn't stopped all morning — very few bookings,' commented Pat as she looked from Monique to Ben and Peter as they sat around the desk in the back office.

'I'm sorry, but thank you for coping so marvellously. I really don't know how we'd cope without you,' said Monique.

'Nonsense,' replied Pat brusquely. 'However Ailsa phoned and offered to come in for a couple of hours each day when she's off duty.'

'She's certainly keen but I'm sure the Reardons aren't very happy that she's leaving,' said Ben and then added, 'Apparently the old man sounded rather gruff when he phoned this morning but understood that Monique wasn't taking any personal calls.' That had been Pat's idea, one with which Ben and Peter had agreed. As anticipated, Vere had wanted to come down immediately but Peter had persuaded him to wait until the afternoon, while Esme Levrier and Mrs Le Page, in addition to conveying their condolences, had both enquired if there was anything they could do, now or even later, and Ben had spoken to the two ladies, looked at Pat questioningly and said that perhaps later there was some way in which they could divert Monique's attention. Roslyn, who for some reason had again delayed her return to England, and Carol Cummings had spoken to Peter and received the same reply. Gerald waited until midday when he just reached for Monique's hands and stammered, 'I'm...I'm so sorry.'

There were numerous calls from local people who were either regulars in the bar or ate at the hotel when Pat and Ben had been relieved that all had left their names and expressed their condolences. Both had experienced and been curious about the person who seemed overcome with emotion and rang off without speaking.

'Did your husband have any relatives or friends who will be coming over for the funeral?' enquired the minister.

'Not to my knowledge. He never spoke of anyone and there were no names in his address book.' Peter and Ben had agreed that the funeral should be held on Monday, but did not agree with Monique that very few would attend.

'You're well known, people will want to support you, show their affection,' said Ben.

'I was so overwhelmed at the number who attended Dad's funeral, I couldn't cope with that again.' It was whilst the choice of hymns was being discussed that the phone rang.

Ben automatically answered it and turned to Peter, 'Excuse me, it's Nevill – he sounds very upset.'

'That's putting it mildly,' thought Peter, at first unable to stem the flow of words; then at last he managed to say, 'Calm down, please.'

'That's impossible! I know Monique told me earlier but I can't accept Noel's death. It shouldn't have happened, why didn't he recover from his injuries?'

'I'm sorry, I can't tell you. I'm not a doctor.' Aware that Ben and the minister were looking at Peter curiously Monique mouthed, 'Do you want to tell Nevill we're making the necessary arrangements for the funeral? Has he any preferences regarding hymns or anything else?'

Within minutes everything had been finalised, the trio were alone and Monique sank on to the settee, but a moment later looked around and said, 'This is a lovely bungalow, Dad's favourite pieces of furniture are here and make it feel special; but sometime I'll have to go back to my own place.' Peter had noticed Ben's concern for Monique ever since the accident and now noted that he was gazing in his direction with raised eyebrows; then all of a sudden Ben was saying, 'You don't have to move back.' And still looking at Peter, 'There's no reason why Monique shouldn't live here, is there?'

'Of course not,' and together they asked, 'Would you like to do that?' They were all staring at each other wordlessly when there was a knock at the front door, which was still ajar, and Vere's familiar voice called out, 'Can I come in?' Monique jumped to her feet. 'Of course,' and Ben, glancing at his watch exclaimed, 'I'm supposed to be at Cheryl's. She's moving in this afternoon.'

It was while they were having tea, which was complemented by a delicious Victoria sponge that Vere had brought with him, that he said, 'I hope I haven't spoken out of turn but Julia Mostyn stopped as she was passing, said she had heard about Noel and wanted to know if it was a rumour or the truth. I had to tell her, of course, when she went off in a rush, muttering to herself.'

'The number of phone calls this morning was incredible,' said Monique, 'however it'll be in the paper tomorrow.'

*****

'This is a really fantastic place, you must be very proud of what your father achieved,' said Cheryl as Ben approached the hotel and turned towards the bungalows.

'Yes, but it's only recently I've realised that and, as you're now aware, my whole attitude towards it, Monique and Peter, has changed.'

Cheryl nodded. 'You're not the only one. I've done a lot of serious thinking, especially since my parents' accident. I've been a fool spending so much time and money at The Sparrow's Nest, it's not surprising I look such a mess and my clothes all hang on me.'

'I'm sure you'll soon look better. However, how did your parents react to your moving out?'

'They weren't annoyed. In fact Mother admitted I should have looked for a job as soon as we arrived here, and found my own flat, and Dad agreed. I don't know what the doctor said but they haven't been out since their return from hospital. Mother seems to be taking an interest in the house and is talking about a live-in housekeeper; she could have my flat.'

As they stopped outside Ben's bungalow Cheryl continued, 'Have you heard, do you know what happened at The Sparrow's Nest last night?'

'No,' replied Ben slowly, relieved that Cheryl had not visited the popular nightspot for eight days.

'Apparently there was a definite police presence out there.'

'How do you know all this?' asked Ben as he unfastened his seat-belt.

'I had a call from a local girl who uses the place three or four times a week. She told me that Louis Bellamy, the cashier was caught passing sachets of drugs at the same time as their winnings, while Max Bellamy and Godfrey Reardon were in the office emptying a briefcase and putting more in the safe.'

'My God!' exclaimed Ben. 'I haven't, or rather we haven't heard anything about this out here, is it really true? Who is this girl, how well do you know her?'

'I don't know her name but she was always friendly, wore smart expensive clothes, well-spoken and has a responsible job – in fact I was surprised she frequented a place like that and before you ask, she hadn't seen me for ten days and wondered if I was ill. It was then she blurted out about—'

'Are you two going to sit there for the rest of the afternoon?' called out Monique when Cheryl said quietly, 'Don't say anything about all this. It'll be in the paper soon enough.'

Within minutes Cheryl had been introduced to Vere; her case, several dress bags and two large holdalls had been deposited in the spare room in Ben's bungalow, and they were sitting in Matthew's lounge, drinking tea.

Meanwhile Detective Inspector Le Tissier and Detective Sergeant Batiste, who were both anxiously awaiting the report from the graphologist, were still jubilant that the fingerprints, although blurred by the use of gloves, on the saw, pliers and on the French window of Matthew's lounge, were the same.

Owen Mahy had been questioned again and repeated that he had not needed the saw that week and had last seen it on Tuesday.

Vere admitted he had not noticed the fence was damaged on Wednesday or Thursday morning. He and Matthew had met as usual – that was on a different part of the path – and exchanged a few words. Although he had offered this information before, Vere repeated that as usual Matthew had continued until he reached the turning leading to the bungalows, when he would walk straight through to the main road, along that for a short distance, turn into another lane and then a path which leads down to the hotel grounds, thus avoiding the hill.

Vere had continued down the path, steps and through the hotel grounds using the same route as Matthew but in reverse. It was because he hadn't met Matthew that Vere had stopped to look over the fence, seen a body on the beach and then, for some reason, glanced down and noticed the damaged palings.

Le Tissier and Batiste had also heard that there had been a substantial haul of drugs at The Sparrow's Nest the previous evening, that the Bellamy brothers, who had been kept in custody overnight, and Godfrey Reardon were still being questioned, and Batiste now said, 'It's fortunate Cheryl Laval wasn't there. She's moving down to the hotel, Ben's bungalow, this afternoon and, according to Peter, she's keen to help wherever needed. She hasn't any hotel training but it was Monique's idea that she should work on a colour scheme for the redecoration of the first floor bedrooms. It's amazing how she and Ben have changed.'

'That often happens after a family bereavement.' Le Tissier continued, 'Matthew was always known as a fair but good employer. We've seen for ourselves the number of staff who have worked for him for a number of years, and I'm sure they'll remain loyal to Monique.'

'Even so, it's a big responsibility for a woman of her age, who's very attractive and could be happily married with a family,' commented Batiste. 'However, we can only hope her family, friends and staff will continue to—' At that moment the door opened, Emile Girard's head appeared, a broad smile on his face, and he asked, 'Can you spare a minute?'

'Of course. More than that if it's relevant to our case.'

'Unlikely, however we now know how a regular supply of drugs was being brought in – young Reardon's involved.'

'That'll upset the old man,' said Batiste and quickly added, 'He always wanted Godfrey to marry Monique.'

Emile nodded, 'I know.' His explanation that the drugs had been brought in during the summer months by the regular courier for the day-trippers who lunched at The Valley View, French golfing parties who flew in for long weekends and also stayed at the hotel, and on occasions picked up from a French yacht by Max in Godfrey's boat, was received with interest.

'This means Godfrey's really involved,' said Le Tissier while Batiste asked, 'Does he have a financial interest in The Sparrow's Nest?' and in the same breath, 'Does he personally handle the drugs?'

'Only to take them from the hotel to the nightclub which will, of course, implicate him. The Bellamy brothers may be released later today, their passports confiscated, their movements discreetly observed,' said Emile.

'Are any locals involved in the importation or distribution?' enquired Le Tissier.

'Further interrogation will resume in 15 minutes. I'll keep you informed of anything that's relevant.'

*****

'You fool! How could you be so stupid?' It was late that same afternoon and Howard Reardon, holding a glass of whisky, glared at Godfrey who said, 'Oh come on, Dad. It's not that—'

'Of course it is. You allowed drugs to be brought into the hotel, not just once, but on several occasions. How do you think I felt when three men and a sniffer dog from the drug squad arrived and spent the afternoon in the office? And although they didn't find anything, except the correspondence regarding the lunches and the name of the courier (which they probably already knew), they're coming back tomorrow morning. Judging from the number of complaints received it's obvious you don't care about the hotel, you're never here; and now Ailsa, who's the most competent and reliable member of the staff, is leaving.'

'I'm sure there are other good receptionists around. We'll soon find someone else.'

'I'm afraid I don't share your optimism,' said Howard. 'Guests, if they return, which I very much doubt they would want to in our case, like to see the same faces.' Howard swallowed the remaining whisky and held out his glass, 'Pour me another one,' and in the same breath, 'When did you last go upstairs, inspect the bedrooms and corridors? The bedspreads and carpets are all in a shocking state and almost all the rooms need redecoration.'

'Oh don't be so fussy, Dad. If you could see some of the people's homes they're probably...'

'Probably in a much better condition than what we're offering...' Then, in a disapproving tone, 'Don't be so mean with the whisky. And as for the quality of the meat we're serving – it's a disgrace. I'm not surprised the residents and chef complain. If the bills were paid regularly – and why aren't they? – the butcher would be glad to supply us with some decent meat.'

'Oh for God's sake, Dad, don't keep on,' muttered Godfrey under his breath.

Although Howard didn't enjoy good health his hearing was perfect and he quickly said, 'Don't rile me. Running this hotel successfully is for your benefit as well as mine. If I was a younger man and you were really interested I'd refurbish the bedrooms, but with this drug fiasco hanging over our heads I'm reluctant to spend any of the little capital I do have.'

'Why must you go on and on about the damn place,' grumbled Godfrey. 'Don't you ever think of anything else?'

'Yes. I'd like to drive round and call on Monique but I'm sure she doesn't want any visitors. Now, if things had been different and you'd got in there before Noel, and I really don't know what she saw in him—'

'But I didn't,' interrupted Godfrey angrily.

*****

Monique is a really amazing woman, thought Gerald as he looked across the dining room, to the corner table. She had coped with her father's violent and unexpected death with courage and resourcefulness and now had to cope with Noel's death. Gerald's gaze travelled from Monique to the very thin blonde who sat beside Ben. He knew she was Cheryl Laval and would be involved with colour schemes and the refurbishment of the first floor bedrooms. She was also prepared to help wherever necessary in the hotel.

But enough of that, thought Gerald; he was more concerned about the phone call he had received from Julia Mostyn the previous afternoon. She had spoken briefly about

Noel but sounded agitated and had asked, in fact insisted, that he call on her the following afternoon.

There was something of great importance that she had to tell him. Gerald glanced around at the few remaining guests who were lingering over their coffee, at the same time wondering what Julia was talking about and what could be so important.

Chapter 29

'Yes!' Inspector Le Tissier's voice was almost a whisper and then louder as he reread the e-mail handed to him by Sergeant Batiste. 'The handwriting is Julia's, which means it's time we paid her a visit to pick up the navy blue pullover and shoes.'

'It's the middle of the afternoon, she may not be in,' said Batiste.

'We'll soon find out.' Le Tissier reached for his jacket which was draped over the back of his chair and continued, 'Julia's not stupid. She probably realised her meeting with Henri Naftel wasn't entirely coincidental. She might feel the need to talk to someone, possibly tell Gerald.'

'But why did she do it?' asked Batiste.

*****

'You're my mother!' exclaimed Gerald; then moving closer he scrutinised Julia's face.

'I know it's been a long time since I saw you. I often wondered how and where you were, if you were alive, but to discover that you're actually here!' Gazing intently at the smooth skin, discreet make-up, Gerald continued, 'You certainly didn't look like you do now. You were always thin, painfully thin but now—' Gerald shrugged, 'Your hair, your skin—'

Julia nodded. 'We haven't seen each other since you left home,' and with a rueful smile she continued, 'Life wasn't easy with your father. He was a selfish, difficult man. However it's amazing what the love and kindness of a very caring man, and cosmetic surgery can do to a woman. And Quentin was that man. He wanted, begged me to tell you.'

'He...he knew?'

'Yes, so did I, as soon as I saw you and heard your name. Naturally you'd changed, matured and resembled Matthew when he was your age.'

'Why didn't you say something? Make yourself known at the time, not wait all those years?' asked Gerald.

'Each time we came to the hotel and saw you Quentin asked that question, when I told him I was afraid you wouldn't want to acknowledge me. I hadn't been in touch since your father died. It was Quentin's dying wish that I should tell you but now, as usual, I've left it too late.' Whilst talking Julia had taken The Book of Ebenezer Le Page from the bookshelf, and opened it, when Gerald gazed, speechless and open-mouthed, at a photograph of a dark-haired chubby five year-old. Then: 'That's exactly like the photograph I've seen of my sons.'

'Who obviously resemble you but unfortunately I won't ever see them.'

It was then that Gerald remembered and asked, 'What did you mean, 'I've left it too late? Is there something wrong with you, are you ill?'

'Why don't we sit down and have a cup of tea?' Julia indicated the delicate cups and saucers, 'I should have time to tell you before they come.'

'Who?' Gerald had also sat down but now leant forward. 'What's this all about? You phoned and asked me to come up, who else are you expecting?'

Julia poured the tea, ignoring Gerald's question, handed him his cup and saucer, and indicated that he should help himself to cake, still talking: 'I've been a fool, a jealous fool.

Many years ago I was jealous of Iris. She married Matthew and like a fool, although I didn't love him and it certainly wasn't a happy marriage, I married Roger – his brother. Later, much later, I returned to the island with Quentin to discover that Matthew, who was still good-looking and an extremely successful hotelier, had married Maureen and had two grown-up children, Monique and Ben who both worked in the hotel. I also learnt that he and Iris had a son, Peter, who lived in England and had his own hotel – I was so envious!' Although Quentin was very ill he enjoyed going down to the hotel, seeing and meeting different people. The cancer spread, Quentin died, Maureen died and then last year I did the most stupid thing – I wrote to Matthew. Not just once, but every month.'

Gerald sat completely still, his cup in one hand, slice of cake in the other. Absorbed with what he had heard, and Julia with the telling, neither had realised that the gate and front door had been left open and there were two men standing in the hall, able to hear every word. Julia continued: 'I then did another stupid thing. It was after—' There was a pause. 'I broke into his bungalow. I wanted to find and retrieve those letters.'

'What!' exclaimed Gerald, shaking his head, 'That was a stupid thing to do. Why did you take such a risk? You could have been found in Matthew's bungalow.'

'I realised that and didn't stay long.'

'But long enough to create chaos – leave fingerprints.'

'I wore gloves.'

'The same as you'd worn when—'

'Yes,' interrupted Julia and ignoring Gerald's attempts to criticise: 'I had always loved Matthew – Quentin knew and accepted that. I thought and hoped that after Quentin's death, on the occasions that I lunched or dined alone at the hotel, Matthew might pause at my table for a brief conversation, but he merely smiled and nodded.' Julia sighed. 'I'm sorry. I'm digressing. Trying to explain why I wrote those letters. Why I did it.'

Confused, Gerald leant forward: 'What are you talking about?'

'I was angry. Matthew had barely acknowledged me that lunch time, or any day that week.'

'Just stop and tell me what this is all about,' interrupted Gerald. 'What have you done?'

'I was on the cliff path. I knew about his nightly walks, had observed him from a distance on several occasions, but he was always alone, never met anyone. That night I was standing under a tree but crossed the path as Matthew approached. His surprise turned to contempt as he demanded, 'What are you doing here?' Then curious and muttering, 'What are you looking at, you stupid woman?' he moved closer to the fence and using his torch, peered downwards towards the cliff and beach. At that moment my anger turned to fury, and determined that he would never ignore or taunt me again, I gave him an almighty shove.'

There was a moment's silence then, 'Oh my God!' groaned Gerald as he covered his face with his large hands.

'I always loved Matthew but,' Julia gazed across the room at the two detectives who stood in the doorway, and in a low but clear voice uttered four heart-breaking words: 'he never loved me.'